FLAWED

FLAWED

J P Blake

T

Copyright © 2025 J P Blake

The moral right of the author has been asserted.

Apart from any fair dealing for the purposes of research or private study, or criticism or review, as permitted under the Copyright, Designs and Patents Act 1988, this publication may only be reproduced, stored or transmitted, in any form or by any means, with the prior permission in writing of the publishers, or in the case of reprographic reproduction in accordance with the terms of licences issued by the Copyright Licensing Agency. Enquiries concerning reproduction outside those terms should be sent to the publishers.

The manufacturer's authorised representative in the EU for product safety is Authorised Rep Compliance Ltd, 71 Lower Baggot Street, Dublin D02 P593 Ireland
(www.arccompliance.com)

This is a work of fiction. Names, characters, businesses, places, events and incidents are either the products of the author's imagination or used in a fictitious manner. Any resemblance to actual persons, living or dead, or actual events is purely coincidental.

Troubador Publishing Ltd
Unit E2 Airfield Business Park,
Harrison Road, Market Harborough,
Leicestershire. LE16 7UL
Tel: 0116 2792299
Email: books@troubador.co.uk
Web: www.troubador.co.uk

ISBN 978 1836281 665

British Library Cataloguing in Publication Data.
A catalogue record for this book is available from the British Library.

Printed and bound in Great Britain by 4edge Limited
Typeset in 10.5pt Adobe Garamond Pro by Troubador Publishing Ltd, Leicester, UK

For S & C

ONE

I sometimes sit at my kitchen table, drinking my coffee, slowly remembering the past. Names of people I've long forgotten pop into my head. Like Charlotte or Sophia, both from boarding school, both crazy and wild. I wonder if they're still haunted by those throwaway insults the nuns would hurl our way to keep us in order or if they've created new demons for their thoughts to battle with. I dealt with my own demons years ago when my therapist told me I needed a plan. That's the thing about a goal. As long as you believe in it, clarity appears out of nowhere, even if you've got it wrong.

My name is Persephone Adelard, I'm thirty-two years old, and I'm a freelance investigator. This sort of work doesn't pay much, but it's interesting and I'm good at it. My Uncle Alfred used to say that I hid so many secrets I should've joined MI5 like he did. But with the breakdown, the suicide attempt, and that mix-up about me burning down the science lab at school, it was never going to happen.

It's three in the afternoon on a rainy October day, and I'm parked at a petrol station a few miles outside of Bath, on a job. I crank up the heater. Hanging around like I do, waiting, watching, it can seep into your bones until all you want to do is wallow in a steaming-hot bath with your feet messing with the taps, wondering when the hot water is going to run out. I close my eyes, hold my hands up to the heater as the warmth dances over my fingertips.

I spot him and quickly sit up. Months of tracking and here he is, right before my very eyes, in his top-of-the-line Maserati. Back from Monaco, back from gambling, back from his elaborate hidden life.

The telltale shot of adrenaline kicks in, and I'm poised, camera in hand, lens trained on the subject like I'm a sniper ready to finish him off. Which, in a way, is exactly what I'm going to do.

He parks in front of the large temperature-controlled garage he secretly constructed a year ago. Inside, he's got a two-year-old Rolls Royce silver; a navy Ferrari; and my favourite car of all time, a Mercedes-AMG G 63 Magno Edition, which retails at around £200K. It's the Jeep that's sort of square and makes you feel like you should be on safari bumping over ragged hills and jungles somewhere close to the Hindu Kush Mountain Range instead of on a B-road on the edge of Wiltshire and Somerset.

I zoom in.

He skilfully navigates the car and parks inside the warehouse-type building, then steps out and straightens the jacket of his crisp grey suit. He wanders around the vehicle, and I zoom in so close I can almost see the pores in his skin, which look remarkably clean for a sixty-year-old man. Spa treatment, no doubt. Without thinking, I drop the zoom to his nails: manicured. Of course they are. I swing back up to his face. It's smug. The Germans have a word for his type of face. *Backpfeifengesicht*. Look it up. It'll explain everything.

He turns and looks in my direction. I've done my homework; he might see a car but there isn't a hope he'd spot me with my camera, but I slink down anyway.

He stands, looking up and down the road, shoulders back, legs astride, chest puffed out. The thoughts going through his head are really easy to read. *I'm a warrior*, he's thinking, *master of my own universe*. It won't last long, and for a second I kick myself for feeling just that little bit sorry for him for the fall he's about to take. He's busted. He would've gotten away with it if it wasn't for his vengeful soon-to-be ex-wife who spilled the beans to her divorce attorney when he tried to screw her out of millions. With what I've found out, justice will be imposed, fairness will be restored, and he'll get his comeuppance. Jail time, for sure. I get it, justice. Some people say that fairness is hardwired into the human brain. I'm not so sure. For all those people he messed with and are now living in poverty, I bet revenge sounds kind of sweeter.

He walks around the side of the building and disappears out of sight. I rest the lens on my half-opened window and wait. I'm not nervous that I'll lose him because I know exactly what he's doing. He's in a small room changing, just like the other times when I've followed him here. Ten minutes later, he comes back into view in a different outfit. He's ditched the fancy suit and opted for sweats like he's ready to do the late shift at the petrol station. If it weren't for the Rolex on his wrist that his hubris won't allow him to take off, the role switch would've almost worked.

He gets into a beaten-up old Mini and speeds away. I scan my photos, decide which one tells the story the best and settle on him in his sweats, getting into a Mini; that's what the rags will want when he's picked up for fraud. The headlines will torture him, come up with something funny yet telling like the last one I read, 'Homeless man under house arrest'.

Out of the corner of my eye, I see another car parked about fifty yards away, its headlights facing me. It's a sleek black Alfa Romeo with an unusual license plate, starting with the letters

YEE. I'm sure I've seen this car before but can't place it. Is someone following me? I shift gears and slowly drive towards it, but whoever is driving shifts gears too and speeds into the main road. Before I can figure out what's going on, my boss calls and I pull into the side.

"Got something for me?" he asks eagerly.

"Yeah, just about to send everything to you now."

"Perfect. How much money do you think he's spent?"

"Including the cars and bling?"

"Bling? Sounding a bit trendy there, Persy. You know you're a bit old for those sorts of words, right?"

I laugh out loud. He's a great boss, lets me do my thing. The word bling has to be at least twenty years old, and, if anything, it dates me. I say nothing. I like his banter.

"He's hidden over six million. But you need to advise your client they need to act fast. He's spending money like—"

"Don't say water, Persy. Please don't say water. You know how I hate overused words." He was a writer years before he became a lawyer. I've read one of his manuscripts and couldn't put it down. He's got loads of talent, but he's rubbish at finding an agent.

"Got it. My point is he's spending a lot of money, fast." I quickly grab my little notebook so I can reel off some examples. Uncle Alfred taught me to be ready to back up every point I made. "In the past week, he's spent £7K on tennis shoes. What's weird, I don't think he plays tennis. Do you need tennis shoes to go on a yacht? It doesn't matter. Then there's £15K on cigars and over £200K on travel."

"£200K on travel? Are you kidding? Where is he going? To the moon? You know what? I don't care, as long as you've got proof."

"I've got it. Check the photos I've sent."

"Good," he says. "Job done."

I pause, ask myself if I should say anything. I grit my teeth. Integrity at work, it's what I pride myself on. "I think I was being followed too. I'm not sure. It's a gut feeling."

"Don't worry, Persy. Even if he's twigged that we're onto him and he wanted to know who you were, we are done. It's over for him. Sorted."

Relief floods over me. It's one of my things. I hate people thinking I'm stupid. Marion, the woman who loves to make it clear I'm adopted, always said I was a disappointment. When she said it at first, I waited, thought she hadn't finished her sentence. Like she was going to say 'you're a disappointment in Geography' or something like that. But she never added another word. That was her point. I was a disappointment.

"That's it? Job over then?" I always feel deflated after a job. A hobby might fix the emptiness. Something like golf or squash, or mountain climbing. I strike the last one. I don't like heights.

"You sound let down," he says. "Do you need more work? Are you short of cash?" He laughs at his joke. He knows I come from money. He likes to tell me that my wealth is the source of all my problems. He's never told me what those problems are, and I've never asked because I don't have the guts to hear the answer. Denial is a rosy place to live. "I tell you what, Persy, let me take a look and I'll call you as soon as something comes up."

I sit in the car in silence. Adrift. I'll end up back at home opening cabinets for no reason, switching from channel to channel, always ending up on a home shopping network, watching a middle-aged woman talk about the latest stretchy dress that doesn't crease and can be thrown in the washer and the tumble drier and all for £10.99, postage included. Once, I timed a woman on the show who was talking about the zipper sewn into the side of a dress. She went on about it for exactly three minutes and fourteen seconds. That's impressive.

The buzz of my phone breaks through the silence, and I cross my fingers that it's my boss telling me he'd forgotten about another job on his books. The caller ID puts paid to any sense of optimism. It's her. Marion, the woman who is so proud to tell everyone how she adopted me. Although she's rich and horrible, I still wouldn't mind calling her Mum, but I don't because she wouldn't like it; plus, it would be an insult to the position.

I shove the buzzing phone into the pocket to drown out the sound. I whisper the mantra my long-ago therapist taught me: "I am an independent woman. She does not control me." In the rear-view mirror, I catch sight of my eyes. They're not buying it. I move the mirror. The phone stops. Then rings again and again and again.

"Nope, nope, nope," I whisper.

The picture of Uncle Alfred, Marion's brother, pops into my head because if I don't answer, she'll start calling him, and he doesn't deserve her crap. He's the only one who's ever given me any good kind of attention. Like when I broke my arm after jumping out the window to get away from Marion, he was the one who took me to hospital. She pretended it hadn't happened.

The phone rings again and I really want to sling the damn thing out of the window, but I take a deep breath, just like I've been taught, clear my thoughts, slowly take the phone out of my pocket and look at it. A warmth spreads through my body, like the smell of chocolate chip cookies that have just been pulled out of the oven. It's not Marion. It's him. Scooter. Ex-boyfriend, ex-CIA, now a private investigator working for me, searching for my biological parents. He'll never find them. Marion has covered her tracks too well. I think he knows that too, but we keep on following leads, as if it's the only way to keep us together since I moved back from the US.

"Anything?" I say.

"You're never going to…"

The line crackles with static. I can't hear him. I mean, I can hear some things, but his words are getting chopped in half, and I don't know what he's saying. He's a freelancer and still takes on covert ops. He could be calling from the States or another country, in a plane somewhere, or who cares where he is, but on my side of the pond, all I've got is dead air.

"I can't hear you," I shout. "Scooter? Are you there?" I want to hear his voice, that confident, low, baritone that to this day sends chills down my spine.

He doesn't answer. I start to call him back, but he's calling me back too and the shock of the ring startles me enough that I physically jump, sending my phone tumbling to the floor. I move too quickly, and the seatbelt grabs hold of me, tightening across my chest. I fumble with the lock until it snaps open and lean forward and to the side and kick the phone into my open hand.

The green light is on and he's still on the phone. I utter a little giggle. "Find a better fucking place to call!" That's our thing. Pretending to be rough and ready.

"I beg your pardon."

"No, no, no," I whisper. It's not Scooter. It's her. The dreaded Marion. I go all weird and throw the phone onto the passenger seat. I'm all of a tizz. It's like she's caught me again peeing in that horrible plant of hers in the drawing room. I don't know why I did that either, some kind of weird revenge? I remind myself that if I ever pluck up the courage to go talk to another therapist, I need to get to the root of that.

With my eyes closed, I imagine being on that beach on the Amalfi coast, the one that's supposed to calm me down. For a nanosecond, it works, but then it doesn't because Marion's showed up on the beach and she's shouting at me. I stare at the phone; it hasn't hung up; she's there, shouting through the thing.

"Hello? Hello? To whom am I speaking?"

I lean over, stab decline, but my fingers are too sweaty, and the phone isn't doing what it's told. She's getting louder and higher, saying words like, "Are you there, Persephone?" She stops. Then I hear her shout, "Answer this phone immediately. Do you not know who I am?" The last time she said that, I tried to be clever. Said if she didn't know who she was, I wasn't going to tell her. She slapped me across the face for that one.

I can't pick it up. I won't pick it up. I spot the kiosk in the corner of the petrol station. Ever so gently, I ease myself out of the car, wanting, for some reason, for her not to hear me. I tell myself I'm invisible, I can do this. I get out, press the door shut, and walk away.

I buy a bottle of Coke and a bacon sandwich as my eyes flit back and forth to the car as if she's an evil genie who will find some way to appear out of the phone. I knock back the Coke, bite into the greasy sandwich, tell myself this is ridiculous. I'm not a kid anymore. What can she do to me? Lock me in the toilet in the barn with all those snails and spiders again? Nope. Those days are over. Not on my watch, buddy.

I straighten my shoulders, lift my head, stride back to the car and get back in. In the mirror, my eyes tell me I can do this, and I want to believe them. I grab the phone, put it to my ear; I can handle this.

It's dead. Marion has gone and in my head I hear the gentle hum of the song 'It's a Wonderful Life'. The universe has my back.

Scooter calls back.

"Sorry about that," he says. "I'm in West Virginia. Coverage is bad. I'm on a landline. So, here's the thing, are you sitting comfortably?"

"It's been a rough day. Just tell me what you've got?"

"I've found them," he says.

He hasn't. I know that. Plus, he's said those exact words when he thought he'd found them before. There's been five already. But I play along because this is what keeps us together.

"You always say that," I say.

"And you always say that too. But I'm telling you. We'll get there. Don't give up. But this time, I'm sure it's them."

"What makes this different?"

"You're the spitting image of her. Same crazy curly hair, not as red as yours, but she's older, so I figure it's faded. They've been together forever. I'm telling you, it's them."

"Go on." I tell myself to sound upbeat and excited because I want to support him.

"They've just retired. From State. Low-level admin. They own a small house on the outskirts of Maryland. They're doing okay. Not great. But okay. Pleasant life."

"Do the dates match?" He knows what I'm talking about. Over the years, Marion has given me bits and pieces of information which I've passed on to him. I don't think the clues I've given him will lead to the truth, but who knows.

"It fits. When Marion was teaching at the university in Bath, she told you she knew an American couple who gave you up. This couple was travelling around Europe in their twenties, like a couple of hippies having a nice time. Ended up doing menial labour for cash at the university, hourly work for a cleaning contractor, that sort of thing. Then, they went home to the States. It's exactly as Marion said. And, like I just told you, you're the spitting image of her. It's weird."

"It sounds possible," I say.

"I know what you're thinking. Here we go again. This is another wrong road and you don't want to get your hopes up. I mean, I remember how devastated you were the last time. And you can feel that way. In the past, there was always something that wasn't quite right, but we followed it through. This time, everything Marion has told you, it all fits, I'm telling you."

It's not possible. Marion lies. If it fits, he's missing something.

"And get this. They left England a month after you were born. How old were you when Marion adopted you?"

"She told me I was a month old."

"And before you ask, there are no papers, no birth certificates, no documents. But get this. They were in England with no money, right? Then, within a month of getting back to the US, they had enough money to buy a small house. They paid $50K back then. Where did they get the money? There was no inheritance. I checked."

"You think from Marion," I say. Would she have gone that far?

"Exactly. Marion paid them to give her their baby with no strings attached."

Scooter thinks Marion bought me. He met Marion years ago; he knows what she's like, and he's a good judge of character.

"This is them, Persy."

I open the glove compartment and look at the letter Marion gave me when I was in my teens. I'd been going on and on, asking to know anything about my biological parents and there, out of the blue, she handed me a letter from them. It was bogus. I checked her handwriting against the letter; it matched. She'd written the letter herself to get me off her back. I carry it with me everywhere to remind me just how horrible she is.

"You're reading that letter, aren't you?"

I smile. He knows me better than I know myself. I didn't tell him I thought Marion had written it. That would be one step too far.

"I'll get the first plane out," I say. I'm excited and imagine getting off the plane, running into his arms, the two of us following the investigation through.

"Whoa there, cowboy," he says. "You won't believe this, but you don't have to."

"I don't have to what?"

"Come to the US. It's their anniversary, and they're going on a trip. A knock-your-socks-off, bucket-list kind of trip."

"Okay…"

"They're going to be in England."

"You're kidding me."

"I kid you not. They are going to England. On a tour. They love all that history shit you guys like to show off about. They'll be at Stonehenge."

"I live near Stonehenge." I don't know what else to say.

"Exactly."

"When?" I ask.

"One week. They leave the US tomorrow. Then to Paris. Then to England."

"Will you be coming too? I mean, it would be great if you were here." I mentally cross my fingers. The searches have brought us closer together but the distance has never helped. If he thinks my parents are going to be here in England, shouldn't he be here too?

"I wish, Persy, but I can't. I'm on another job. But you promise me you'll take this one seriously? The last time I thought I'd found them, you went all weird on me."

"Because it wasn't them, was it."

"It wasn't. But these are them. I feel it. I know it. Don't bail on me. Okay?"

"If you don't bail on me, I promise I won't bail on you."

"There it is, then. It's us. Together against the world."

I smile. That's what I really want. Me and him. Together.

"What are you going to do about Marion? Are you going to tell her? I mean, it will come out at some point. She'll want to know how you found them."

A couple of beeps sound through the phone; he's got another call coming in and I'm glad; I don't want to deal with what I should or should not say to Marion.

"Persy, I've got to go. I'll call you later, okay? I'll send you what I have."

In the mirror, I catch the look in my eyes. Resigned? Sad? I crunch them shut. He's excited, he wants to get to the truth, and whatever happens, I know it will end up with him coming to England. This could be it. The springboard to our life together. I hold my breath for the count of five, push a smile onto my face. I can do this. I can be the woman he wants me to be. A surge of confidence slowly threads its way through my body and when I look at my eyes again, there's a sparkle in them that I've never seen before. The couple he thinks gave birth to me are coming my way and I'm going to be that girl who meets them. I'm ready to be that girl who's just found her biological parents. Out of nowhere, the excitement changes. I will meet them, tell them my name, they'll google me and see my picture in the newspaper. The one after the accident. Me behind the wheel, my head to the side, blood all over my face, the airbags disabled, something I'd done myself to make sure that I'd succeed. Which I hadn't. Marion was right about that too. Failure. I force myself not to look in the mirror.

My phone buzzes, Marion's name pops up, and something strange happens. I don't swear to myself, roll my eyes, or steady myself for her nasty, bitter words. And I know why. Because I'm doing something that will really annoy her. She can take her misery and shove it.

With a lightness of heart, I pick up the phone.

"Hi, Marion. Is everything okay?" My voice is almost

sing-songy. It doesn't sound like me. I'm about to tell her that Scooter thinks he might've found my biological parents then change my mind. I want to see the look in her eyes.

"Persephone," she says with that plum-in-her-mouth drawl. "Is that you?"

"Yep. It's me."

"It is I," she enunciates robotically.

"What?"

"It is I. That is the correct English usage. The finest boarding schools in England did not clarify the difference between an object pronoun versus a subject pronoun?"

My eyes stare back at me in the mirror; they've gone black. *No,* I tell them, *don't do something you'll regret. You're better than this. Let it go. She's a different species.*

"Persephone. Are you there or not?"

"I am," I say.

"Good. There's a dead body. You need to take care of it."

TWO

At first glance, everything seems normal.

Marion is sitting in her favourite chair, a George III number bought from Athelhampton House for £36K in the late '50s. The cashmere blanket draped over her lap is close to slipping to the floor, so she sets her cup of tea on the coffee table beside her and puts the blanket right. The place whiffs of eucalyptus and mould, which has gotten worse since her seventy-year-old housekeeper died a year ago, but I don't mention it. If Marion wants to live this way, so be it.

She's sipping from the Harrods tea set I gave her when I was seventeen. I'm thirty-two now, and it's the first time I've seen it used. She's trying to manipulate me. She's pretending that she cares.

Sitting right next to the sugar bowl by her half-drunk cup of tea is the little vial of Nembutal, her secret insomnia fixer. Any other day of the week, it's hidden in one of those old Elastoplast things, all rusty and worn, kept under her pillow in her bedroom. She's left it out on display to prove some sort of point.

The lipstick stain on the cup matches the lipstick on her

lips. She's a stickler for cleanliness; that cup was lipstick-free before she used it. She said this was an emergency, yet she's had time to redo her make-up. I should applaud her theatrics.

I fold my arms tight against my body to give me a bit of warmth. She lives in a big old house that goes back to the thirteenth century called Jefferson Manor. I've asked her so many times to get heating installed – she's loaded, and she can afford it – but she won't. Too self-indulgent, she says. So, she sits in the sunroom, day after day, with its large windows and heavy curtains, all wrapped up with her blankets and her slippers with her little heater just by her feet, which has to be broken because I've never seen it on.

My fingers are numb, and I'm shivering with cold, but my coat is behind me, thrown over the back of a chair. I should grab it and put it on. But I can't. She'll assume I'm heading home and I'll never hear the end of it. No one leaves the manor unless she says so. Arrivals and departures are her domain.

"There's a dead body," she says. We stare at each other like it's a game of chicken. "And you need to take care of it."

Her tone is the same as she used on the phone. Unapologetic – no, I'd go further; it's as if she's saying 'I'm somewhat bored, and now I'd prefer to get back to the paper'. I should be shocked, but this is Marion, a woman who believes the words 'entitled' and 'arrogant' are compliments. If she were driving a double-decker bus that knocked you down, she'd complain that you'd damaged the bumper.

I look around because I can't see a body. The last one she covered up with a blanket and left it behind the sofa. I look from one corner of the room to another. It's not behind the big plant plot, or the writing desk or the coffee table with the lamp on the top. Where is the dead body?

"I can't *see* the dead body," I say.

"Outside somewhere," she says. "Maybe the shed?"

She's enjoying this, making me play her cat-and-mouse game.

"What do you mean outside somewhere?" I ask.

"Is your hearing as slow as your intellect?"

I know better than to answer that one.

"This is tiresome. You need to finish this whole thing off," she says. The lipstick stains on her teeth look like blood. Maybe she's a vampire. No, I would've noticed teeth marks on the necks of the others.

I'm about to reach for my coat when she abruptly asks, "Have you put on weight?"

I self-consciously pull my sweatshirt a little lower and marvel at her ability to simultaneously hold two conflicting emotions. My tummy versus a dead body; she has a gift.

"You said she's maybe outside?" The word 'she' pops out of my mouth too quickly to pull it back in. She hates the word 'she'. Likes to say, 'Who is she, the cat's mother?' I don't know what this means. We've never had a cat – at least, not a live one. "The body," I self-correct.

"What about it?"

Has she forgotten she got me over here to get rid of the dead body? "You said it might be outside?"

"Yes." There's a mean little scowl on her face, and she says the letter 'S' like 'sh' and I'm listening to Sean Connery for a minute. She's drunk, something that happens all too often, and she's got that red and blotchy skin to prove it. She's a badly worn seventy-two-year-old; dementia has started to age her, and time confuses her – at least, that's what the doctor said when the forgetfulness started.

I watch her. She watches me. It's a game of chicken. Both of us staring each other down like it's part of an elaborate act that fools everyone into thinking neither one of us knows what's going on. That she doesn't recall the dead bodies or how they got inside her house. I look away. She's got me beaten. If there were a Nobel Prize for lying, it would be hers, hands down. She'd probably win it twice. No. They'd change the rules, retire the award, tell the world they'd never seen anyone who could lie like her before and would never know this level of achievement again. Ever.

She grabs her stick hanging from the back of her chair and flinches as she stands. Arthritis is in her knees. I should feel pity, but I don't because I sometimes think she fakes that too, another one of her ways to manipulate people. One of my many therapists once told me I needed to be more sympathetic, that Marion's childhood must've been abusive and dysfunctional. I told her Marion never talked about growing up, and the therapist said she was probably like that because of some deep-seated trauma. I get what she was saying; I mean, it's not that complicated. That we're all a product of our childhood. But a rotten upbringing doesn't give you the right to be a rotten human.

Marion looks at her watch and then back at me in a haughty, my-chin-is-higher-than-yours kind of way. I'm being dismissed. Okay then. Fine.

I say, "I'm going to the shed or somewhere outside to look for a dead body that may or may not be there."

"Well, if that's what you feel you must do, far be it from me to stop you."

I grit my teeth. She's not going to get the better of me. Not today. I'm full of confidence; I've got a secret she knows nothing about. I feel powerful.

"What is that silly smirk on your face? Are you not feeling well?"

I don't know what to say.

"Go on then," she says. "Get on with it."

"Uncle Alfred? Have you told him about this?" I already know the answer to that but I want to needle her. When she called me, she said the dead body was in the living room; now it's gone. Only Uncle Alfred could've helped.

"Absurd," she says, "I suggest you complete the task at hand."

I'm not going to let her get the better of me. "Maybe next time you 'find' a dead body, you could call the police. How does that sound?"

Her eyes turn evil black. "Don't push me, Persephone. It won't end well."

I don't answer her because she scares the hell out of me, and if she puts her mind to it, there's no knowing what she might do.

"I'm leaving," I say.

"Which I have already asked you to do. Now. Turn off any lights once you're done. The electricity bill has been unnecessarily high. That is, of course, unless you wish to debate any other trivial matters before I go to bed."

I don't answer.

"And have you done your puzzle today?"

She's gone back in time. When I was seven, I fell from a tree and hurt my head. She'd read that puzzles help the brain and improve problem-solving skills, and every day after that, she left a puzzle at the end of my bed. I couldn't have breakfast until it was finished.

"I've done the puzzle," I lie.

"Good. Preventative. Proactive. Restorative."

I make a move, hoping the list of words she's spouting out will stop. I grab my coat, stroll outside and slam the door behind me.

My movement alerts the motion detector, and the back garden is flooded with light. On the patio, the granite table and wrought-iron chairs are littered with damp leaves blown in from the Japanese maples. The air holds the faint aroma of pig manure, and the spitting rain lands in my eyes. I blink and squint. The space looks cold, unloved and unkempt, and I tighten my coat around me.

I hurry across the flagstone path that winds across the grass like a serpent, slip through the narrow opening of the tall, manicured hedge at the far end, and find my way to the shed. It's not really a shed. It's a £50K eco-office, but the word shed will do. I grab the pretend stone with the key hidden inside, unlock the door and go on in. I look over my shoulder and through the window I see Marion watching me. Good. I'll do exactly as she suggested.

The shed is large enough for two sofas, a dining table and a desk if you want it. Marion doesn't – she hates clutter. Two comfy chairs are sitting on top of one huge Persian carpet. One has its back to me. There could be a dead body sitting there. There's nothing. No body, no skeleton, no little old lady. Just empty chairs in a big, miserable room. I walk to the far end, to the wall-to-wall cupboards, with the secret door with the bathroom behind. Maybe the body will be there, crumpled on the floor or draped over the toilet, her matted hair dripping onto the tiles. I hold my breath again and yank open the door.

It's empty. No body.

I turn around and take a long look at the room. I flip up the corners of the Persian carpet. Of course, a body wouldn't be under the rug, I'd see it, but I'm playing her game.

There is no body. She's already taken care of it and she's messing with me. I glance in the mirror on a hook near the shed's door. Marion is right: I am putting on weight. I promise myself tomorrow is the day: no more pizza. I take one last look around, then lock the shed up. Before heading out, I sneak a peek back at the house and the sunroom. She's still standing there, watching.

I get into my car that's parked at the back gate to the garden to drive down to Uncle Alfred's. He lives alone on Marion's estate at the end of the dirt track and spends his days caring for his pigs. He loves animals; he even had a lion in a cage once, a big old thing he bought from the safari park when it was going out of business. He didn't keep it. He ended up giving it to the Big Cat Sanctuary in Marsden within two days of delivery; seeing the animal pacing around, all enclosed with no freedom, he couldn't cope.

The moon is high and bright, and it shines a spotlight on the old Ankerwycke Yew tree. I turn on the engine, snap on my seatbelt and press play on the radio. The Mamas & the Papas are belting out 'My Kind of Music' and I belt out the words with them and I don't give a damn if nobody else sings along.

I expertly manoeuvre the car and the three-point turn becomes a two-point turn, another sure sign that all is well with the world. The muddy lane to Uncle Alfred's is rutted and slippery, but my hands are steady on the steering wheel. A rabbit hops out right in front, and my foot jumps into action. I slam on the brakes, and, with inches to spare, the bunny disappears out of sight.

I move on, but the back wheel bumps over something.

The rabbit?

I didn't actually see it with my very own eyes hop away.

I toy with the idea there's something wrong with the car but discount it: six months old, it's not likely. I get out and feel sick; the idea I've run over a rabbit creeps me out. I take a look and find the culprit: it's just a rock, not much bigger than a rugby ball, all grey and black and splattered with mud. The bunny is alive. Yet another good omen. It's probably making its way to safety in one of the century-old trees that dot Marion's estate. I remind myself to tell Uncle Alfred. He'll like the story.

The moon sprays a beam of light so bright that it makes

the droplets of rain sparkle from one surface of the hedge to another, and the intoxicating smell of smoke and pine needles drifts over from a bonfire someway off. I ease back into my car, the engine hums into gear, and the headlights flicker on.

Two shiny objects glisten in the rain, maybe four feet ahead of the car. Jewellery? Something Uncle Alfred has dropped?

I get out again to see what it is.

Shoes.

I get closer and peer into the dark, damp undergrowth. In the shoes are a pair of feet – old feet.

It's her. Marion's dead person.

I want to say I'm shocked, but why would I be? After all, – getting rid of Marion's dead bodies – been there, done that, got the Nembutal-stained T-shirt.

THREE

I crouch down to get a good look at Dora from the care home where Marion volunteers and donates a load of money each year. Marion forces me to volunteer there, too. Dora is one of Marion's special friends, invited back to the manor loads of times and fawned over like a precious trinket. And now she's here, waiting to be disposed of. The woman was close to Marion and now she's dead. It's not hard to get the picture.

Pulling her body along isn't a problem because she's little and the wet ground is not too hard or too mushy, so dragging her isn't that hard. Without a hitch, I zig-zag my way to the car, her feet under my armpits. She looks pretty. A miniature, not-quite-so-rich version of Marion. She's tiny, can't be much more than five feet, and has grey curly hair long enough to get caught in her mouth, which I notice when I drop her legs to the ground. I gently pull the wisp of hair away and tuck it behind her ear. Then I open up the boot, climb into it, crouch down, and stretch out my arms so that her body is easy to reach. I haul her up and over until she's lying in the boot. I take a breather, look around, feel the cool air against my skin, climb out of the car and slam the boot shut.

I drive down the bumpy lane to Uncle Alfred's pig farm.

Marion must've called earlier in a rare moment of clarity because he's waiting with a wheelbarrow. He's wearing overalls, a waterproof coat, and a pair of green wellies. He's standing legs akimbo, his arms folded, and he's shaking his balding head in dismay.

"We have to do something about this," he says as I get out of the car. "It can't go on, Persy, it really can't." His lips are tight, his jaw clenched.

It's a worthless conversation. We've been here before. He brings his wheelbarrow up to the car, then helps me lift her out of the boot.

The squeaking and bumping of the barrow being wheeled across the ground gets the pigs all wound up, and they run towards us, grunting and oinking and poking their shiny little snouts between the wooden slats of the fence. They sound happy. They've been here before.

In 2012, in Oregon, a farmer's false teeth were found right beside his hog enclosure. His body, that was long gone. It's not that they crave human flesh; it's about what's available. And if push comes to shove, they've got no problem making a happy meal of Homo sapiens. Uncle Alfred's pig farm is Marion's ace in the hole.

He sets the barrow down and waits for me to go through the old lady's pockets. I find what I'm looking for – an envelope folded in two. Inside is a poem:

> *There is a strain to live among the hills,*
> *The old and full voices of men and more*
> *Of some free stream, whose miserable presence fills*
> *The solitude of sound: I shut the door*
> *Ever such is my yearning to die*
> *This is the scene for which I can't shy.*

The poem written above is a reflection of how I feel. I no longer wish to exist on this earth and want to end my life. No one has helped me. I do this of my own accord.
Yours truly,
Dora Haslea

I hand the letter to Uncle Alfred, then cup my nose and mouth with my hand, a useless attempt to get away from the smell of pigs. He reads the poem and spits out a sort of derisory cough. "We both know who wrote this."

I nod. His question doesn't need an answer. We should talk about this, the two of us, but we don't. We all know what's going on, and maybe delving into it would be too painful, so we all go along with it, sort of crossing our fingers that the deaths will stop.

"Who is plagiarised this time?" He looks at me as though I'm supposed to know. As it happens, I do. For a few terms, I studied literature at university before the breakdown.

"Felicia Dorothea Hemans," I say.

"Not Wordsworth?" There's a glint in his eyes; he loves it when he sees that I know my stuff. "I thought the preference was Wordsworth."

"Hemans wrote it to Wordsworth."

Uncle Alfred glances over the wheelbarrow's body, shifts his feet, and ends up staring at me as though I've got some dark secret hidden in my breast pocket.

"I will finish this off," he says.

I hesitate. Dora is very small, but still. "I don't want you doing this on your own."

"Please. I'd rather you weren't… involved."

It's a tough call. There's no one in this world I care for more than him and I try to push away the truth that he and Marion come first. I force myself to remember the good times;

it's the best way to go. He was the one who picked me up from boarding school, took me to my doctor's appointments, or came to watch me play tennis. Marion used to get angry about it and said I needed to be independent, but he wouldn't have it. Now he's getting thinner and more stooped, partly to do with the heart attack a year or so ago.

"I'm here now. I might as well…"

His eyes are determined, and he's gritting his teeth so tightly, little waves of skin bunch just under his cheeks. He shakes his head, puts his arm around me, and draws me towards him so that we stand together, side by side, my cheek resting gently on his shoulder, watching the pigs move and shove and grunt. It's a regular Hallmark moment.

He stands a little straighter. "Best to get this over and done with." He picks up the handles to the barrow, and the wheel squeaks and squelches in the mud. His arms look strong. He can handle it.

As I trudge back to the car, the cries of the pigs are getting louder. I shove my fingers into my ears. I pay close attention to my breath, a meditation trick, a way of putting aside what's happening, but it's not working. *Death is death*, I tell myself. *We all have to go somehow.*

Uncle Alfred shouts at me, and I turn back. He's rubbing his chin with a worried frown.

"Are you okay?" I ask, walking back towards him.

"Sorry, Persy. Sorry to state the obvious. But will you take care of the other side of this?"

I nod. Nothing else needs to be said. He's talking about the care home and the need for me to make sure no one connects our family to the dead woman. I've done it before, and I'll do it again. It's what I do. Maybe it's the only thing I *do* do for Marion, and I know why. It's not for her. It's for him, Uncle Alfred.

My phone rings. It's her again. I thought she'd gone to bed, but no such luck.

I'm tempted to ignore it, but Uncle Alfred must've heard the ring, and he's let go of the wheelbarrow handles and turns around to see who it is. I smile, put up my hand to let him know it's all okay, and answer the phone.

"Have you seen Uncle Alfred?" Marion asks.

I'm looking at him, picking up the handles, pushing the barrow towards the sty. She knows I've seen him and sent me here, but jealousy is one of her things. She hates it when I spend too much time with him. Used to lock me in my bedroom when he would come around, just to keep me out of the way.

"Yep," I say. "He's in front of me."

"Can he hear this conversation?"

He's walking closer to the sty, maybe six feet away.

"Why?"

"Answering a question with a question. Research shows this is the first sign of a declining mind."

It isn't. She makes up stuff like this, then puts the word 'research' in front of it to make it sound more persuasive.

"He can't hear."

"Good. I'm concerned."

Her words are almost laughable. *She's* concerned? She's not the one who's just had to tidy up a body.

"Dora. The dead woman. Alfred knew her."

"Okay…?"

"You're not listening. He knew her *very well*. And she is now dead."

"What do you mean by that?" I whisper. I turn my back to Uncle Alfred, cover the phone and my mouth with my hand and dip my head.

"Are my words not clear?"

An image of my clenched fist smashing her in the face pops into my brain. "*You* knew her. Not him."

"Persephone. Are you listening to me?"

"Don't," I hiss.

"Don't what, Persephone?"

"Don't try to point the finger at him."

Uncle Alfred has set the barrow down and is walking towards me. "Persy. Are you alright?" he asks.

"I'm hanging up," I tell her, and I do.

"Is anything wrong?" There's a crease between his eyebrows.

"Not at all," I say. "Sorry, a difficult case at work. One of the guys I'm following might've left the country." Uncle Alfred is one of the few people who knows what I do. He also knows it's confidential; he'll let it go without more questions. That's what he's like. He gets things.

"You looked rather anxious."

He ruffles the hair on the top of my head, and, for a moment, the smell of old spice washes away the smell of the pigs. "We are very proud of you, you know?" he says.

"I know," I say. Over his shoulder, I see that Dora's legs have flopped out of the front of the wheelbarrow.

He follows my gaze. "Oh dear. Don't worry. I will take care of everything. Off you go." He squeezes my shoulder. "Do you think this will ever stop?" he asks me.

I kind of shrug because I really don't know.

I drive away slowly. In the rear-view mirror, he's standing, legs wide, arms folded, watching me. If this were ever to get out, I don't doubt for a moment that she'd try to make either me or Uncle Alfred the fall guy. But that won't ever happen. I'd rather kill *her* first.

I head home, the tightness in my shoulders gradually easing. After a couple of miles, I see the sign for the Hope and Anchor. I'm hungry, and the place has great food, but I drive on by. The idea of seeing smiling faces biting into sausage and mash is just a bit too much.

Marion calls again. Why the hell won't she go to bed? I remind myself that Mum and Dad are on their way and everything is bound to get better. I can be stronger because I don't need her anymore. If she ever tries to put any blame on Uncle Alfred, I won't stand for it.

"What you said before, on the phone, about Uncle Alfred, it wasn't right."

"Are we on Greenwich Mean Time?" she says.

"What?"

"Greenwich Mean Time, GMT. Are you not familiar with the concept?"

"Yes!" I sound defensive.

"It's dark. And it's only eight-thirty in the morning," she says.

It's the evening; she's got the time of day upside down.

"Yes. We're on Greenwich Mean Time."

"I assumed I was correct." She hangs up, and I'm left holding on, as usual, listening to dead air.

FOUR

I'm sitting at my desk, in my office, on the phone, on hold. I rent a small space in the city. I don't always use it, but sometimes working outside of my place feels better, so I keep it available, just in case.

Roger the Dodger, our nickname for our thirty-years-plus family lawyer, is on another call. We call him that because he's not dodgy at all; if anything, a kind of stiff, upper-crust, by-the-book sort of person. I suppose that's why the nickname is kind of funny. His assistant knows us well and asks me to wait a few seconds so that she can interrupt him. I've already figured out what I have to say and how I have to say it. If she hadn't pushed me over the edge by pointing the finger at Uncle Alfred, this would never have been necessary.

Roger coughs into the phone. "Persy. How pleasant to hear from you. What can I do for you?"

Roger Penrose. He's known me since I was a child, from the time Marion sent me to spend the day with him to learn about investments and how to manage money (I was six). He was kind; he just handed me a book and told me to read it when I was older. For the rest of the morning, I sat playing computer games. I never read the book. I'm not even sure I took it with me.

"A quick question. Has Marion said anything to you about Uncle Alfred?"

"No. Should she? Is there a problem? I only spoke to her two days ago, but she didn't mention a word."

I tap my fingers on the desk, acting the part even though I know he can't see me. Just a concerned daughter, trying to plan for the future. "I think we might need to have a discussion."

"Is there something worrying you about Alfred, Persy?"

"No, no. It's Marion." I allow a pause to hover in the air. "Sorry, it's just that she has been doing some rather odd things. I just want to make sure that…" Again, I stop for effect. "Actually, I don't know if Uncle Alfred has spoken to you about this already. Marion's dementia?"

"Dementia?" He sounds surprised.

"Marion was diagnosed a while ago. I'm so sorry. I'm not sure if I should be talking to you about this…"

"Persy. Please. This is exactly the kind of thing you *should* be discussing. I suggest we have a family meeting to review the situation."

"Marion isn't ready to admit how serious this problem is. In fact, I'm not sure if any of us are, really."

I feel a slight stab of guilt. It feels wrong to be using Marion's illness against her in this way. But Marion knows exactly what she's doing. Or maybe she doesn't. Who knows? But it doesn't matter, she's putting him at risk. With a bit of luck, it's only me she's spoken to about Uncle Alfred, but who might she talk to next?

"It's important to face up to these issues, Persy. You are doing the right thing. Now, tell me, how serious is it? I haven't seen Marion in a few years. We do everything by phone."

I know all of this already. Marion loves to say it: "Under what scenario would I allow the hired help to enter into my home as a guest?"

"She's been… well… saying some rather odd things."

"For example?"

I toss any nagging thoughts of remorse out of the window. This has to be done to keep Uncle Alfred in the clear. I trot out a few bits I read about when I googled Marion's problems. "She sometimes thinks that she's being held prisoner."

"Prisoner?"

"Exactly. Says someone tried to break into her bedroom, but luckily the guard at the door protected her."

"The guard? She has a guard outside her bedroom?"

"No, of course not. She's imagining it all."

"Persy. This all sounds rather worrying."

Maybe I've come on too strong. "It is, and it isn't. Uncle Alfred is taking care of everything. Goes in regularly. That sort of thing. If it gets worse, then we might need another conversation. The real problem at the moment isn't so much about what she says or thinks, but who she says it *to*." I give my voice a measured little hitch. "So sorry, it's all a bit upsetting."

"I understand." His voice is kind and understanding and barely above a whisper. "I think we need to chat face to face. Now, shall we put something in the calendar? If you like, I can come over to Alfred's?"

I think about Dora's body at Uncle Alfred's farm. "I'll speak to Uncle Alfred and get back to you."

"Sensible idea," he says.

"One last thing. You remember a couple of years ago we put together a Power of Attorney?"

"Quite right. Quite right. Just before Marion went into the hospital for her knee replacement. Yes. I remember it quite well, in fact."

"Is it still in force?"

"One second." The sound of file drawers opening and shutting. "Good. I thought I was right. Yes. Perfect. It was a

Financial Lasting Power of Attorney, or LPA, in your name, and it ends when the donor, in this case, Marion, dies."

I cut to the chase. The three dead women have all come from the same care home. I need leverage. Just in case. "Marion donates large sums of money to Meadow Bank Care Home. Can I step in and manage those donations?"

"Are you thinking of changing her commitments?"

"Maybe. I'm not sure."

"Are the funds designated to the care home not being used wisely?"

"I don't know. I just want to make sure that we've got all our bases covered."

"Good thinking, Persy. Highly commendable. Let's discuss it when you come in."

I lean back in my chair and put my feet up on the desk that used to belong to Uncle Alfred. When I sit here, like this, I like to pretend I work for MI5. That's the job I really would've loved. I do my usual spin of my failed aspirations. Sure, MI5 may have cooler tech and gadgets, but, quite honestly, I've got enough money to buy the same sort of things. In the past six months, I've bought a scanner that searches for hidden cameras in seconds, a thermal imager so I can see people in the dark at one hundred yards, and a hush device to mask my voice. The one I like the most is Spyera, an app that sits undetected on another person's phone or computer and lets me see what someone is up to from the comfort of my home. It's impressive and only costs me £400 a year.

A call comes through on my landline, but I let it go to voicemail; what to do about the problem of Marion still up front and centre. I listen to the message. It's about a job I did a few months ago, and the man who hired me is giving me an update. "Persy. Your Greek mark, Spyropoulos. He's hopped on a plane, just like you said he would. We're not sure when he'll be back in the country but as soon as I hear, I'll let you know."

I tailed this guy for months, and it was one of the easiest jobs ever. He went to three places – that's it. The supermarket, the little coffee shop just down the street down from his flat, and philosophy class. Actually it's because of him that I go to philosophy class too. At first it was to keep an eye on him, but now I go because I like it. You learn things like, 'you are not your thoughts', or, 'listen is an anagram of silent'. At the last class, Greek guy mentioned he might not make the next few lessons so I guessed that he could be heading off and I left the class halfway through, broke into his apartment and found the airline tickets. I never told my boss how I found out and he didn't ask.

I kick my feet off my desk, slug back the last of the coffee purchased on the way in and check the clock on the wall. Ten-thirty. A good time to go to the care home. It should be quiet because the breakfast will be over, the nurses will be back doing their rounds, and the kitchen staff will be busy cleaning up.

I lock my office door, head out to the car park just behind the building, and drive on out to Meadow Bank Care Home to make sure no one connects the dots to us.

Dora has been missing five days: if Marion was a suspect, we would've heard something by now, I'm sure of it. I toy with telling the world she's killed these women – the image of her in prison clothing is kind of persuasive – but I won't. It'd hurt Uncle Alfred too much. Over the years, he's lied to me too about where I came from, but somehow I'm okay giving him a free ride because he's dominated by Marion too. You can see it in his eyes.

I drive up the hill, pass through the new wrought-iron gates, paid for by Marion, and park by the landscaped gardens with the pretty tables and chairs just waiting for that sunny day, also paid for by Marion. I do a quick 360. No police cars. Nothing.

Inside the main door, I try to wish away the smell of bleach and old. The receptionist, Susie, is sitting behind her desk. She's been there about three and a half years and I can read her mood better than the morning paper. Today must be a good day because her hair is falling loose and she's wearing lipstick. She's also wearing a pair of gold hoops so big they almost touch her shoulders.

"Nice earrings. You don't normally wear any."

"I know. My birthday last week. Larry gave them to me."

"How is he?" I've never met Larry, but she's told me enough that I feel like I know him better than she does. He doesn't like his plumbing job, is overweight and fancies a new Nissan, just like the one his cousin has but not in red. That kind of thing.

"Larry's alright. Well, he was until he found out his boss wants him to do some extra shifts. I don't mind; he gets on my nerves if he's at home. And to tell you the truth, I could do with a bit more in my back pocket; we get peanuts here." I smile and nod. I've never had that sort of a relationship where you just tell each other everything. I'm not sure I'd want it; it'd probably be as boring as it sounds.

I give an exaggerated look around the place. "Is it quiet today or is it me?"

"Darn sight quieter than two days ago. You should've been here. Place was like a train station with all the comings and goings. A bloody mess if you ask me."

"What was going on?"

She leans forward, hunches a bit, and drops her voice. "You haven't heard? Oh my God! You don't know what happened? Old Dora went for a wander. They haven't found her yet."

"Dora?" I pretend I'm running her name through my head,

trying to put the name to the face. "The one who turned a hundred?"

"No, that was Grace. Dora. Little. Curly hair. Marion, your mum, was really close to her. Remember, she was the one in the photograph. With Marion. The one on the brochure they use for fundraising."

"The one with dementia?"

"Everyone's got dementia. The little one with grey curly hair," she repeats. "Marion went with her to the hospital a couple of times, brain tumour, remember?"

"I didn't know Marion went anywhere with any of the patients," I lied. I knew exactly when Marion went with Dora because it was on the same day Uncle Alfred was refusing to go to the doctor's appointment. He insisted on staying at home as Marion showed the woman her ten-year-old hydrangeas.

"You have to remember," Susie carries on. "Marion sent her flowers. Took her out to places. Marion was nicer to her than any of this lot were, that's for sure."

"She went missing? That's awful. Were the police here?"

"Three of them." Her face is animated, caught up in the excitement, absent of any worry about a missing old lady. "One of them was in school with me. He was a little squirt then, and he's a little squirt now. Only difference is the uniform. This one doesn't fit him as well."

"Do they know what happened?"

Susie shakes her head. "I don't think they care, quite honestly. You could tell from the way they were talking. I heard one of them say she was going to die anyway." She raises her eyebrows. "I'm not saying it out of turn. You could see it in their eyes. Old woman, past her sell-by date."

"What happens now?"

"Don't know. They talked to everyone. Who she was friends with, that sort of thing."

"They didn't call Marion. At least, I don't think they did."

She lowers her voice even further. "Probably won't bother. They're onto another case already. It's not as if Dora's been murdered by a serial killer or anything."

I look away. Don't want her to see any thoughts running through my head that might show up on my face.

"Persy, are you okay?"

I use one of my tricks to get my head together. Switch the word 'serial' to 'cereal', and, just like that, a bowl of cornflakes pops into my head.

"Sorry. Yes. Light-headed. I haven't eaten this morning."

"You look like someone just died." She nods in the direction of the kitchen. "You want me to tell the chef to rustle up something? I bet he's still got some toast if you want it."

I shake my head and force a smile. "Thanks. I'll get something in a bit."

"Don't blame you. That chef gives me the creeps." She dips her head, conspiracy in her eyes. "I bet he's not really a chef. Wouldn't be surprised if he was homeless before he came here. We always seem to find the weirdos, if you know what I mean."

An old lady is shuffling towards us, eyes locked on her Zimmer frame.

"Those cops were weirdos too. The little squirt, the one I went to school with, said they weren't even going to bother with Dora. Said she'll turn up one way or another and we both knew what that meant."

"You really don't think they're going to investigate?"

"A kid threw himself off the top of a car park yesterday. The one by the bus station. You know the building, the one they want to pull down?"

I nod, although I've no idea what she's talking about.

"Said it was to do with drugs. County lines, here, in Bath. So, I said, you're going to prioritise teenage kids getting shitfaced instead of a little old lady who's gone missing? Those were my exact words, I swear to you. You want to know what he said back?"

I nod.

"*Nothing*. Absolutely damn nothing. He just shrugged." She leans back so hard in the chair that it creaks. "Nothing. What do you think of that? Old Dora. Paid her taxes. Did her bit, and this is what happens. It's bloody shameful."

She turns at the sound of the old lady with the Zimmer frame steadily making her way past us. "Sadie, you're not allowed here, remember? Go on back to the library." She rolls her eyes then tosses a sneaky grin my way. "They lost Dora at Longleat Safari Park. Can you believe it? She might've been eaten by the lions for all we know." She giggles, then catches herself, as if laughing wasn't quite the right thing to do. "Just wandered off. Actually, they're not sure *where* they lost her. Twelve on the bus, only eleven came back and there were four stops in between. And the driver was Edith – never driven the bus before, only did it because Jenny was off sick. She feels terrible about it. She's taken a week's leave."

"Awful," I say.

"You know what makes me really mad? They've already gone and got someone coming in for Dora's room. Just like that. Gone and cleared her stuff out. I heard Derek tell them to get her room repainted and fumigated. Fumigated. Can you believe that? As if she wasn't clean. She took a shower every day. He's so horrible; he doesn't care."

"Derek, the manager?"

She nods. "Son of a bitch. You should hear the things he says about the people here. Calls them wrinklies under his breath. He's disgusting."

"He's having her room painted?" The thought creeps me out.

Susie nods. "Pretends it's a spring clean."

"But what if she turns up? Does he think she's not coming back?" I hold my breath.

"I sure as biscuits don't know." She looks up, and I follow her eyes to the clock on the wall. "We've got someone coming in for a tour. Be here any minute." She checks her watch to make sure it matches the clock. "Looking for a place for their aunt. They'll probably get Dora's room, won't they?" She leans over on her chair just enough to get a clear view out to the car park.

I turn around too. In the car park, a man is getting out of a navy-blue Ford.

"Wow. I hope that's the guy who's coming in to talk about his aunt. Look at him." Susie straightens her shoulders and, without seeming to know it, pushes her shoulders back so her boobs are front and centre.

He's confident, strides rather than walks. And when I get a better look at him, I swear I do exactly what Susie did.

FIVE

Derek, the manager, is doing his rounds. I choose the perfect place to wait, smack in between the reception area and the new handy-dandy coffee machine, which is right opposite the hall that goes down to Derek's office. As soon as he walks by, I'll see him, and I need to talk to him to plant the same seed I planted with the lawyer.

I could've made an appointment, but I wanted it to seem more casual, to kind of bump into him, nothing really to worry about, a quiet word in your ear sort of thing. By the time I'm done with him, he won't believe a word that comes out of Marion's mouth.

The good-looking guy who got out of the blue Ford is chatting with Susie. I press the buttons on the coffee machine and make a steaming-hot cappuccino as snippets of their conversation waft my way. His aunt is okay now, but she's not as strong as she used to be. She's social and likes people. Enjoys bingo. She has a quirky sense of humour and used to have a cat, but it died a year or so ago. He's tall, over six feet with wavy black hair and a naturally athletic build. He's wearing a white button-down shirt, open at the top, a navy suit jacket, jeans and a very cool pair of well-worn brown suede wingtips. The whole getup looks completely effortless.

Susie waves him towards the coffee machine. He turns and looks at me, straight in the eyes, and lifts his hand. At exactly the same time, Derek the Manager comes waltzing by. I glance back at good-looking guy; I want to stop and chat, it's not often I fancy someone, but he's gone. When I turn back, Derek has passed me by and has already gone into his office and slammed the door shut.

I hurry down the hall and turn the handle to his office to go on in, but it's locked. It's never locked. He prides himself on his open-door policy, literally.

Derek is shouting. I check no one is watching me, crouch down and peer through the keyhole. Man, is he angry. He's pacing, red-faced, lots of gesticulating. I put my ear to the door. Hear bits and pieces. "I can't," "not right," "bullshit." That sort of thing.

I've never liked him, it feels good to see him so angry.

"No," he shouts. "Of course I know Dora is dead."

I take a couple of steps back. He said Dora. He said dead. How does he know? *What* does he know? Who is he talking to?

"Yes," I hear him shout. "I've got the damn address." He writes something down on top of a stack of Post-it notes.

Inside his office, it goes quiet. Through the keyhole, I see him slam down the phone and look in disbelief as he kicks the hell out of the beanbag the staff bought him as a Christmas gag gift. He stops, takes a breath, his shoulders low, his head stooped. He stands by the window, his back to me, shaking his head. Then he turns around, rips off the top Post-it note and shoves it in his pocket. He walks towards the door and throws it open. I jump to my feet.

We're standing face to face. Does he know I was listening?

"Persy?"

I step back, caught off guard. "Sorry. I hoped we could have a word."

He doesn't move, just stands there, his body sending the message that there isn't a hope in hell I'm getting into his office. "Have you been waiting long?"

I shake my head. "Just arrived."

He raises an eyebrow. "Good. Great," he says. "But I'm afraid I'm on my way out." He steps into the hall and locks his office door. When he turns, I spot the little Post-it note sticking out of the top of his pocket. There's a number on it, 27 something. "My uncle. Just died," he says. "I have to leave."

"I'm so sorry," I say, following him up the hall. He's lying.

"Me too." He strides ahead of me. "We can meet this afternoon. Call Susie." And he's gone.

I wait in the corridor. Check my watch. I figure three minutes max and he'll have left the building and be on his way down the drive. I go into the bathroom opposite his office and slip the tools of my trade from my bag. I wait another three minutes, leave the bathroom, check the corridor in both directions, and with a few quick manoeuvres I'm inside his office and locking the door behind me. I'm in my element; my heartbeat slows, and I'm ready to do what I do best. Spy.

From the window, I see his fancy BMW heading north, up towards Combe Down. The car is new and has to be worth over £50K. How can he afford that? I know his salary; it's not enough for that sort of lifestyle. Where is he getting his money?

At his desk, his screen is still up; he hasn't logged out – rookie mistake. I grab the spare USB drive on my keyring and insert it into his computer to download everything he's got. While I wait, I open drawers and go through files. In the bottom drawer is a bottle of whisky, expensive, half gone. It's a Dalmore, the antlers on the front give it away, a King Alexander, has to be worth a couple of hundred pounds. I don't drink whisky, don't like the taste, but Uncle Alfred's got a sixty-year-old Macallan scotch that Marion bought for him, her way of trying to get him out of her house when she's up to no good. So many times he's tried to get me interested and has taught me enough to know when a spirit costs a lot of money.

The rest of his desk is just plain messy. They should've given him a drawer organiser rather than the bean bag. At least it wouldn't have been kicked to death.

From out of nowhere, heavy footsteps are coming my way. I shove myself against the wall; I can't remember if I locked it behind me. If the door opens, I'll hide behind it. It can't be Derek, I would've seen him drive back him. My eyes dart to the car park. His car isn't there.

I hold my breath and clench my fists.

The doorknob turns slowly, and the person on the other side pushes the door as if trying to come in. The door is locked. I wait. The footsteps move away. My head drops, and I force myself to take deep breaths. I need to be better.

With the download complete, I grab the USB drive and shove it in my pocket. I grab the stack of Post-it notes I'd seen him writing on and take it too. I leave.

Susie looks surprised when she sees me walking towards her and mutters something about thinking I'd already left. The logbook is sitting on her desk. All calls into the care home come through her. Whoever Derek was talking to, if they called him instead of him calling them, she'd have written down the name.

"Has Marion called?" I ask. "Would you mind checking?" As she scans the page of calls, I step closer, glance at the names, and try to see what she's written. Since I arrived, only two names have been written down. I point to the last one and give her a knowing smile.

"Is that the good-looking guy? What's his name?"

"No. That's some guy who called and spoke to Derek.

Geraint Williams. Sounded Welsh. I had to make him spell it. Pronounced Gurr-rant. That's how he told me to say it. He was a bit of a jerk, really. Made me feel like an idiot."

I smile. "I hate men who do that."

"Me too." She looks over my shoulder and suddenly sits up straight, tossing her thin hair ever so slightly. It's him again: good-looking guy. I slip my hand in my pocket, make sure that the Post-it notes and the USB drive are still intact, then give Susie a quick wave and head out.

Before the door closes behind me, a man's voice shouts. I spin around.

"Could I ask you a question?" Good-looking has followed me out and is standing in front of me, a warm smile on his face.

Over my shoulder, Susie is having a laugh, making all sorts of rude gestures. Who knew there were so many referring to sex?

"I assume you live here?" His grin is mischievous, his eyes are sparkling, and he seems kind of nervous. His accent is from the North, maybe Lancashire? I took a linguistics class once; they used the word rhoticity, something about the letter 'R' and if it's audible or not. His is. Mine isn't.

"I do," I say. "In fact, I really shouldn't be out here now, but I needed a break. Too many parties, too much socialising. You should try it."

"I'm in," he says. "Name the day."

We both laugh awkwardly, and then there's an odd kind of quiet, like neither one of us knows what to do next.

"Susie said you volunteer here and your mother Marion donates money?"

I want to scream, *she's never been a real mother!* But I don't. It would reveal more about me than it does about her.

"I was just wondering if maybe you'd have some time. To chat about the place. It's my aunt, you know…"

"Do you want to know anything specific?"

"To tell you the truth, I'm winging it, coming here today. She really can't be on her own anymore, especially as her place has stairs and she needs a stick. Plus, she's isolated, lives in a small cottage down a road that's almost impossible to drive down, and I'm too far away to check up on her. If she fell, it could be days before anyone would notice. So, I think she needs somewhere but I'm not really sure what I'm looking for."

I can hear Marion's I'm-so-damn-clever voice in my head. *Well, if you don't know what you're looking for, there isn't any reason to be here, is there?* The thought takes me by surprise; unsettles me. Are we more similar than I care to admit?

I smile. "I think it's best to just get a feel for a place. Do exactly what you're doing, check a few options out." His eyes don't leave my face. "Talk to some of the residents. Ask the receptionist for a couple of names."

"That's a good idea. Thank you. What about you, would you want to move in here? If you were older?"

"That's a good question. I hadn't ever thought about it." Which is a lie. Of course I've thought about it. It's a permanent cruise for me. I'll sail the world, forever.

"You're smiling," he says.

This happens to me a lot. I get caught up in my thoughts, and reality disappears.

"Sorry. Sure, I'd come here, why not? But listen, right now, I've got to go. Maybe another time?"

"Coffee, lunch, dinner?" His confidence is disarming.

"Susie will give you my number. We can figure it out."

"Great. And I'm Andrew," he says with a grin. "Andrew Cooke."

I hurry away, and he stands by the door, watching. It feels nice. When I was a kid heading back to boarding school,

Marion never waited or watched. And because she wasn't sticking around, she wouldn't let Uncle Alfred either.

I make a promise to myself. If ever I have kids, I'll never walk away from them like that. I'll wait, and I'll wave, and my feet will stay rooted to the ground to make sure if they turn around, I'll be there, watching, showing how much I care. Snow, rain, a category-seven hurricane: I won't give a damn; I'll stay.

SIX

Uncle Alfred calls. "Just checking in."

"I'm leaving the care home."

"Nothing to report, then?"

We both know what he really wants to hear. That the disappearance of Dora won't come back to the Adelard family. He won't ask me outright if it's all okay; he doesn't have the capacity to say, 'Hey, Persy, have they any idea at that geriatric centre that Marion's a monster?' We have a silent agreement, years in the making, to avoid saying the truth out loud. It's a complicated dance, our thoughts working together in unison, never actually saying too much. What is the dance he does with Marion? It's too tricky to tell.

I remember, a few years ago, finding a box with an old newspaper inside and some old photos. Snaps of the three of us. Me with Marion or Uncle Alfred. Outside the Musée de l'Orangerie in Paris on my fifteenth birthday. Me skating on the ice rink in Manhattan when we'd gone there one Christmas. Holidays, birthdays, special events. But why had she hidden them under the bed like the photos were a nasty secret? So, I took them, cut my face out, then put them back, and waited for her reaction. Nothing. Maybe she hadn't seen them, but I'd bet a million bucks she had and refused to give me the pleasure of her telling me she knew what I'd done.

The memory of that moment spooks me and splinters of anxiety appear out of nowhere. I quickly pull into the side of the road, get out, and lean against the car, dipping my head, taking in deep breaths, and doing exactly what the last doctor told me to do when this bad feeling takes over me. The harsh contrast of the cold and rain against my skin feels good, and the air expands my lungs, and, bit by bit, the nausea slips away.

I don't want to go home.

The Post-it notes I'd stolen from Derek's office are tucked inside my pocket and I pray there's something on them that will give me something to do. Sure, I write little notes to myself all the time, usually a reminder: 'buy some bread' or 'go to the post office' or 'five pounds heavier', but I don't rip them from the pad then kick the shit out of my furniture. Purpose has returned. I jump back in the car, grab a pen, and gently shadow over the indents left by his writing.

27 Laycock Drive, Tetherton.

Tetherton is known as the bully area of the city. I've never been there, but most of the crime reported in the local rag, like petty theft and drugs, occurs there. I think it's about time for me to visit and see for myself.

I google the exact address, zoom in on the picture. A run-of-the-mill, nothing-special, semi-detached house in a row of other exactly-the-same houses. Maybe Derek was telling the truth. Maybe his uncle really is sick and this is where he lives. The thought disappoints me; I need to be on the trail of something.

I log into the land registry, enter the address and wait for the details of ownership to pop up.

The small, luminous screen shows me the name of the

owner and for a second I have an out-of-body experience because it can't be possible. A surge of nausea ripples through my stomach and that light-headed feeling I'd just got rid of comes back with a vengeance.

The owner of the property is Dora Haslea.

It's not possible. I have to be wrong. I check the dates, thinking the information might be years old and out of date. It isn't. The information on the screen was last updated three months ago.

There's no mistake. Dora owns the house, which means she had assets. This doesn't make sense. Meadow Bank is a care home for people who don't have enough money to pay for themselves.

Something is wrong. This is wrong.

Could it be that the house is worth nothing? Is this the reason behind what's happening here? Perhaps the value of the place is below the threshold for financial assistance. Maybe it is located on a fault line, and there's a possibility that the ground might open up and swallow it, so it's worthless.

I do a quick price check on Zoopla. The house right next door, the one attached to Dora's, sold two months ago for £400K.

I want to call Uncle Alfred, tell him we have a problem, but what could I say that wouldn't push him to an early grave? *Hey, Uncle Alfred, guess what. Dora owns a house. Which means she has money and someone somewhere will want it. And the first thing they'll do is dig really deep to find out what happened to her in the hope she really is dead so they can sell her home and grab the cash?*

With the address on my satnav, I navigate through winding roads and tall trees, and I finally arrive at her neighbourhood. The houses are all identical, with matching gardens and no obvious differences between one street and the next. Everything is too perfect, too uniform. It's like a carefully constructed replica of a town with no individuality or character.

I spot Derek's sleek BMW, check the number of the house where he's parked and see he's outside Dora's house. I slow down, look around and find a place to park that isn't in his direct line of sight if he comes out or looks through the window.

I grab my camera, attach the zoom, make a few adjustments, and start clicking away.

Her house has white net curtains that look clean and well-maintained. The front door is painted dark green with no nicks or scratches, like it's only just been painted. The front garden, with its small patch of grass, is regularly mown, with the mower marks clearly visible. The roof looks uniform and in good condition, without any patchwork. The place has been well taken care of, even though she's not living there.

I spot a couple of kids coming towards me, kicking a football from one side of the road to the other. The ball hits a car; the alarm goes off; they run off screaming and laughing. Derek comes out of the house, checking the street as if to make sure the car is not his. Another man comes out of a different house and looks out onto the street. The neighbour lifts up his keys, points them at a car parked behind Derek's, and the alarm stops. He walks down his path, wanders around the car, satisfied that nothing is wrong, and then goes back in and closes his front door.

Derek doesn't go back in. He just stands there, turns around, and is clearly talking to someone inside the house. I can't see who it is.

Derek is coming out of Dora's house.

I train the zoom on his face and start clicking. He's holding something in his hand. It's flat and white. An envelope? A cheque? He walks down the path, shoulders back, confident stride, and glances up and down the street as if unfamiliar with where he is. He slips into his car and drives away.

Another man comes out of Dora's house. He goes to the corner of the lawn, grabs something, and then pushes it around the back of the house – a lawnmower.

I need to talk to him to find out what's going on.

I start to get out of the car, then stop myself. It's too soon. I don't have a plan.

The man comes back around, and he's holding a chair. No, not a chair. I mean, it's a chair, but the place where you sit isn't on it. You'd fall through the hole if you tried. He disappears again and comes back with a box – a toolkit, for sure. He's taking the chair apart. He's going to fix it. He leaves again and comes back with three other chairs, all with the seat missing. He sets a tarp on the ground, puts the chairs and toolkit on top, and sits down.

I know how I can handle this.

The phone rings. It's Scooter. "If something is wrong, you need to tell me."

"Why are you whispering?"

"I'm not whispering," I whisper.

"You're whispering, but I don't care. Nothing is wrong. Did you look at the emails I sent?"

"No. I didn't know you'd sent any."

"Then look. It's your parents."

Excitement washes over me. The moment of anticipation when it's me and him, working together, searching for something important enough to change a life.

"I'll stay on the phone," he says. "Put me on speaker. Take a look."

The man in the garden of Dora's house is settled into his work. He's not going anywhere.

I open my emails and click on the link he's sent. Right in front of me is a photo of two really happy people. They are laughing, holding hands, standing on a beach. It has to be summer. All around them are people in swimwear lounging on towels on the sand, under umbrellas, their bodies glistening in the sun. Mum and Dad are not in swimwear. She's wearing a white floaty maxi dress with thin straps and a hat with a wide brim to shield her face from the sun. He's in a polo shirt, pale blue, and shorts to the knees, the sort you can swim in. Their feet are bare.

"Talk to me," Scooter says.

I take a quick look at Dora's house. The man has a hammer in his hand, bashing some nails into one of the chairs.

I make the photo on my screen larger. Mum's wavy hair looks a little dry and is a dusty fading red. My wavy hair looks a little dry, and it's a brighter red, but it will fade. I smile to myself; using the word Mum, it's a bit premature, but getting into character, why not.

Her eyes are blue, unusual for redheads; it's one of the rarest colour combinations of all human beings. My eyes are blue. The similarities are uncanny.

At a guess, I'd put her height at around 5'9". I'm 5'10". When I'm in heels, standing next to an average-sized person, I look quite tall.

Last, she's smiling, and her hair is down, not up.

When I'm happy, I leave my hair down, too. When we meet, I make a mental note to ask her if she lets her hair down when she's happy. I giggle to myself. I've just said *when* I meet her, not *if*. I think about Scooter. I really want him to be here with me when we both find out the truth.

"Persy, are you there?"

"Yes, I'm looking at them. Give me a few seconds." The man in Dora's garden is holding onto something in his teeth. I think it's the nails he's hammering into the chairs.

I study Dad. Spot the slight gap in his front teeth.

I have a slight gap in my front teeth.

Not only are my maybe Mum and Dad still alive, but also still together, which means they value loyalty, just like me. I think guiltily about my conversation with Roger the Dodger about Marion's dementia; that wasn't too loyal to Marion. I feel bad. But I was loyal to Uncle Alfred. I feel better.

"It's them," I say with a catch in my voice. "You really think it's them."

It's not them. Marion's ability to deceive is stronger than my or Scooter's ability to detect. I'm sure of that. Like all the other maybe parents, we'll find that out, but for him, for me, I need to believe.

"I know," Scooter says. "That's what I've been telling you. Proof of the pudding, as you Brits like to say. I always thought that was a weird kind of saying. Why would you eat something if you're not sure what it is? But then you eat weird stuff anyway. What's that weird thing, hagget?"

"Haggis," I say.

"That's the one," he says.

SEVEN

The man is still in Dora's garden, although now he's lying on his back, his hands under his head like it's sunny outside. It's not. It's cold and miserable. He doesn't move. Is he asleep?

I take my hair out of the ponytail and tussle it so it's falling to my shoulders, just like Mum's. I put on some lipstick and a touch of mascara. I grab the clipboard that I keep in the back of the car. With a clipboard in your hand, you can fool anyone.

I can't stop thinking about Mum and Dad. What on earth would they feel if they knew what I was doing? I bet it would make Mum laugh. Dad would probably be concerned: is this the sort of thing our daughter should be getting involved with? I can even hear his voice. It's deep and a bit monotone, sort of Jeremy Irons. But not as Scar; Dad certainly isn't evil.

The man is now standing up and going into the house. I wait. Hear the front door shut behind him.

I walk up the path surrounded by the smell of newly cut grass, my clipboard tucked under my arm, and ring the doorbell. A loud, aggressive bark comes from inside. How come I hadn't spotted there was a dog before? I step back. I like huge dogs, but this one sounds angry or hungry or maybe even ready to kill.

The man opens the door. Up close, he's got long hair in a ponytail, mid-forties, clean-shaven, and a T-shirt stretched over his large belly. If pressed, I wouldn't be able to explain it, but something about him doesn't seem quite right.

The dog has stopped barking and is behind a little wooden gate that it seems to be trying to chew through.

"I'm looking for a Mrs Dora Haslea?"

"Why?" He folds his arms and puffs out his chest.

I can work with this. It happens every other day in my line of business. "We did some work on the house. She never paid."

"I'm not paying." His chest puffs out even more. "*She* owns it. I don't have to pay a thing. And what has she had done? I've been here two years; I painted the door. I keep the garden nice. She hasn't done a damn thing. If anything, she owes me."

I flip some pages on my clipboard. Every page is in the same format: Excel spreadsheets with names and addresses to make it look kosher.

"Okay. Here we go. The roof." I smile up at him. "Two and a half years ago. You're right, and it was before your time."

"Told you so."

I look at the dog. "What a beautiful animal. What breed is it?"

"Bulldog crossed with a husky." He turns to glance back at it, and I see his face soften into a smile. The dog must see it, too, because it wiggles its bottom, moves back a bit and sits. It has a dark patch over one eye, and one of its ears is forward.

"He's so cute," I say. "What's he called?"

"Rocket."

I laugh out loud. "That's a great name. Anyway, I'm sorry to have disturbed you. If you can let me have the owner's contact number, I'll go directly to them."

"It's not them; it's her. And I don't have it," he says. "I just go through her agent."

"Her agent?"

"Hold on a second." He steps over the gate that's holding the dog back. The dog looks at me, winks, I swear it, then follows him out of sight.

When the guy comes back, there's a card in his hand. "Here you go. I pay the rent to this new company. Before, it was easy. Then the lawyer left a message on my phone, saying I couldn't pay him cash anymore; I had to pay it to a new company. I told him straight that ain't happening without some real paperwork."

"Smart," I say. "A lot of people get scammed that way."

"Shame you weren't here half an hour or so ago. You would've seen him. I told him straight. I want legal documents." He starts to laugh. "That made him jump. When I said that to him on the phone, he got here quicker than greased lightning."

"Good for you," I say.

"You want to see the documents?"

"Sure," I say, and he disappears again.

I look at the business card he handed me. Derek Pringle, Xanadu Holdings. Lawyer. It's one and the same. Derek Pringle, the manager of the care home. Now it's Derek the Lawyer. Who will he be next? Derek the Chef? Derek the Postman?

He comes back with a bundle of papers in his hand. On the front is the name Geraint Williams.

"Your name is Geraint?" I try to pronounce it exactly the way he told Susie at reception when he called the care home.

"You've gotta be one of the first people in a long time who knows how to say it." He beams with pride as if it's the two of us together. "Welsh. Means 'old man'."

"You don't look like an old man." I laugh. He likes what I just said. I can read it on his face. I flick through the documents and spot Derek's name again on the last page. There's an account number right under it. "You know what," I say, "I'm going to contact the lawyer directly." I snap a photo of the document.

"Where are you off to now? You want to come in and have a cup of tea?"

"I wish I could. I'm on the clock. Another time?"

"Any time you like. Just come on round. I'm here all day, every day. On benefits. I hurt my back. Can hardly move." I think about him moving the mower across the lawn and carrying the chairs onto the lawn. Bad back, my ass.

"You know what," I say. "Maybe I will come back. Thank you."

I turn away and walk back down the path, knowing his eyes are still on me. At the end of the path, I turn around and wave. He grins, nods, then steps back into the house. The dog's face is peeping out from under the net curtains.

I get into my car and drive away.

I pull into the car park of a small pub, log into my computer, get into Companies House and insert the name of Xanadu, the company Derek had written on the card the guy gave me. It pops up on the screen. In business for three years. Real estate. One director: Derek.

I log into the care home website and bring up Derek's profile. He was appointed manager ten years ago. I think about his fancy BMW. Is this his con? He secretly takes people into the care home who actually have money and then makes sure he takes control of it. He has to believe Dora is dead, and he's cleaning things up. Right about now, I bet he's putting ownership of the house into his name.

And nobody is checking.

Which means that, dead or alive, he's going to get her money.

I call the care home and ask for Derek, and Susie puts me right through. "Gosh, Derek, sorry, I thought I'd leave a message. You're back already. How is your uncle?"

"Fine. Thanks for asking."

"It must've been a shock – the look on your face when I saw you! And you were in such a hurry. The news must have been so awful for you." Putting him on the spot like this feels good.

"It was, Persy. Getting news like that, someone dying, it's never nice."

"How old was he?"

"Seventy," he says without missing a beat. "Quite young nowadays." I hear a well-rehearsed sigh. "But there you are. Now. I know you didn't call to talk about my uncle. What can I do for you?"

"I need some of your time. Are you free now?"

"I'm not sure I—"

"It's about Marion's donations."

"Aah," he says, his words now clipped and professional. "Of course. Later this afternoon?"

"I'm actually in the area. Now would be great."

"Then now it is," he answers.

I drive down to the care home with the radio on, the Beatles singing 'Here Comes the Sun'. Marion calls. I stare at her name on my phone. What will Mum and Dad make of her? They would've known her back in the day; she probably told them they weren't doing a very good job, but now, what would they think? I'd bet they won't like her.

I answer the phone with that burst of optimism typical of someone who believes they have some leverage.

"Persy here," I say, my voice light and airy. She hates the name Persy. She always corrects me. Persephone. I'm giving her the gift of insulting me. *Go ahead, Marion Adelard*, I tell myself, *knock yourself out.*

"Who in God's name gave you the authority to discuss my mental health with my lawyer?"

EIGHT

My heart is racing as I hear the familiar click of the phone slamming down. Marion's volatile emotions always catch me off guard. It's like the weather in England. Wait five minutes and it's bound to change.

I have to call Uncle Alfred, but I don't want to because I didn't tell him that I was going to call Roger to discuss Marion's dementia. He'll be disappointed in me for not asking him first, but I need to speak to him because I don't know what Marion may or may not have told him.

"Marion just called," I say.

"Good. Did she tell you we had a wonderful morning?" Uncle Alfred sounds upbeat, and if he knows Marion called to shout at me, he's not giving it away.

"A wonderful morning?" I repeat.

"Marion and I walked to the mausoleum; you remember that place? I don't think you've been there since you were a child. Scared to death of it, you were. You wouldn't even step inside the door. You used to stand outside in those little flip-flops of yours. Remember them? They were pink, I think. I wonder what happened to them. But no matter, both Marion and I found it quite peaceful."

"I'm glad you had a nice morning. But Marion wasn't calling to mention your walk. She called me because she was furious."

"Because?"

I take a breath. "I called Roger."

"Roger the Dodger?"

"Yep," I say. "I was worried at some of the things Marion was saying."

"Really? Like what?"

I can't bring myself to tell him that Marion was trying to give the impression that it was him who killed Dora.

"That's not important. The important thing is that she's been saying some odd things, and I need to make sure that if she says the wrong thing at the wrong time to the wrong person, they won't get the wrong impression. Especially right now, with all that's been happening with Dora."

"I see," he says, but his voice tells me he doesn't.

"I'm trying to protect her. Protect us. That's all."

"That explains why she was a tad angry with me too."

He's doing his doublespeak. A tad angry tells me she was probably going insane, and he's trying to downplay it.

"What did she say?"

"It's not important." He's using my tack, pushing my concerns away. Did I learn everything from him? "Suffice to say, Persy, I'd lay low for a few days if I were you. There's no stopping her when she has a bee in her bonnet."

She called him and went nuts; his words confirmed it. "I'm sorry," I say. "I just wanted to get ahead of a potential problem."

"You know, we sat on the marble steps. I made a couple of sandwiches; it was marvellous."

Why is he talking about the damn mausoleum? I rub my forehead with my hand, trying to push away the headache this conversation will create. Why can't he tell me exactly what she said? And why mention that damn place. I hated it. Marion said it was a place for the dead, and when I was a kid, all I could think about for months was all of the ghosts inside, wandering around, all bumping into each other, and there wasn't a hope in hell I was going to let any of them bump into me.

"Anyway," he says. "I will let you go because your work is very important. Far be it from me to get in the way of a talented young woman doing a very serious and responsible job."

Why is he buttering me up? He used to say that sort of thing when I was at boarding school. Marion would be in the car watching us as usual; he'd start off saying something nice, then tell me that Marion had booked the two of them on a cruise for three months during the summer holidays, so I had to stay at the school because there was nowhere else for me to go. At least he bothered to tell me. Marion would've just buggered off.

"Are you two going somewhere?" I ask, the trigger of that memory making me ask the obvious question.

He laughs. He used to do that, too. "My dear Persy, why would you think that?"

"Are you?"

"No plans to travel anywhere. Those days spent zig-zagging across the globe are behind us."

I think he's lying, but I know him well enough to know that once he decides not to tell me something, he won't change his mind.

"I'm sorry about what I did. Calling Roger. I bet Marion chewed your ear off."

"What a delightful expression. Although nibbling might better suit."

I laugh out loud. "What about peck? She was pecking your ear off."

He's laughing now, too, and I'm glad. "Perfect," he says.

"She was pecking my ear off. Although, I suggest, in the future, we strategise before any further action is taken?"

He's telling me I shouldn't have spoken to Roger without checking it with him, and I think he's right. "Agreed," I say.

"So, Persy. Brighten my day. What is going on with you?"

"You remember Scooter, my friend from the US?"

"Ex-CIA, if I remember?"

"Exactly. Well, he thinks he might have found my biological parents."

There's a pause. "Do you think that's wise, Persy? Have you told Marion?"

"I haven't. Should I?"

"You decide," he says. "Maybe leave it for a few days."

"Because?"

"Good question," he says and I hear his intake of breath. "Let her get over the situation with Roger."

I'm not sure if I should push him. I've tried before and all it's done is to make him upset and the image of his frail face comes into my head. Part of me aches to send over the photo Scooter sent me, to get his reaction, to see if it squeezes some new information out of him, but I toss the idea away. I've been at this for decades. Nothing is going to change.

"Okay," I say.

The large, white sign with bold letters proclaiming 'Care Home' looms in the distance, standing tall against the dull grey sky. I park and walk inside as the smell of antiseptic and aging hits me. My heart races with a mix of anticipation and anxiety as I prepare to meet Derek to figure out how best to handle him.

Susie is at reception. We toss a couple of sentences from one to the other, and then I head down to Derek's office. I slow down before I get to the door to give myself time to rehearse what I need to say, and before I know it, I'm sitting across from him at the desk I ransacked just a few hours before.

"So sorry about your uncle." I watch him.

"I know. Awful. Terrible thing." He manages to look sad. I mean, really down. It's a masterclass in acting. Will he look like this when I prove how he scammed Dora? I want to spell it out to him, here and now, see the change in his snaky eyes. But it's too early. Marion is the priority. It is best to wait until the story of Dora has long been forgotten.

"Thanks for seeing me," I say. "Much appreciated."

"I think I know what you want to talk about." His face is serious. "Dora's disappearance."

His words hit me like a bolt of lightning. He's taken the wind out of my sails. I don't like it. I'm left speechless. If *I* were scamming some older woman and I'd just been up to their house to steal even more money, I wouldn't immediately bring the name up. I don't understand. Is it possible I've got this wrong?

"Dora?" I ask, keeping my voice nice and steady. I stare at him, search for a darting of the eyes, an uncomfortable swallow, a covering of the mouth by his lying fingers, but there's nothing. Cool as a damn cucumber.

He says, "Marion must be very worried." I swear he's watching me the way I was watching him. What's going on?

"How do you mean?" I ask.

"Marion was particularly close to Dora." He tilts his head, eyes set on mine. "And Dora was very close to her. She would've done anything for Marion." He runs his hand through his hair and flashes me a quick grin. It's like the tables have turned, but I don't know what they are. "Please let Marion know that I will not rest until we find out exactly what happened to Dora." His chair creaks softly as he leans back.

I want to swallow, but I mustn't. "I'll tell her of your concern." There's a slight wobble in my voice. I clear my throat, sit up, and lean forward. "Derek, the real reason I am here is to discuss Marion and her donations."

The smirk disappears from his face. "Is there a problem?"

It feels good to have him on his back foot. "Maybe," I say.

"She isn't going to pull her donations, surely? We have an agreement." He's gone a bit pale.

"Not yet. No. I'm not here to discuss what may or may not happen in future. It's something else. I'm sorry. Marion has dementia." The look on his face makes me think he truly has no idea. "It was diagnosed a couple of years ago, but Uncle Alfred and I decided not to mention it. To keep it private."

Now he's frowning like he doesn't know what to make of this news. I guess he's trying to figure out what angle to take and how to keep the money rolling despite Marion being sick. "I'm… um… sorry, I didn't know."

I look down at my lap, then look back up, making sure the picture of a daughter saddened by this awful news is clear for him to see. "At first, I thought she was just saying odd things because she was a little forgetful. It was Uncle Alfred who realised there was more to it."

"Saying odd things?"

He knows something; it's written all over his face. Maybe a memory, a little event that's happened in the past and now that I've mentioned dementia, he's putting two and two together. This is precisely what I need him to do.

"She's said something unusual to you?"

"A few weeks ago. She was saying the names of old patients. People who have long gone."

My pulse is racing. Was she talking about the other victims? Could there be more than the three I know about? It's too horrible to think about.

His cell phone buzzing breaks through the silence, causing him to jerk suddenly. He grabs it, answers it, and tries to act nonchalant as he mutters something about calling the person on the other end back, but his voice sounds guarded and uncertain. He opens a drawer in his desk and shoves the phone inside. Why is he being so secretive?

"Look," I say briskly. "I won't take any more of your time. I just wanted to let you know that I will be taking over more of our family's financial aspects. And with Marion's dementia, can you just let your staff know that if she says anything odd, to disregard it? And maybe let me know. It would help me get a grip on how serious this whole thing is."

"She was speaking German," he says.

I spit out a laugh. "She what?"

"German. When she was talking about the patients."

"Marion doesn't speak German." I don't know many of the signs of dementia, but I'm pretty sure the spontaneous ability to speak a foreign language isn't one of them.

He must've seen my disbelief because he answers quickly, with a kind of apology in his words. "You know what, forget it. Maybe I misheard. Who knows? Don't let it worry you."

"What about Susie? She sees Marion whenever she comes in. Has she mentioned anything?"

He's got a smirk on his face. "Like speaking in tongues?" He's trying to be funny, but it's way off the mark.

"I'm sorry?" I say.

"Apologies, Persy. Gallows humour. It's part of the job. It's how we deal with difficult situations."

"Really," I say in a way that he has to see I'm pissed off with the remark. I stand up. He stands up, too.

I take on a tone of quiet authority. "Could you ask Susie? *Now?*"

"Now?" Being told what to do isn't something he likes.

"Is it a problem?" I pause for effect. "Given the extent of Marion's donations, you would want to make sure she's protected from embarrassment."

He doesn't know what to say.

"I'll stay here," I say. "Or should I follow you?"

"Fine, fine. No problem. Whatever you want." He marches off with uppity little steps.

I stand by the door and watch him go. As soon as he turns the corner and is out of sight, I hurry round to the other side of his desk, grab the phone he put in the drawer and stuff it into my pocket. My bag is on the floor, and I kick it hard enough that it scoots behind the leg of the chair. I nip across the hall into the bathroom. I sync his phone to mine, flush the toilet and head back out, his phone tucked into my jacket pocket.

Derek is sitting behind his desk. Alone. I make a point of looking around. "Where is Susie?"

His phone vibrates in my pocket.

He must hear it because I can hear it, and I'm only a few feet away from him. He raises his eyebrows as if he thinks it's my phone and he's okay if I need to answer it. "It's not important," I say. "I'll get it later."

He motions for me to sit down. "Vera fell. Susie is helping her. But I asked Susie if she knew of anyone saying anything about Marion being confused or saying odd things, and she said absolutely not. I asked her to keep an eye out and explained what you told me." He nods his head towards me. "And, of course, at the next staff meeting, I'll mention it. With discretion. We'll keep on top of this."

"And you'll let me know of any concerns."

"Of course." He steers me out of his office and up the hall.

"My bag," I say. "I'll be right back." I hurry back into his office, slip his phone back into the drawer, grab the bag from behind the garbage bin, and head into the car park.

I ease back into my car, keeping my eyes on the care home, looking through the window to see if Derek is inside, watching me. He's not. He's gone. I pull out of the home, take a right, drive less than a mile, and then pull into the side of the road. I call Uncle Alfred.

"Does Marion speak German?" I say without missing a beat.

There's the briefest of pauses. "Why would she speak German?" His voice sounds weird. And that's not an answer. A yes or no would've done it.

"No reason. Something Derek said. If she did, I think I would've known, right?"

"Absurd," he says. "She was probably talking about music. She mentioned Bach or Beethoven or even Schumann. Derek's knowledge of culture has often struck me as rather pedestrian. Maybe one day she was asking if they had some sauerkraut to go with her meal." He starts to laugh. "Could've been anything."

He's right. And maybe she does speak some German; she's a well-educated woman who's travelled the world. I speak some French and have never used it. Uncle Alfred speaks Latin, and I've never heard a word. As for Derek, he speaks fluent bullshit.

NINE

I sit in my flat, drumming my fingers on the desk as the USB drive with the contents of Derek's computer is downloaded onto mine. It's seventy per cent done.

I hate waiting when you know something will take less than thirty minutes. There is not enough time to start something new or to take a nap. I stretch, walk to the window, and look out, invisible to the tourists and the locals who meander right in front of me. Watching without being watched is reassuring.

The owners of Le Bocage walk by, their dog on a lead. It's a local interiors place that's in the top one hundred in the country. They sell their services, furniture, china, and wine and are trying out a coffee shop. They have some of the best pastries in town. The place is perfect. You can wander around, buy something, eat, and drink; it's got it all, and their Georgian building is gorgeous. I check my screen for the millionth time: all done. I snap the laptop shut, shove everything in my bag, and head to Le Bocage. I do my best work in public spaces.

Fifteen minutes later, I'm sitting on the first floor, coffee in my hand and pain au chocolat in my mouth. It's perfect. I open my laptop with a quick crack of the knuckles and a long, deep breath. It's time to figure out who Derek is.

It takes less than a minute to get a handle on him: impatient, disorganised, and undisciplined. I've seen it too many times before. Documents with random names, no organisation, no dates, and a complete lack of knowledge about how the computer could work for him. The screen is packed to the brim with documents, some overlapping others. I click away. Some files have nothing in them. One of the files he's named 'Think About'. Inside are random bits of information that must've piqued his interest at some time or another. Healthy eating habits; clothes to wear to keep warm when it's raining; an article about Siberia. Another file he's called 'Aspirational'. I click into this just for the heck of it. Photos of boats; tall, long-legged blonde women (he's under 5'6"); and, best of all, pictures of castles. Castle upon castle upon castle. I close the file, tell myself to go through my own computer at some time to see what it says about me.

An hour later, I've gone through maybe fifty per cent and I've found nothing. I order another coffee and another pastry and switch to his emails. They're even worse. He can't decide how to sign off. 'L8ter'; 'G2G, Bye'; even 'Fare thee well'. You couldn't make this crap up. Even better, he's got one folder that's titled 'Passwords' and inside is exactly what you'd expect of the name. Now he's an open book.

I'm bored, need to take another tack, decide to investigate the emails based on the size of the document and the attachments. This is more interesting, throwing up insurance policies, lawsuits (one of the patients claimed the home was keeping her children from visiting – sadly, I doubt that was the case) and several reports from the Care Quality Commission.

How would I get tripped up if someone was looking at me? Nah, that doesn't work. I'm meticulous. The stuff you'd find out about me would be trivial. My toothpaste; how I like my coffee; maybe a list of people I knew at school or university. I've been well trained. Dead bodies, remember?

I wonder if he knows about deleted files? A trick of the trade. People delete files but emails, attachments, it's easy to forget that even when you delete them, they hang around. When I was a kid, I used to keep a diary. It wasn't every day, it was more about specific events: a showreel of highlights of the crappy things Marion did to me. Like restricting food because I was getting too chubby, or taping my mouth shut when I was too loud. I'd told a lie. To this day, I won't even go swimming unless the water is up to thirty-seven degrees. Because Marion was a snoop, I'd write my thoughts in an email and send it to myself, and then I'd delete it. There it would sit, in the deleted file, which Marion had never considered looking into.

I click on 'deleted' and then 'attachments'. Then I spot it: the Excel document labelled 'investments'. Bingo.

The spreadsheet is easy to read, standard, and nothing sexy. It has four columns: name, amount, code, and ID.

The names column is easy. It's a list of insurance companies.

The amounts are just as easy – ranging from £50K to £150K.

The code section has all the same two letters. LI. I don't know what that means.

The last column, ID, combines letters and numbers, each not exceeding seven digits. It could be some code, but I'm not sure. My gut tells me if it is code, it would have to be pretty rudimentary. Given that Derek inserted it, my sense tells me to ask a kid in elementary school to figure out the code, and they'd get it immediately.

I download the spreadsheet.

I sort the insurance companies so they now sit in alphabetical order. One company dominates. It's the one Marion uses. They're big. I know them pretty well; they're on speed dial and handle our cars, homes, furniture, and even personal liability. Our account is significant, and our dedicated agent cares for everything. He's good, goes by the book, and is dedicated enough to make sure he doesn't give out any information he's not supposed to. I take a sip of my coffee. He'll give me *something*, I'm sure of it.

I call him.

After we chat about this and that for a couple of minutes, I ask him how much it'll cost to insure if I want to buy a Bentley Flying Spur for Uncle Alfred. He laughs at the question because he knows Uncle Alfred would never drive it; he even reminds me of the vintage Porsche that sits in the garage year after year without moving an inch.

Eventually, the conversation tails off. "There's another reason I'm calling," I say. "It's about Marion."

"She'd definitely not drive it." He laughs.

"Thank God," I say with a giggle. "But a quick thing, and I'm sorry to have to bring it up, but Marion hasn't been very well. It's early days, but it's dementia."

"Persy, I'm so sorry." The tone of his voice changes immediately.

"Thanks," I say. "We're getting on top of it. I'll be taking over more and more of the financial responsibilities. But that's not why I'm calling. I need your help."

"Anything," he says.

I cross my fingers. "I'm at Marion's now. We were going through some files. She's just gone to bed because, quite frankly, this is exhausting. Anyway, there's a spreadsheet of policies, and I swear I know nothing about them, and she couldn't remember a darn thing either."

"You want to send it to me so I can take a look?"

"That would be great. It was in an email she'd printed, but I don't know where it came from. I want to know if it's important or not. Do you know what I mean?"

"Have you got it there, in front of you?"

"It's here."

"Send it now."

"Hold on… Done," I say.

"Great. Give me fifteen minutes."

I close my laptop and wait. A young couple in their thirties are sitting in the coffee shop a few feet away from me, not talking. He's looking at his phone. Her arms are folded, and she's staring out the window. Neither of them seems happy. I check their hands: wedding rings. What must they think of me, sitting here by myself?

After about ten minutes, he calls back. "Okay," he says. "None of this has to do with Marion. So, you've got nothing to worry about."

"Why would it be on her emails?" I ask, trying to get an answer from him.

"It's to do with the care home. I'm sure you know this already, but thanks to Marion, we now handle all of their insurance needs, too. She was probably sent a copy. She's a trustee, isn't she?"

"Yes. Exactly. She is."

"I really wouldn't worry about it. It's nothing to do with her."

I push a little further. "Got it. So… the code, in the third column, LI, what does that mean?"

"Life Insurance."

I laugh. "Of course. Sometimes I can't believe how stupid I am. And what does the last column, the numbers and letters, mean? I haven't seen anything like that on our insurance."

"The first four letters are references to the policy. I don't know the last three numbers. At a guess, and don't quote me on this, it probably reflects a name coded for confidentiality."

"Got it," I say. "Thank you so much. One question, and I don't want to put you on the spot, but is one of those insurance policies for a Dora Haslea? You must have heard about her in the papers. She's gone missing. When I tell Marion what the spreadsheet is all about, she's bound to ask."

"I can't tell you the details, Persy, but I can confirm that is one of the policies."

"I'll keep my fingers crossed the beneficiary is the care home. Money is tight. I mean, a policy would have a beneficiary, right?"

"Hold on."

I hear the clicking of keys.

"Yep. It's got a beneficiary."

"It's Xanadu, right? That's one of the vehicles I've heard her mention."

"It is," he says, his voice almost a whisper. "You didn't hear it from me."

I put down the phone. I should feel as pleased as punch, but I don't because I know what that slimeball is up to. He's the beneficiary of life insurance, probably those in the care home who have no family and are too vulnerable to disagree with him. It doesn't sit well. How could he do it? And how *does* he do it? Does he sneak into the person's room, close the door, and tell them to 'sign here' as he holds the pen in their trembling hands with the cracked skin?

It doesn't matter, I tell myself. *I've got him. Whatever he has on our family, I've got it covered.*

Out the window of the coffee shop, I spot a familiar face. A man is walking this way. It's him, Andrew – the good-looking guy visiting the care home looking for a place for his aunt. I sit straighter, grab the lipstick from my bag and put some on. He's coming in. I click out of Derek's computer, click into mine, pull up an old spreadsheet and stare at it like the elixir of life is staring back at me.

He comes in. I watch him over the bannister: the set of his shoulders, the comfortable swing of his arms as he wanders towards the counter. He orders a coffee and a pastry, and, suddenly, the guy behind the counter gestures up to my floor and tells him there's space up there to sit. Andrew swings around to follow where he's pointing and sees me sitting there, staring down at him like a prat.

"Persy," he says. "I'll come on up." He smiles at the man behind the counter and bounds towards me like he's pleased to see me.

I shove the laptop into my bag, cross one leg over the other, and try to create an air of composed relaxation. It's not working. I'm grinning like a teenager. He puts his coffee and pastry down, and, suddenly, we're in an awkward hug. When he sits down, I see he's changed his brown suede shoes to blue ones. I don't know what to think about that. Cool? Weird? Musical? Different colours to match different socks?

"Do you come here often?" he quips, then takes a sip of his drink. "Sorry," he says when he wipes his mouth. "Can I get you anything?"

I shake my head. "I'm good."

"My office is just around the corner; I love this place."

"It's handy for me, too. I live pretty close." There's a weird silence, which I feel compelled to fill. "You mentioned your office. What do you do?" Lots of people hold off on asking those kinds of questions because they think it's disrespectful. The years I've spent in America have made me more direct and open. I think that's a good thing.

"Consultant," he says. He gulps down some coffee. "What about you?"

As always, I lie. Following people to uncover fraud is a serious thing, but most people don't understand it and think I'm some kind of government stooge – a bit like being a traffic cop. "I'm an editor," I say.

"So, you work from home?"

I nod. I could tell him about the office in Queen Square and how I follow people and get to know them better than they know themselves, but I don't. Who needs another complication?

"Your job is a lot like mine," I say. "Self-employed, relying on the next gig."

"Exactly."

"What sort of consulting do you do? I hope it's more lucrative than my editing. I'm lucky if I get three jobs a year."

"Business," he says. "I studied accounting." He takes another sip of his coffee.

He's interesting. He avoided the question of what sort of consultant he is and tossed out such a wide explanation it's impossible to know exactly what he does. Business, what doesn't that cover? I toss it aside, a question for another day.

"Have you decided on the home for your aunt?" I ask.

"Not yet," he says. "Probably Meadow Bank, although there's one problem."

"Which is?"

He throws me a mischievous glance. "Your mother Marion Adelard's money. The manager gave me the Annual Report. Without her, I'm not sure it would survive."

"There are always other sources of money. Marion today. Another wealthy benefactor tomorrow. Grants. There are many options as long as the home has a strategy."

"*Does* the home have a strategy?"

"Marion's commitments cover ten years. They'll start looking for alternatives in the next few years, and they know the score."

"Will she honour those commitments?"

He's done his reading. Good for him. "There isn't a legally binding contract. It hasn't been pledged that way, but there's an informal understanding. Which, quite honestly, if she reneged, might or might not stand up in court. But Marion is…" I laugh. "Well, she's many things. But she's a woman of her word. She's in for ten years, for sure."

"Why is that?" he asks. "I mean, why the care home?"

I have to look away. Exactly. Why? Years ago, I asked her the same question. All she answered was, "Well, why wouldn't I?" Conversation over. On a good day, I tell myself she's worried about her own mortality and feels the pain of other elderly people. On a bad day… hell, I don't have to spell it out. Three of them ended up in the pig pen.

"She's always feared getting old," I lie.

"What about Derek? What are your thoughts on him?"

His question catches me by surprise. Until all this happened, I never really gave Derek a second thought besides thinking he was a bit of a slimeball. Andrew's question suggests that he's spotted something off with him already.

I nudge my computer bag under my seat and give a kind of half-grimace, a not-sure kind of face. "I don't know."

"A bit dodgy, if you ask me. Have you seen the BMW he drives?"

I need time to figure Andrew out. He's observant and more into finding out about the home than I'd expect. "He does his job. He knows what he's doing. I haven't heard any complaints."

He sets down his coffee and leans towards me. I'm holding my breath, wondering where the conversation is going. And then, locking eyes with me, he asks, "Are you seeing anyone?"

I burst out laughing. "You're going right there?"

"If you snooze, you lose."

That sort of confidence, I'm not going to lie, it's a turn-on.

"I'm not seeing anyone." I smile, pretend to be coy. "Why are you asking?" The grin on my face is getting wider by the second.

"The waiter downstairs was asking."

I can't help but laugh again. "Clever."

"Then you'll have dinner with me?"

I bite the inside of my cheek, trying to stop him seeing that there isn't anything better I'd like to do. Coming on too strong is never a good thing. I also need to slow this down. I feel a little out of control.

"Is that glimmer in your eyes a yes?"

"Sure," I say. "Why not."

He finishes his coffee and stands up. "I'll call you." Then he kisses me on the cheek and walks away, leaving the scent of Penhaligon's Blenheim Bouquet in the air. I know it well. The first boy to put his hand up my skirt behind the bicycle shed after a chaperoned school dance always wore it. He'd taken it from his dad's bathroom. It's one of the good memories.

He disappears back down the street, and I pack up and leave. I've sat there too long and feel obliged to shove a big tip in the jar by the till. It's pretty cold, but the sun is shining high in the sky, and the people in the streets seem to have smiles, a skip in their step, and a laugh in their eyes. Is that what love does for you? Does it brighten your day?

As soon as I get home, I hear the landline ringing. I check my mobile: five missed calls from Marion. I'm buzzed enough to pick up the phone without any fear whatsoever.

"Yes?" I say.

"Is that Persephone?" Her tone is officious, as though I'm someone of no significance.

"Yes. You know it is."

"Alfred explained the reason you spoke to Roger about my health."

I hold my breath. What did he tell her?

"I had hoped you would have learnt to control your emotions by now. You should not pick up the phone in a panic whenever you feel slightly concerned about my health. It's ridiculous. The next time you feel the compunction to take action regarding my affairs, I suggest you pause, communicate to me those thoughts, and await my response."

Smart thinking, Uncle A. Now Marion thinks I'm worried about her, and it's annoyed her so much that any suspicion about me trying to take control has turned into that ever-so-frequent irritation with her disappointing daughter.

"You're right. It won't happen again." I mentally erase the things I've already said about her dementia to Derek and Susie and the insurance company.

"Good. As long as we understand each other."

"We do."

"Then I'll say goodbye."

"Okay. I'll see you later."

"Why will you see me later?"

She hates colloquialisms; I need to think quicker. "A turn of phrase," I say.

"Good. Because I have an event this afternoon."

"What event?"

"A tea party."

There's no tea party. I would've known – I would've had to have done the shopping.

There's a clinking of what sounds like china in the background.

"A young man is coming around," Marion says.

"What young man?" I ask and immediately feel bad. If she wants to fantasise, why do I need to push it so far? Let her fantasise.

"A policeman."

My stomach drops. "A what?" I say stupidly.

"A policeman, Persephone. Do you have problems with your ears?"

"You're kidding."

Now it's her turn to laugh. "Of the many things you might attribute to me, I believe 'kidding' is not one of them."

"Why on earth is a policeman coming for tea?"

"Why wouldn't a policeman come for tea?"

I should hang up now and move on. These circular conversations only end up one way: with me feeling slightly insane.

"What is his name?" I ask.

"What is *your* name?"

I can't do this. She will outwit me every time. She's more than twice my age, and, in seconds, she reduces me to a child who hasn't yet learnt the ability to think.

"He'll be here at three," she continues. "And I have rather a lot to do. And, quite honestly, at your age, you should have a lot to do, too. Certainly more than asking silly questions." She hangs up.

A therapist once told me that Marion sounded like a narcissist. I wasn't interested in a label. I just needed to know how to cope. She told me that it would be best if I believed that whatever came out of her mouth, truth or lies, was her reality, even though it may not be fact. I still can't grasp what the therapist meant by that.

TEN

I am sitting in my living room and can't stop chewing my nails. It's a habit I thought I'd kicked years ago. My mind is all over the place, torn between Marion's claim about a policeman coming to tea being true or not. The being true side is winning and all I can see is Uncle Alfred and me in the dock, desperately trying to explain that everything that's happened is a complete mistake and Marion has made it all up.

I can't trust Marion.

A little voice tells me I'm overreacting, but that voice is quickly smacked down by a way bigger voice that's screaming at me, telling me not to listen to that dumbass voice who doesn't know anything.

Maybe it's dementia rearing its ugly head, and she's unwittingly stumbling towards the bear pit?

Should I call Uncle Alfred?

No. I don't want to worry him. He'll get anxious, probably hightail it to Marion's, and then she'll slap him down just like she did me.

Why did she say a policeman? She didn't mention the name of a policeman. If it were true, wouldn't she have said something like, I don't know, 'Inspector Bloggs is coming for tea. He's a policeman, you know.'

I tell myself off. Be logical. Rational.

There might be a police officer going to visit Marion.

There might not be a police officer going to visit Marion.

There is only one way to find out. Period. Done. Over and out.

My clone app on Derek's phone dings so loudly that it shocks me out of my thoughts. I hurry to my computer, put on my headphones, and listen in.

It's his bank. Calling about a loan. The woman sounds fed up. The mortgage hasn't been paid. Again. He jumps in and tells her there's nothing to worry about and that he'll have the money in two weeks. The woman's not buying it – it sounds like she's heard it all before. She asks him for specifics and wants to know when they can expect payment because her senior manager will want the details. She tells him she must justify why they are not taking legal action. I like her immediately.

"I'm about to come into some money," he says.

"Could you give me some more information?"

"Inheritance."

"From whom? If you could give me the details, it would be appreciated."

"My grandmother just died." He doesn't even bother to feign sadness.

"And the name of your grandmother?"

"Dora," he says. "Dora Haslea."

I don't want to listen anymore, and I don't want to think about how horrible some humans can be. Another thought overpowers that thought. Derek is sure of himself. Dora's body hasn't been found, but he's telling the woman in the bank that she's dead.

"What was the date of her death?"

My heart stops. What's he going to say?

He clears his throat. "I'm so sorry," he says. "Can you hold on?" Silence, then he's back. "Apologies. We have an emergency here. You have all the information you need." And he hangs up.

I throw the headphones onto my desk, lean back in my chair, and take a deep breath. He has no idea if Dora is dead or not. He's hoping. That's all. And if he doesn't know if she's dead, then he doesn't know her death is connected to Marion. The world, all of a sudden, seems lighter.

I catch sight of the clock on the other side of the room. It's two-thirty. It's nearly time for Marion's tea party.

I shove the chair back, grab a coat and run down the stairs to my car. Real (or imaginary) policeman is (or is not) on his way to Marion's – time to figure it out.

When I open the front door, Marion stands at the end of the corridor. She's confused, does a kind of who-what-why gape, and is speechless for a rare moment.

She usually wears a black turtle-neck sweater and a grey skirt. Today, she's dressed up.

She's wearing a moss-green plaid skirt with an orange stripe and a moss-green turtle neck with a moss-green gilet on top like she's in a photo shoot for Orvis. Around her neck is a vintage Hermes scarf she bought on a trip to Rome. I remember it because it was a bank holiday weekend. I'd come home to find the place empty.

Her hair is swept back off her face. She's got good hair, wavy and thick, and when it's back like that, it looks elegant and effortless. Regal. Like a duchess. In her hand is the 1895 walking stick with the ivory handle, a present from me years ago.

She glances into the drawing room, and when she looks back, her eyes are as black as thunder, her jaw is clenched, and she's bearing down so hard on the stick it's wobbling. She looks again to the left, changes the expression on her face, and says something like, "I'll be right there," and her voice sounds sweet and kind like she's Mary friggin' Poppins. She steps forward and shuts the door so whoever is inside can't hear.

She beckons me forward. "What on earth are you doing here?" she hisses.

"You said tea. Am I not invited?"

"Duplicity is not your strong point. Please do not participate in such behaviour with me. You were *not* invited, as well you know. You were *informed*. Do you know the difference between being invited and being informed, or is this something whereby you require further instruction?" She's saying 'S' like 'sh' again. She's been at the sauce.

"Oh well, I'm here now," I say, ready for this moment when I walk into an empty room. Or not. If it's a policeman, he'll be sitting up straight, a notebook ready on the table, a little pencil in his hand. Maybe in uniform, maybe not. I'll swan in, like I'm just passing by. I've practised the look on my face in the car over here – surprised, but not overdone. A look that says it's not unusual for some form of dignitary to be in the house. In her day, with Marion's wealth, who knows who might've swung by. And I'll apologise, explain that I can't stay long. And I'll hold out my hand to shake his, nothing to worry about here, Officer. Nothing at all.

Marion is paralysed by fury. I take my chance, dart around her, turn the doorknob and rush on in.

My eyes lock onto the man sitting there.

This can't be. I'm on another planet. I'm living in a parallel universe.

He's perched right there, at the table, and the look on his face is odd, a sort of look of surprise – but not overdone. The same look I was supposed to be wearing on *my* face.

"Andrew?" I ask in shock.

My mind is trying to make sense of what's happening. Is it really him? Were we really having coffee together just a few hours ago? Maybe I dreamt it. I sometimes do that – have a dream so vivid I think it actually happened. Like the time Marion said there was a baby rabbit in the horrible mausoleum. There wasn't – she only said it to get me in there. And now I don't remember whether that was a dream or whether it was real.

Marion walks in front of me, makes a big deal of leaning on her walking stick because it's wobbling even more, as if her arthritic knee has gone from bad to worse within seconds.

"Persephone. Let me introduce you to Officer Andrew Cooke." Marion couldn't have heard me mention his name and assumes that I don't know him.

"Nice to meet you, Officer Cooke," I say, emphasis on the *officer*. "I'm Persy Adelard." I hold out my hand. I don't want to touch his lying son of a bitch fingers, but I've got no choice.

"Her name is Persephone," Marion corrects.

Andrew stands up. "Andrew Cooke. And I apologise, Marion, there seems to be a little bit of confusion. I am not a police officer. I was, many years ago, but not now."

"One never stops being a police officer." Her tone is superior and oh-so knowledgeable.

"Actually, I did." He glances desperately at me. "I am *not* a police officer. I am a consultant. Nothing more, nothing less. You can check me out. Call the station."

"Indeed," Marion says, as though she doesn't believe a word of it.

"Why are you here?" I ask.

"Persephone," Marion says. "Please allow our guest to relax before you start bombarding him with questions."

I sit down, my eyes taken away by how she's set the table. A starched, pristine, white table cloth, the expensive blue-and-gold Versace tea set, but the food – the only word I can use is flabbergasted. It's so not her. No genteel cucumber or salmon sandwiches. No delicate desserts. She's cut up store-bought cold sausage rolls, pigs in blankets, pineapples with cheese on sticks. The stuff she makes fun of. Pigs in blankets? She'd rather die than allow those words to pass her lips. Let alone the food itself.

"Where are the scones?" I ask.

Marion glares at me, then says something about needing another cup and saucer for me. She raises her eyebrows and stares at me, her secret way of making sure I follow her. I toss a mock, polite smile at Andrew and follow Marion out of the room. She orders me to close the door behind her.

She walks ahead with no limp at all and waits for me at the end of the hall. "Persephone, that was most ungracious."

I don't know what she's talking about.

"The comment about the scones."

"I'm not following."

"His accent." She stares at me as though I'm stupid. "He has a north country brogue."

I'm still not following, but I keep my mouth shut.

"North country," she repeats, her nose is wrinkled as though she smells something bad. "Scones and sandwiches just won't do. He's probably never had a high tea in his life. Better to offer him sustenance with which he is more familiar."

I don't know how to answer her. "Everyone in England knows high tea."

"Silly girl," she says. "Of course they don't. We should not make those lesser than ourselves *feel* lesser than ourselves. Dignity. Class. Show some."

She stalks back into the drawing room, and for the first time since she ordered me out of the room, I see she doesn't even have the walking stick. I follow her.

Andrew looks confused. "I thought you were getting another place setting." He nods at her empty hands.

"I'm getting so forgetful. The nicer china is right behind you." She feigns embarrassment. "Persephone, would you mind getting one from the cabinet?"

"I'll get it," Andrew says. He tosses me half a smile. He's trying to get back on my side. It won't work. Why didn't he tell me he was coming here?

We sit around the table, all of us upright and uncomfortable. I pour the tea. My hand hovers over the plate of sausage rolls to pick it up and pass it around. I can't bring myself to do it, embarrassed by Marion's explanation and why she'd put them there. Marion seizes the moment, leans in, grabs the plate and holds it towards Andrew. The plate shakes in her hand.

"Let me help," he says, lifting it away from her. He takes a couple of sausage rolls, then offers the plate around.

Marion shakes her head, an expression of horror in her eyes. "Oh dear, no, not for me," she says. Unbelievable.

I follow Andrew's lead and take two.

"So," Marion says after a sip of tea. "What are you here to investigate?"

The word investigate is so strong given what Marion has done; how I don't spit out my mouthful of dry sausage is incomprehensible. I cough to hide my shock and use my napkin to cover my mouth. Marion shoots me a look like I'm an embarrassment. Andrew remains calm, chewing and swallowing.

"Investigate?" he asks, wiping his mouth with his napkin.

"A policeman with an interest in a care home. There has to be some agenda, no?" Marion stares into his eyes. Then looks straight into mine. "Persephone, do you think we need Uncle Alfred to be here?"

I don't know what she's playing at.

"Is there something to investigate?" Andrew answers.

She gives him a nod of approval. "A man used to giving

nothing away. That, I must say, is somewhat beguiling." I can't look at either of them. "Are you suggesting I have something to hide?" she continues.

Andrew gives an easy laugh and takes another bite of the sausage roll.

I can't stand it. They're playing this weird game that I can't follow. I snatch up the plate of pigs in blankets and shove it towards him. "Andrew, please." But I'm too eager, and three or four slide off, three into his lap, and one onto the floor. I can't look at Marion. He picks them up and holds them. I take them from him and put them on my plate.

"So, Andrew," I say. "I suppose you're here to talk to Marion about finding a place for your aunt at the care home?"

There's a pause. He looks at me, and I see a look of panic in his eyes. I don't understand why. Was the discussion about his aunt a secret? Was I not supposed to mention anything about her?

"How do you know he has an aunt?" Marion asks.

The panic on Andrew's face now comes into focus. If I didn't know Andrew, how would I know he had an aunt? I look at Andrew. He's picking up a sausage roll like he doesn't have the guts to look into my eyes.

"What?" I say stupidly.

"You said he has an aunt," Marion says.

"What?" I say again.

"Persephone. Please stop. You were very clear. You said his aunt is interested in the home. How would you know that?"

There's no point in continuing this farce any longer. "I saw Andrew at the home. The other day. He was talking to Susie, who told me she was about to give him a tour. I caught a glimpse of him."

"So, you know each other."

"No. We don't *know* each other. I saw him at the home. Susie explained why he was there."

Andrew jumps in. "Persy's right. And that's the reason I asked to meet you." He wipes the side of his mouth with a balled-up napkin, which I'm pretty sure is hiding a mouthful of sausage roll. "Whatever home she goes into, she will probably be there for several years. Derek and I talked about it. That's why he suggested I come here. To talk to you." His words are getting faster and faster. She's scared the hell out of him too. "I wanted to get to know the place a bit better. I think Derek was right. Is it okay that I came here to discuss the home with you?"

Marion ignores his question. "And did you like the home?"

"I did. Yes."

"You think it will be a good place for your aunt?"

I don't know what's happening. We've gone from interrogation to pleasant conversation in the blink of an eye.

"Definitely," Andrew answers.

"Do you have any questions? I seem to remember, when Derek called me, you were concerned about the finances. Or did Derek misunderstand your concerns?" Her tone has suddenly hardened. I think she thinks Andrew's question is impertinent.

"Only that the home seemed to depend on your contributions. It was a casual question, nothing more."

"Then let me ask you this in return." She smiles. There's a spot of lipstick on her teeth again. I have to look away. "Can you imagine any reason why I might not continue with my donations?"

There's a pause that seems to stretch for eternity.

"I can't think of any reason at all," he says, trying to sound indifferent but failing.

She fidgets on her chair a little. Then, out of nowhere, she leans in, grabs a sausage roll and takes a bite. She smiles. "Good. I can't either. So, yes, it's fair to say the donations will continue. These are quite tasty, aren't they?" The Marion I know has disappeared out of sight, and someone else has come out to play. I wish I knew who it was. "And I apologise, Andrew," she continues. "This time of the afternoon, I often begin to feel a little tired and become, what would you say, Persephone, rather grumpy?" She smiles at me. I have never used the word grumpy in her presence. She'd wallop me with that walking stick.

Andrew's demeanour changes as well. "I apologise, too. What you do for the home, it's remarkable. I'm sorry if it seemed like I was being nosy. Maybe I crossed a line."

"We're all allowed to cross lines from time to time." She's beaming at him now. "Part of being human, I think. I know I have crossed rather too many lines in my time."

The little hairs on the back of my neck stand up.

"I'd like to hear about those times," Andrew says, and they laugh together.

I have to change the subject. I'm scared she might blurt out some of the lines she's crossed, but I can't. I'm out of my depth.

"I think we need more tea." Marion gives him a genteel little smile and moves her chair. He stands up to help her, and she says something about how kind he is and the importance of manners; then, she wanders out, leaving her walking stick behind. Again. Not a wobble in sight.

Andrew picks up the teapot that's sitting on the table. "Doesn't she need this? Shall I go and take it to her?"

I shake my head. "I don't know what she needs."

"She's interesting."

I don't answer.

"At first, I thought she was baiting me, trying to trip me up. By the end of it, she seemed okay." He smiles the smile of a man who knows nothing. "I think she likes me. What do you think?"

I sip my cold tea; I don't want him to see the embarrassment in my eyes. Marion doesn't like anyone. As always, she's fooled him into thinking that, deep down, she's just a sweet, harmless old lady.

"I think I threw her off at first. That was my fault. I was trying to impress her by saying I used to be an ex-cop. I shouldn't have said that."

"You didn't tell *me* you were a cop." I try to keep the defensiveness out of my voice. After all, we've only had one coffee together; why should he have told me?

"In the whole scheme of things, it's not important. It just felt like the right thing to say to her."

"And what about me? Is this why you asked me out on a date? To find out more about Marion's money?"

He looks horrified. "No, no. I swear!"

I watch him. There's a saying I like to keep in my head: 'when someone reveals who they are, believe them'. What has he revealed to me now? He picks and chooses what information to give to which people. Is it him who gets to decide what part he will show at any time?

"Why did she suddenly think your Uncle Alfred should be here? Actually, who is Uncle Alfred? And why am I calling him Uncle Alfred? It's not as though he's my uncle."

"Don't worry about it," I say. "He lives on Marion's estate. I think she suddenly felt bad she hadn't invited him too. That's all." I'd like to know the answer to that, too.

He leans in. "And what's with the food? Sausage rolls and pigs in blankets? I feel like I'm getting ready for Christmas."

"Stop," I say. And I mean it. I'm allowed to stick it to her. That's a given. But hearing him, I don't know, it sounds wrong. I look over my shoulder, half-expecting her to be standing by the door, listening. She's not. "I'm going to check on her."

He holds onto my arm. "You'll come back, right? I mean, you won't disappear and send in Alfred the enforcer?"

"Funny," I say and leave the room.

In the kitchen, Marion is standing by the kettle. She's making a fresh pot of tea in the white china teapot she hates, with stains and a crack in the spout. I grab a nicer one from the row of teapots on a high shelf. "Here," I say. "Use this one."

As I pass it to her, I notice the little bottle of Nembutal on the windowsill. The lid is off and on its side as though it's just been opened and discarded too quickly. I see a tiny puddle of liquid in the chipped white teapot.

"You've got to be kidding me," I say.

Marion looks at me blankly. Then she puts the lid back on the Nembutal and leaves the kitchen without a word. She walks down the hallway towards the sunroom, and I hear the door open and then slam shut.

I want to run after her, ask her what the hell she was doing. Was she going to kill Andrew, was that what this was all about?

ELEVEN

When I come back, Andrew is in the drawing room looking at the rows and rows of leather-bound books, pulling the odd one here and there out. I apologise; I explained that Marion wasn't feeling well and had decided to take a nap. He mumbles something like, "Okay," but he seems more interested in looking at the myriad subjects in the hundreds and hundreds of books.

"Who's the polyglot?" he asks. "What have you got? Arabic, French? Are some of these in Latin?"

"First editions," I say. "Every book in this room is a collector's item. I wouldn't be surprised if she's got something in Swahili if it has value."

"Have you read any of them?"

"Never," I say. It's not strictly true. I used to love books, and you couldn't get them out of my hands. And I'd read anything. At eight, I'd already consumed a dozen or so biographies. But she didn't like me touching the ones in here; it was about oily fingers on the covers. It made me furious because if they were that old, plenty of other people would've touched them already, which made me want to touch them more. So, I'd sneak the English ones out and hide them under my mattress. Until she found me out, went wild, took every book from the shelves in my bedroom and locked me inside. The next day, she came up and handed me one book – *The Diary of a Young Girl* by Anne Frank. I was emotionally too young and, after I'd finished it, I cried for days. If I have kids, I'll never let them read that book.

After that, I never touched another book in her house.

"You didn't read them as a kid?" He turns away from the books and looks at me. "You'd never have got me out of here."

"I was always on my bike," I lie. "Or running around outside like a demon."

"I can imagine that. You could ride around this place for days. It must've been fantastic living here. Did your friends come over and play hide-and-seek? It must've taken you ages to find each other!"

I nod and smile and pretend to access some false memory. The one time we played hide-and-seek, Marion sent me off to hide but never came to find me. I was hiding for hours until it got dark. They'd already had supper when I came out of my hiding place. Marion told me off for missing it and sent me to bed hungry.

"I'd better head off," he says. "You fancy dinner tonight? 'Cus I've got to tell you, I'm starving."

"You don't want any more of this?" We both look down at the dismal display of food.

He laughs. "I'll pick you up at seven-thirty?"

"Done."

"Text me your address."

"One question," I say, pulling a Columbo on him as if this one last question will reveal the truth of everything. "I can see why you didn't mention being a policeman. But why didn't you tell me you were coming for tea?"

He looks down at his feet, then back up at me. "I… I wanted to see her on her own."

"Why?"

"Look. I'm familiar with your wealth. Susie filled me in. They told me Marion was a bit of a ball-breaker. I suppose I was intimidated. I thought I might be out of my depth. I didn't want you to see it."

It's a good answer. If it's not true, it's a great lie. Admit to a vulnerability that suggests he wanted to look good in my eyes. Who could resist?

"But I was bound to find out at some point."

"I know that. I just wanted to understand who you were and how you lived. I've never known anyone with this kind of money."

I walk him down the hall and watch from the top of the steps as he drives away. "Can I trust you?" I murmur to myself.

I wander back into the house and stand in front of the Italian Renaissance mantel surrounding the marble fireplace in the drawing room that's rarely lit – another symbol of everything I despise about this house: grand but useless.

The one time I saw it lit was when I was a kid. For no particular reason, I went downstairs and found the door wide open and the hearth covered in ash. I picked up the little brush from the wrought-iron set to clean it up, but something moved when I got to my knees. A cat? There. In the fireplace. And I think it was dead or dying. I mean, it must have been.

Marion appeared out of nowhere, chased me away, snapped at me, and shouted that this had nothing to do with me. The memory is real, I'm sure of it. Except I can't remember what I said to her. I must've said something because it would've upset me. It upsets me thinking about it now. But that bit, I can't remember.

She walks in as I'm standing there, staring into the grate. "This place will be yours one day. All of it." Her lipstick has gone, and her hair is flat on one side where she must've fallen asleep against the chair. "Would you like something to eat?" she asks.

I shake my head.

"Maybe not the best choice of food. Would you agree?" She raises one eyebrow.

"I would."

"I was merely trying to make him feel at home."

"Were you?" I think it's far more likely that she enjoyed showing him up. She loves making people uncomfortable and then acting like she's innocent.

"What will you do with it? The house, I mean. Once it's yours. I would imagine new heating. You will have enough money to do exactly what you'd like. You know that."

I want to tell her I plan to raze it to the ground and get rid of everything. The land I'll give to the little church across the field. It's small, Norman, with floor-set brasses, old wooden pews, and the smell of incense. They've been running out of space; there's no more room to bury people. It seems oddly fitting.

"You've always loved this house. I think you'll make it so very cosy."

Cosy is not a word in her vocabulary. This new Marion is someone I'm not used to.

"New heating, new water tank, new roof. What about an extension? Indoor swimming pool, heated, of course. Something Italianate, I'm thinking. Elegant. With Greek statues. Base it on the Roman Baths."

I feel so tired. All of this is just rubbish, and I want to yell. It's just stuff. It's not *life*.

"You'd need a much bigger tank for that, of course. I do find it a little annoying when we run out of hot water. Not that it happens with only me rattling around in this big old place. But I'm sure when you're living here, you'll have all sorts of interesting people coming to stay."

I've never brought friends here, and if she hadn't invited Andrew, I would never have brought him here either.

"I need to leave," I say. I grab my coat, waiting for the inevitable ticking off from Marion for leaving before I'm given the okay. Today, she doesn't say anything. Maybe she's tired of it all, too.

I'm tempted to ask her what point was she making by trying to poison Andrew. The moment feels right, her guard is down and maybe we could have an honest conversation for once. But what's the point? My brain sometimes tricks me: let's pretend this is a new day, and you'll get a straight answer. More fool me.

I head home. Halfway back, the phone rings, and I tell myself if it's Marion, I will not answer it; I'm drained and don't have the energy. I check the caller ID. It's Scooter.

Fear grips me. The arrival of my mum and dad is too big for me.

"You want the good news or the bad news?"

"Bad," I say.

"Good. Because there is no bad." He laughs so loudly I have to pull the phone away from my ear. It pisses me off. "Remember I told you they're going to England after Paris? Well, they've changed their minds. They're going to England first."

I don't get what he's telling me, and I'm still upset by his dumb prank.

"What?"

"They are going to be at Stonehenge the day after tomorrow. Can you believe that? The damn day after the damn tomorrow."

It's all happening too fast. "I don't believe it."

"They're on their way, Persy."

I'm too taken aback. I'm in a dream-like state, and any moment now, I will wake up.

"Scooter, listen to me, we're not even sure it's them."

"Persy, it fits everything. But sure, there's always a possibility that it's not them. I'm not going to bullshit you. You need to think of it the other way around. What's the likelihood it's not them? The odds are better that way."

"How could we prove it?"

"You know the answer to that. DNA. But you know how I feel about that."

The last time I went along with him finding a couple, I went over to the US, secretly grabbed a glass with their fingerprints on, paid over the top to get the DNA. Except I'd picked up the wrong glass and messed everything up when the DNA came back as mine. It was a mess. He was livid. We made a pact. Anyone we found, consider them, meet them, DNA them but only if they wanted. They had rights too, he'd said.

A car overtakes me, and I slow down to let it pass. The car is blue, similar to the colour of Andrew's vehicle.

"Scooter," I say. "Something different. Can you find out as much as possible about someone?"

"Of course."

"Andrew Cooke," I say. "Ex-police. I want to make sure he is who he says he is."

TWELVE

We're in a cute little bistro in the centre of town, Andrew and me, at a table for two in the corner right next to the window. The place is half empty; it's the middle of the week, and the servers in their white shirts and dark aprons are happy to mill about and smile and check up on us a bit too frequently. I'm wearing tight white jeans cut just above the ankle, a pair of brown suede ankle boots with a nice, thick, effortless heel and a silk blouse that buttons at precisely the right place to tease the eyes towards my boobs. Andrew is wearing jeans and a round-necked sweater topped off by a leather jacket tossed over the back of the chair. He looks cool.

A bowl of oil and balsamic vinegar sits in the middle of the table, and we take turns dipping chunks of warm bread. It's intimate and natural, as if we've known each other for years.

"So," Andrew says. "I guess I should tell you why I was kicked off now." His eyes have a sparkle that tells me he doesn't mind admitting what went down.

"I didn't know you were kicked off."

"I didn't mention that?"

"There's quite a lot you didn't mention, *apparently*." But I'm smiling as I say it.

He grins and blushes. "Okay. Sorry. Let's start again. I was kicked off the force. Do you want to know why?"

"Sure," I say.

He edges in on his seat, puts his elbows on the table and leans towards me. "So, Jake, one of my friends, irritating kind of a guy, short, always making a thing of it – like, 'I can get through that window', or how great he was at football and skiing because he was lower to the ground. That sort of stuff." He hunches forward and looks over each shoulder as if he doesn't want anyone else to hear. "So, we were on a case. Taking down a drug gang. They had a load of dry-cleaning shops, all a scam, that sort of thing." At this point, the memory is so funny that he can barely control himself. "Sorry, sorry. So, we were in one of their launderettes. Their machines were huge, and they were for hotel laundry and industrial. And we all betted that he couldn't get into one of the dryers."

"He didn't get in?" My voice is all astonished.

"Not only did he get in, but he was also waving through that little glass window thing and telling us to turn it on."

"You didn't."

He can't stop laughing. "The look on his face was so shocked, the drum going round and round, him peering out at us…" His eyes are tearing up from the memory.

Now I'm laughing too.

"And we all took photos." He sniffs back his amusement and takes a couple of breaths. "But one of my mates, Jack Hughes, put it on social media because it was so damn funny. It went viral." He scratches the back of his head and leans back a little. "Behaviour not becoming of an officer." He kind of shrugs. "But you know what, I think we had it coming. Got a bit big for our boots."

And there it is again: that self-awareness, that disarming honesty. There's something else too. He's told a story that should be easy for me to check. So, presumably, it has to be true.

"But you know what, enough about me. What about you?"

"Nothing as funny as that," I say. And I manage to come up with a few stories, not mine, ones I've read about. Like the time I got locked in a shop when the owner left for lunch (I didn't; it was in the newspaper) or the time I was at a gardening centre, didn't realise the time, and they closed the place up with me and my car inside. I had to wriggle under the gate, get a cab, and then go back the next day to pick up my car. The centre gave me a complimentary cream tea for that. That didn't happen to me either. I had overheard it in a café, but I liked the story. It makes me feel normal and a bit silly.

I don't tell him any of my actual stories. The time Marion left me waiting at a bus station for three and a half hours because she was having lunch with a friend. Or the time she gave me sleeping tablets because she couldn't bear listening to me cry.

He's funny and smart and easy to talk to. He's also a great listener, attentive, and keeps eye contact, which makes me a bit self-conscious. Is my hair too wild or, like Marion always says, has he spotted I'm a bit on the chubby side? And every time my head goes to that useless, I'm-not-good-enough place. I use one of my tricks to push the thoughts away. I focus on his face and take mental measurements of his features. His nose must be about 2.2 inches long, his face is about five eyes wide, and his eyebrows are thick and well-shaped but not like a woman's; they're not plucked. I figure there has to be over five hundred or so hairs in any given brow, but he probably has more than that because they are bushy. He has a nice smile and white teeth.

This is what I've found out about him so far: his wife died, no children. He was a soldier (military police), and because he started at eighteen, he was eligible for a pension at thirty, so he left. The army paid for university, where he studied accounting but didn't like it. He switched to criminal psychology and then joined the Met. Two years later, he was suspended for the prank he had told me about. He's forty, eight years older than me. He has worked as a volunteer fireman, a security guard, a personal bodyguard and a PI, which is a real coincidence because, as an investigator, I'm as close to a PI as anything else. He's consulting now, which has something to do with business and IT. He was living in London, felt isolated, and moved to Bath to be closer to his aunt. He still has a place in Islington that's worth just over a million (he bought it for £180K twenty years ago) and is rented out to a couple of idiot investment bankers who pay him £6K per month, which is why he can afford to be self-employed.

This is what he's learnt about me: I'm thirty-two, dropped out of university for reasons unknown. I don't mention the breakdown, the suicide attempt, or the building where I live that I own. I want to tell him about my real job, but it's too soon because I'm not really sure exactly who he is.

By the time his steak and my salmon arrive, we've already polished off a bottle of wine.

He chews and swallows. "Are you going to tell me the real truth, then?"

The question shocks me. I keep my eyes down and cut through the salmon. "How do you mean?"

"About the home. What is it about that place that keeps Marion giving?"

Why are we back on this already? "I think she's afraid of dying." I fall back on the same half-truth I told him earlier.

He says, "I don't think she gives a damn about dying."

My head shoots up. He's watching me.

"I mean, and I apologise for saying this, but she seems so out of touch, so removed from reality, I don't think she would give dying another thought."

"Why do *you* think she donates money?"

"I don't know. That's why I'm asking you."

It feels like I'm being interrogated. I shove more salmon in my mouth and tell myself to think about something else, so I don't look guilty. Mum and Dad, that's a good thing to focus on. What will they think of me? What about Andrew? Would they like him?

"She has a lot of money," I say. "She gives loads away. The care home is just one of many." The care home gets about eighty per cent of her total donations, but I won't tell Andrew that. Plus, I don't know what it is about the home that keeps her so engaged. Maybe guilt about her own mother, the one she refuses to talk about?

As if reading my mind, he says, "Do you think Marion's parents were poorly treated in their old age, something like that, and she's trying to make up for what happened to them?"

"Who knows? I don't know anything about them."

"You know nothing about your grandparents?" He sounds amazed. "One look at Marion and I'd say you were from a long line of aristocrats or something."

Then it hits me. He hasn't heard. Relief floods through me like a hurricane; this is the perfect way to switch the conversation to something that won't trip me up.

"You didn't know. Sorry. I'm adopted."

He stops chewing.

"Sorry," I say. "I can never remember who knows and who doesn't. Marion has told everyone at the care home."

He puts down his knife and fork and wipes the edges of his mouth. "Persy, I'm sorry. I didn't mean to pry. I mean, you call her Marion; I thought it was, I don't know, a being-rich thing."

"Do you think the royals called the King Charlie boy?"

He cocks an eyebrow. "You're comparing yourself to the royals now?"

I start to laugh. "Maybe they've got a bit more money than Marion." We grin at each other.

"How do you feel about that?" he asks. "I mean, being adopted?"

I take a deep breath, bite my lip, and try to look like I'm thinking. Which I'm not. The way I feel about being adopted – not just adopted but adopted *by Marion* – is something that sits inside my chest like a stone every day of my life. "Water under the bridge, really," I say casually. "I've had a lot of time to get used to it."

"And your biological parents? Have you ever tried to find them?"

I meet his eyes and try to read them. Does he know something?

"Tried and failed," I say.

"Really? I don't think I'd ever stop looking if it were me."

"Do you mind if we don't talk about it?" I lower my eyes, pretend sadness. This isn't a conversation I want to have with him. His stare is sometimes so intense I swear he can read my mind.

"Done," he says. "The care home. That's where we were."

"I can't remember what it was about the home you asked about."

"Why Marion donates," he says without skipping a beat.

Why do we keep coming back to this?

"I think we've already beaten that one to death."

"What's her relationship with Derek, the manager?"

"With Derek?" It's like I'm the ball in a pinball machine. Bouncing from one question to another. Except there's a common denominator: the care home. "How do you mean?"

He shakes his head like he can't quite make up his mind. "I don't know." He pauses. "There's something about him; I can't put my finger on it."

"He does his job."

"But he's a bit sleazy. It was a bit too cosy with the patients and the staff. Don't you think?"

He has no idea how close to the mark he is. "All this after just one visit. You took a lot in."

"I can't help it. I sum things up too quickly. Sometimes I get it wrong. But Derek, I don't know, reminds me of some of the scum I nicked." He drops his napkin on the table and leans back.

"Should I discuss this with Marion? I mean, if you think something isn't quite right…"

"I don't know," he says. "Not yet."

And there it is. Two little words that open up a whole new line of thought. Not yet. He's got something on his mind and he's going to keep digging.

"What do you mean?" I ask.

He gives me a soft smile. "I need to look at other homes. I really don't know what I'm talking about. Maybe I'm overreacting."

Or lying.

I hold his gaze. "Look," I say. "I wasn't going to say anything, but honestly, I should mention it. My power of attorney will kick in at some point, and I'll be responsible for those donations. It's *me* you should be worrying about. Not Marion."

"Seriously?" If he's surprised, his face doesn't show it.

"Marion has dementia. Couldn't you tell?"

"I'm sorry to hear that. But no. I'm not sure. Maybe. Sometimes, she seemed slightly off, but I thought it was who she was." He fixes onto my face. "Poor Marion."

We share a bowl of ice cream and brownies and end up talking about growing up, more him than me. He tells me about London and the city and his parents coming from a housing estate. I'm never quite clear why people share that sort of information. I think they're trying to tell me they were poor, as though it's something to be embarrassed about. Or perhaps they're proud of it. But either way, I can't relate. My feelings about my childhood are so tangled that I can't imagine wanting to share the truth with anyone.

We leave the restaurant with two bottles of wine demolished and a little giddy. Instead of walking straight home, we take the scenic route. Down and around Bath Abbey, across to the Weir, down to the Holburne Museum, back up past the fire station. Then we take the little slip road towards The Circus where I live. It's dark, and the calm wind makes my eyes tear up. By the time we get to my door, the care home and Marion seem far away.

"You want to go for a drive?" I ask.

He looks at me as if I'm kidding.

"Come on. It's only nine. Show me where you live."

He's not sure where I'm coming from. And I'm not sure where I'm coming from either; all I know is that I don't want the evening to end.

He tells me he's parked a few streets away, and we walk up Brock Street into Margaret's Building. He stops at the glittering glassware shops and talks about the woman who owns the shop, how talented she is, how she makes everything herself, and always has the time to chat. We walk a little further and stare into the Le Bocage's windows, where we bumped into each other. We stay close, my arm through his, our steps in unison, our bodies leaning into each other.

"Here's my car," he says. "You want to go for a drive?"

I give him a 'come on, let's have some fun' grin.

We drive towards Larkhall, to his place, and I can tell he's proud of knowing everything about the small village. He points to the little church that turns into a pub on a Friday night, past the deli that sells individual meals for people who, like him, tend to eat alone. We drive down the little road, and he points to the place where he lives. He slows down.

"What do you want to do now?" he asks.

"Have you ever been to the top of Lansdown?"

He shakes his head.

"You know what?" I lean forward and look up into the night sky. "Keep driving up this hill. There's a place to pull in where you can see the stars. It's beautiful."

"Okay," he says.

We drive up the hill, past the Hare and Hounds pub, the golf club, and the racecourse. I point to the turning on the left.

"Into that little road?"

It's more like a dirt track. "There's a place at the end, just before the trees; you can pull in there."

We get out of the car and lean against the bonnet. I turn to him and pull him towards me. As his lips meet mine, I feel his tongue pressing forward. Then he pulls away and picks me up ever so slightly, so I sit on the bonnet, the metal warm against my thighs. Slowly, he eases my legs apart, cups his hands around my hips and pulls me closer. One of his hands cradles the back of my head while the other finds its way inside my trousers, and I feel his fingers penetrate me. He whispers some words in my ear, but I don't know what they are because I can't concentrate. I scoot off the top of the car and take off my shoes, trousers, and pants. He turns me around so my ass is bare to the sky, my stomach pressing against the car, and my toes digging into the cool, damp grass. He drops his trousers, and I feel him inside of me.

Thirty minutes later, he drops me back home. I don't ask him in because it doesn't seem right, as if somehow it would make what we'd done seem normal and every day. I stand on the pavement and watch him drive away.

I want to say it was fantastic, that it was the best sex I've ever had, but I can't because the moon was bright enough for him to get a really good look at my backside, and I know that my ass isn't one of my better parts. Marion always told me so.

THIRTEEN

It's nine-thirty in the morning. The smell of damp hangs in the air, and the drizzle of rain leaves tiny spots on my bedroom window. I've left it slightly ajar to give me some air because my head thumps from the wine last night.

Outside, the trees are swaying gently, and the tourists wandering around The Circus have umbrellas or hoods up as they clutch their coats around them. But inside my living room, with the radiators turned up, I'm toasty and warm in my favourite pale-blue pyjamas and thick robe tied around my waist.

I pad into the kitchen, turn on the coffee machine, and treat myself as a way of keeping the good feelings from last night going. I open the new milk frother I bought a while ago and fill it with oat milk. This day deserves the best, hottest, thickest cappuccino. As I wait, I check my phone. Three texts have come in from Andrew.

First: *You left your knickers in the back seat.*

Second: *If you need them, I can leave them on your car's windscreen.*

Third: *Kidding. I've already left them on the handle of your front door.*

I text a couple of lol emojis and expect nothing in return. To my surprise, he texts back.

I am off to Cheltenham today. I'll text you when I get home, probably around eight.

He's not playing hard to get. I like that. I throw myself down onto the sofa, stretch out as far as I can, then rest my head on my arm and replay every second I can remember of the night before. I cringe at the memory of him seeing my ass but tell myself to move on; with a bit of luck, he doesn't have twenty-twenty vision.

The spyware I put on Derek's phone pings. I set my coffee down and wander over to the computer with a sense that the call is probably nothing: marketing, the plumber, who knows. I listen in.

There's no one there; Derek has already hung up; he probably had the wrong number.

I jot down the number and do a reverse directory, but it doesn't show up. Shall I or shan't I make an anonymous call? I hate doing that because I always feel that the person on the other end knows it's me and can see me standing there like an idiot hiding behind my phone. *Needs must*, I repeat to myself. I block my number and then dial the one Derek just called.

A woman answers. "Bath and Avon Police Station," she says.

I swallow hard. Should I hang up? I've blocked my number, but what if they have the technology to break through? *No*, I tell myself, *I would know if that sort of technology was widely used. Wouldn't I?* I can't hang up. It's too big a risk.

"Can you tell me who I should contact to volunteer with the Police?" I close my eyes and bang my forehead with the side of my fist. There was too much wine the night before, or maybe my ability to think is declining by the minute.

"The website is the best," she says kindly. "We've got a list of what's available. It's quite straightforward. Go there first, and if you need further information, call us back. We're always looking for good people."

I thank her, tell her that's what I'll do and hang up. Then I sit on the sofa, my head in my hands. Why is he calling the police? It's about Dora, it has to be. I'm back to the same questions Derek raises whenever I think about him. *What does he know? Why did he hang up?*

Derek's phone dings again. He's on the phone, calling the same number, calling the police. I hold my breath. Will he speak? Will he hang up again?

He speaks. "This is Derek Pringle from Meadow Bank Care Home. Please put the person in charge of the missing person's case on the phone. I don't have much time." His voice is aggressive and superior.

"Is someone missing, sir?" It's the same woman who answered my call, and her tone says she's not about to take any shit.

"I wouldn't be calling if she wasn't missing, would I?" Derek snaps.

The woman on the phone doesn't speak. She's smart. She was giving him time to think.

"Yes," he says eventually. "Sorry. Yes. Dora Haslea is missing."

"And this has been reported?" He's pissed her off, and she's going to make him pay.

He's finally noticed. "I apologise. I haven't given you enough details. I'm rather upset. So sorry."

"The missing person?"

"Dora Haslea. She went missing from Meadow Bank Care Home just over five days ago."

"I'm familiar with the case. And you are?"

"Derek Pringle."

"A relative?"

"No. I think I said. I manage the care home."

"*You* manage the care home where this elderly woman went missing?" She's trying to make him feel guilty. Like he clearly wasn't doing his job very well. She's perfect.

"Could you please put me through to the officer in charge?" Derek is getting pissy again. He can't help himself.

"Of course. Can you hold?" She doesn't transfer him. She hangs up just like that.

I would've laughed if I weren't so worried about why Derek was calling them. What is his plan here? Given the scam he's been pulling, why does he want them even more involved than they already are? I don't get his agenda, which is a real problem. How can I protect my end if I don't understand what he's up to?

I wait. Derek is waiting, too – there's no movement on his phone. I imagine him in his office, the door shut, kicking the beanbag until the insides spew onto the carpet.

Eventually, he calls the police station again.

"This is Derek Pringle," he says. "I'm calling about a missing persons case – Dora Haslea – and I was wondering if I could speak to the person in charge of that investigation. I called earlier but was cut off."

It's the same woman as before. "No problem, sir," she says crisply. "I'll put you through. It might ring a couple of times, as our system bounces from one desk to another, but someone should answer."

"Much appreciated," he says, the soul of humility.

This time, she doesn't cut him off. It rings maybe seven more times, and then a man with a young voice picks it up.

"Mr Pringle. I understand you have questions about Dora Haslea. We did meet. I was one of the first officers at the care home. What can I do to help?"

"I'm worried."

"I think we are all apprehensive, sir. An elderly lady, missing for several days, we should be."

"But I haven't heard about a search party."

"I'm sorry?"

"A search party." Derek's voice rises.

"I'm still not following."

"Let me be clear." Derek never learns. He's getting aggressive again, making the same mistake he made with the first call. "An old lady has gone missing, and no one seems to be looking for her."

"Why would you say that, sir?"

"Is this a joke?" Derek shouts.

"Sir, you need to calm yourself."

"People should be searching for Dora Haslea!"

"They *are* searching for her."

"Then why haven't I heard it on the news?"

"It's Derek Pringle, correct?" This is the first time the policeman has mentioned Derek's first name. He has to be looking at some notes.

"Yes?"

"Okay, Derek. We have had people searching for her. Every day. A combination of officers and volunteers. I can understand why you are concerned. An older person out in this weather, maybe alone. But a search is taking place."

"Well, I haven't heard about it. And Dora has not been found. And, quite honestly, I think the worst might have happened. This needs to be taken very seriously. There might've been foul play."

Why is he using those words? I don't understand. The penny finally drops. If he wants the insurance money, he needs Dora to be found. Dead.

"Foul play," the officer repeats. "Now, that's an interesting phrase to use. Why would you assume that?"

"I'm not assuming anything. It stands to reason, doesn't it, or am I the only one with a brain? She's elderly. She can't stay out all that time. Something terrible must have happened, and it's obvious you are not taking it seriously."

"Derek, why don't you come to the station for a more thorough update? Since you're so worried. Maybe you have information that might be helpful to us. I have a few questions based on what you've said today."

There's a long pause. "Come down there?"

My hand is over my mouth. If I were that cop, I'd wonder if this jerk on the other end of the phone is involved in some way, too.

"Shall we set a time?" the policeman asks, his voice silky smooth.

"You know what. If you don't take this seriously, maybe I should go straight to the press."

Oh, Derek. What are you playing at?

"Go to the press?" The officer sounds mildly amused, like this isn't the first time he's heard this type of crap.

"Yes. The press. To let them know she's disappeared and no one gives a damn."

"She? Do you mean Dora Haslea? We prefer to put a name to a person in distress."

"You *know* that's who I mean," Derek splutters.

"Good. We're on the same page. To confirm, I'm looking at the logs of this particular case, and if I'm correct, Dora has been missing for just over five days, and this is the first time the manager of the home where she disappeared has called. Is that correct?"

"I'll be speaking to the newspapers," Derek shouts. "Mark my words."

His threat sounds real. He has to be confident that his deceit and taking ownership of her assets will never be uncovered. His arrogance is impressive.

I stand up, sit down again, run my hands through my hair, can't sit still, my thoughts too muddled. Derek is a problem. He's a loose cannon, unpredictable, and I can do nothing about it.

To calm myself down, I finally jump into the shower, turn the water on as hot as possible, take it for a couple of minutes, and quickly switch it to cold. It takes my breath away. I stand firm, arms crossed against my chest and my head under the icy blast. At the count of fifteen, I can't take any more. But I force myself to stay for another five seconds. I quickly switch back to hot. It's done the trick. Calm has returned, and my breathing has steadied.

I tell myself he's not going to go to the press. Why would he? He doesn't want more attention on him. He's threatened something he can't deliver. And all for one reason: Dora's life insurance policy. I almost feel good about the fact that poor Dora's body will never be found. He's going to be waiting a long time for that money.

I get dressed and dry my hair, ready to think. I need to get ahead of this.

I call Susie at the care home. I need to make sure the Marion dementia message has gotten through.

"Susie, I'm just checking in after my conversation with Derek about Marion – I think he talked to you about it?"

"He did. And don't worry, okay? I asked people around here if Marion had said anything to them, but nobody had a bad word. But don't worry, I'll keep on it. Okay."

"I'm not sure Derek understood how concerned I am…" I'm fishing, but Susie likes to gossip as much as the rest of us. Bashing Derek is something she'll respond to, I'm sure of it.

"Ugh. Derek never knows what he's talking about. Sorry, I don't like speaking out of turn, but he doesn't. I swear he barely knows any of the patients. I told you, didn't I, that he calls them wrinklies. I don't know how he gets away with it."

Derek's number is up. His staff hate him. The bank is clamouring for their money. The police want to ask him some questions. He can't go much lower.

"Do you think I should mention that he's not very good at his job to Marion?"

"No," she says quickly. "No, don't say a word. It's between you and me. I need this job. Persy, sorry, I shouldn't have said anything."

"Susie, we're friends. The conversation was between us. If you want me to say anything to Marion, I will. If you don't want me to, I won't."

"Thanks, Persy," she says. "If we could keep this between us, I'd appreciate it. I'm going to get off the phone if you don't mind. If he comes back up and finds me chatting with you, he'll get paranoid."

"Comes back up? Back up from where?"

"The basement. He calls it the archives, but it's just a cellar."

"I didn't even know there was a basement."

"Full of old files, tapes, that sort of thing."

"Tapes?" The colour drains in my face. "What tapes?"

"CCTV footage. We've got cameras all over the place. We only look at them if we need to. Like the police the other day, they looked at Dora getting on the bus to go to the safari park, that sort of thing. It gets stored in the cloud, but we also back everything up."

"I had no idea."

"Yep. It's all down there. The basement has all the old stuff from when we changed systems. He's been holed up there for a couple of days. Probably sleeping down there, for all we know. Don't tell him I said that."

My mind is a jumbled mess of thoughts. What is he

looking for in the basement? As I pace around my apartment, I realise I'm asking the wrong question. It's not about what Derek is looking for. It's about whether something in that cellar could incriminate us.

FOURTEEN

I carefully wipe down the kitchen counter and ensure every crumb and spill is gone. Next, I strip my bed of its sheets and replace them with fresh ones, tucking in the corners tightly. As I run the vacuum over my carpet, I focus on each section and get every speck of dirt. Mundane tasks to try to get my head back in order. It's the only tool I have left to convince myself I have any control.

My logic tells me Derek will find something – not with Dora, but with the others. All it takes is one tape showing Marion acting suspiciously, and Derek is going to start connecting the dots. Maybe he already has.

The jarring ring of the phone annoys me. It's Scooter.

"Hey, what's going on?" I clear my throat, plaster a smile on my face, willing my voice to sound routine in the hope that nothing has gone wrong.

"Before you get all paranoid, your parents are on their way to England, as reported. That's not why I'm calling. I've got some news. About your guy. Andrew."

I breathe. I'd forgotten I'd asked him to check up on Andrew, and my interest had waned. Andrew versus the weight of what Derek is searching for in the basement of the care home – there's no competition. Sure, I spent the evening with him. Sure, it might go somewhere. But there's too much other dark stuff looming over me. Andrew isn't a big deal.

"Are you on your computer?" he goes on. "I've just sent you a photo. Check it."

"Hold on." I step over the vacuum, sit at my computer, and click into my emails. A familiar face appears on the screen. It's Andrew, but a much younger version of him in his police uniform. He looks fresh-faced and naïve. He looks, I don't know, innocent.

"Yep. That's him," I say.

"Okay. He was on the force. He was kicked off. The punishment seems harsh because it was a practical joke, a prank, as you people like to say. But the papers got hold of it. They went after him. The worst thing is that he lost his pension, which sucks."

"He told me all that." Why am I even on this call right now? My thoughts need to be consumed with figuring out how to handle Derek.

"Then he sold insurance. Went on to private security work. He even did a stint as a personal bodyguard for a company that handles high-net-worth people in London. I'm going out on a limb here, but it looks like he doesn't stick with anything too long. Commitment issues?"

"Okay," I say. "Look. It doesn't matter anymore. But thanks."

"And now he's a consultant." I don't think Scooter has heard me. "It's not clear exactly the consulting he does. There's no website. I'd say he's probably a gun for hire. Give me some time, and I'll figure out the details."

Scooter's words pique my interest. "Gun for hire?"

"You know what I mean. Investigation. Cheating spouses. That sort of thing."

Andrew said he was a business IT consultant.

"Who is this guy to you?" Scooter asks. "Is he important?"

"Someone I met. That's all."

"No. Say it ain't so. You mean you're not waiting for me?"

"Funny," I say.

"Why funny? We'd be perfect together."

I don't want the banter. I can't think about Andrew right now, and I don't want to have another complication.

"I've got to go," I say.

"Okay. But if you fancy this guy, you can tell Marion she doesn't have to worry."

"What?"

"Marion. She gets possessive, right? Not with this guy. No skeletons in his cupboard."

"What are you talking about?"

"He's a lucky man: no family. I wish I were like him. You know how bad my family is—"

I interrupt. "How do you mean, no family?" The hairs prickle on my arms.

"Only child of two only children. Both dead. And they lived abroad anyway. He's all on his lonesome. Why? Did he tell you something different?"

"He said something about an aunt." My voice comes out shaky.

"Looks like we've just found that fatal flaw. Is it such a big deal?"

I lean into the computer screen and stare into the smiling, lying eyes of the photo of Andrew. *Yes*, I think to myself. *Yes, it's a big deal. Because if you don't have an aunt, what the hell are you doing snooping around the care home?*

"Persy, are you there?" Scooter asks.

"Thanks," I say to Scooter. "I've got to go." I hang up.

People are doing things they're not supposed to be doing.

Derek hiding out in the basement. Andrew going to view the care home for an aunt who doesn't exist. Why would he do that? My mind offers up dozens of reasons. He was embarrassed; he had some illness, and he'd need a care home for himself. Or, it wasn't an aunt he was worried about; it was a friend, maybe an ex-partner, that he didn't want to tell me about. I don't know, I don't know, I don't know.

I screw my eyes shut. Or maybe it's so much more straightforward than all of that. Perhaps he's just a lying son of a bitch. And if he is, what in God's name is he really up to?

I'm angry. I don't get angry; I get quiet. I get thoughtful. And sometimes, I get irritated. But angry, no, that was beaten out of me years ago by Marion on account of it being too undignified.

I text Andrew. *Am starving. Want to eat?*

He doesn't waste a second and replies almost immediately. *Perfect timing. Back early from Cheltenham. I'll pick you up. You choose the place.*

Did he get back early from Cheltenham, or is that a lie too? See, that's the problem with a liar. No matter who lies or what it's about, you never trust the liar again. Not for a friggin' minute. I make a mental note: two can play that game. It's time to put a tracker on his car.

I change my clothes and wear a power outfit – black leggings, a black turtleneck and a brown, fitted leather jacket. A pair of red suede high heels. It's not for him, it's for me; I want to feel strong and in charge, and nothing does it better than a pair of hooker heels.

I look out onto the street and wait to catch sight of him. There's no way I'm letting him up to the flat; any signals that I want to spend another evening with him must be avoided. I spot his car, grab my keys and hurry on down. I open the front door at exactly the same time as he goes to press the buzzer. We face each other. His face is beaming, glowing, and he's got a little sparkle in his eyes that shouts to anyone who happens to be watching, *I like this woman.*

He throws his arms around me and nuzzles my neck. "So good to see you. I had such a good time last night," he whispers.

I want to push him away, knock him to the floor, kick him in the teeth. "Me too," I whisper back and give him a gentle kiss on the cheek.

He holds my hand as we cross the street and get into his car.

"Where do you want to eat?" he asks.

"Côte, I like that place, and we should be able to get a seat."

"Côte. Excellent. Maybe we can retake the scenic route home."

Our eyes meet, and a sly, knowing smile spreads across our faces. I try to maintain an air of coy playfulness, tilting my head and shaking it ever so slightly as if to say, 'oh, you are such a naughty one', playing at romance. In truth, last night's encounter was nothing more than basic car sex, something any teenager has done and quickly forgotten. *Car sex*, I repeat in my head. Sounds like carsick. Carsick is better: it'll make me feel ill whenever I think about him and me at the top of Lansdown.

We settle down at a table, again with a bowl of oil and balsamic vinegar between us. I order salmon, and he orders steak.

"You realise we're having exactly what we had last night?" He smiles the smile of a man who's just been laid and reckons he's got the gift that keeps on giving.

"What can I say? I like what I like," I say.

"Do you think that's the sort of couple we will be in the future? Doing the same thing over and over again?" He looks into my eyes, as his are brimming with confidence.

One hot and heavy night on top of a hill up against a car, he's already planning our future. If he weren't a lying jerk, it would almost be sweet. No. I take it back. One night of okay sex, and he thinks we're going steady. He's a narcissist; he has to be.

"I don't know," I say. "What do you think?" I'm finding it hard even to meet his eyes.

"I don't know. Sounds nice. We'd go everywhere together. Supermarket, pick up bread, and coffee shop. Always together." He laughs. "Maybe we'll end up wearing the same clothes."

"That's a line that should never be crossed, ever." Being part of this banter is killing me. He needs to learn to read the room.

"No. Come on. We'd look cute. Maybe even have the same pyjamas. Onesies."

I give a forced laugh, but inside, my mind is racing. When am I going to nail him? I can't decide. Food first? I should've googled whether getting the truth out of someone is easier before or after eating.

Andrew offers me some bread. I take a piece, dip it into the greasy liquid, and shove it into my mouth. Last night, it tasted spicy and smooth. Today, it tastes sickly and cloying.

Andrew does the same as me, breaks off some bread and starts to dip. As he bows his head, I see his hair getting thinner on the top and his skin slightly wrinkled. He's not going to age well. By the age of fifty, he'll look mid-sixties. My spirits lift, and I realise my head is tilted, and I'm gazing at him with a smile. I've drifted off into my imagination again.

"Are you okay?" He looks at me.

I wipe my mouth and set my napkin down. I'm ready to confront him right here, right now.

He grabs some more bread and dips away. Then he glances up at me again. "You seem, I don't know, detached?"

I can see his teeth churning the bread over in his mouth. There's a slight slick of oil on his chin.

"Can I trust you?" I ask.

He swallows hard, licks his teeth with his tongue, drops his napkin on the table and rubs his mouth with his hand. "What?"

He's playing for time. I know it. He knows it.

"Trust," I say. "How important is it? To you?"

His eyes narrow, and a sly smirk plays on his lips. "Seriously?" His tone is mocking, as if the question is so absurd it doesn't even merit a response. I can see the gears turning in his head, trying to decipher why I would suddenly bring up such a weighty topic. He leans back in his chair, one hand tapping thoughtfully on the table. "That's quite a heavy subject to broach out of the blue." His voice is tinged with curiosity and amusement.

I resist the temptation to grab him by the scruff of his collar, my hands itching with frustration. "Is it?" I try to maintain a calm and collected demeanour. "I don't think so. I find it quite straightforward."

He looks down at the table and then back up at me. "Persy, what's going on?"

I lean in and say slowly, "You don't have an aunt."

He remains still, his body frozen in place. His eyes are unblinking, and his throat doesn't even quiver. He's a poker player. Best to take care.

"You've been checking up on me?"

"That's the best you can do?"

He straightens up, breathes in through his nose and looks around the restaurant as though he's searching for the way out. If he is, then I've learnt something else. Besides being a liar, he's a coward.

He calls for the waiter. If he's going to run, at least he will pay first. "A large scotch, please." The waiter looks at me to ask whether I want one too. I shake my head.

The space between us is filled with a deafening silence. His gaze refuses to meet mine, his eyes fixed on some distant point. I become hyperaware of every minuscule movement he makes, every twitch of muscle and flutter of eyelashes. My brain functions like a high-speed camera, capturing every nuance of his body language and analysing it in search of answers.

The scotch comes to the table. He knocks it down in one, puts the empty glass back on the table, coughs and finally looks at me.

"And you're not an editor," he says.

I fight the urge to flinch. Of all of the answers I'd imagined in my head, I wasn't expecting this one. I reach for the obvious retort. "What is this? Attack is the best form of defence? I'm disappointed."

"I still have contacts with the police. I checked you out. You follow people. You're an investigator."

We're staring at each other. It's a game of chicken. "Given what you did for a living, you had to have known that it's standard practice not to say what you do in my job. No one admits to being a fraud investigator, especially if there's any involvement with the government." I pause. "Maybe you should tell me who gave you that information about me. It's confidential. It could put me at risk. Whoever is wandering around talking about me needs to be reprimanded."

His eyes are locked on me, unblinking and calculating – his mind races in a frantic frenzy, searching for an escape. I can see it right in front of me.

Our food arrives, but neither of us moves.

"There was no lie on my part," he says.

I laugh out loud. I can't wait to hear how he will slither out of this.

"I mean, no, okay, sure, I don't have an aunt, but it was done for the right reasons."

"Is that the definition of a lie? A lie is not a lie if there's a sound reason behind it?"

"Persy," he says. "I'm sorry. Okay? I didn't like lying. But I had to. I had no choice."

A few months ago, I read an article about men. It said they don't just rank themselves higher than women in terms of how often they lie but also consider themselves better at lying altogether. How screwed up is that? Being proud of their ability to do wrong! Like, I'm good at breaking legs, or I'm so great at knocking people's teeth out, or I'm good at stealing money from old ladies.

"You had no choice," I repeat as if I'm talking to a child.

"I'm a private investigator. Not a consultant. There, you have it."

Scooter already told me this. I can't even be bothered to play the game of not knowing what he did for a living. I watch him and try to translate in my head what Andrew is saying to me now: oh, how stupid of me, I'm so sorry, blah, blah, blah. Does he think I'll buy that excuse?

"Andrew," I say. "Look. Just answer me two questions. First, what has anything you've just said got to do with the fact that you lied about having an aunt? Second, what are you doing hanging around a care home?"

A heavy sigh escapes his lips, his shoulders sag, and he looks around nervously before leaning in closer. "Can you promise to keep this confidential?" His voice is hushed.

"Why? If I don't, you'll have to kill me?"

He stretches his arm and puts his hand on mine. "Persy. I'm serious."

"Sure," I say. "Why the heck not? I'll keep it confidential."

"I'm investigating the care home."

His words hang in the air like a dark cloud, suffocating me. I lower my eyes, not wanting to see his intense gaze. I focus on a speck of parsley that sits on the table. I can't breathe.

"Three families," he says. "Three families have hired me. Something is wrong at that place."

I'm so scared by what he's told me I can hardly breathe. Is he looking into the disappearance of those women who were last seen at Marion's? I don't want to believe this. Could it be happening? Is that why he asked me out? Jesus, the two of us humping against a car at the top of Lansdown and all the time, what he was doing is trying to dig up dirt on what was going on at Marion's house of death? I want to throw up.

I take a sip from the glass. "I'm not following."

"I know it's a shock, Persy. I'm sorry."

What's coming next? Will he make a citizen's arrest? Are Marion and Uncle Alfred already in custody?

"Don't be sorry," I say with a tight, self-pitying smile.

"They think Derek has been stealing money. He is conning some of the patients. I'm pretty sure he is, too. That's why I couldn't say anything."

A weird bark of laughter escapes from my lips, and I clap a hand over my mouth.

"Persy?"

I'm shaking my head and don't trust myself enough to speak.

"Persy?" he repeats.

I swallow. "Just… Run that by me again?" I need time to get my act together, let the fear dissipate, and believe that Marion is clear.

"I know. It's hard to take in. I'm investigating Derek. For stealing."

"Stealing?" Confusion reigns. What's worse? He's investigating Derek, or he's such a rubbish investigator that he hasn't noticed bodies have been disappearing.

"Derek? Stealing?" I'm stuck in a brain loop and sound like an idiot. "Derek. From the care home?"

"That's why I lied. I need information; I needed to get in there to figure out what he's up to."

"Derek from the care home is stealing money from the patients, and that's what you're investigating?"

He nods. "I know your family are close to him. And I'm sorry. That was another reason I couldn't mention it."

"No, I get it."

"Marion is a benefactor, close to Derek. That's why I was so tight-lipped. And then I met you and liked you… I didn't want you to think I had some sinister ulterior motive."

"You thought Marion might be involved in some sort of fraud?" I want to laugh out loud and shout from the rooftops. Marion, fraud, don't be absurd. Now, murder, well, that's a different thing.

"I'm sorry." His face is red, and he stares at me and grips my hand. "But it's clear she knows nothing. She's loaded. Why would she be involved in anything like that?"

"Why would she, indeed?" Who says, indeed?

"I know. It's ridiculous to have even considered it. But I had to make sure."

"Of course you did." I say the words with a bit too much enthusiasm. "I get it. I do."

"Now I need to figure it all out, put the pieces together."

I grimace. "How will you do that?" I think about the spyware on my computer, Derek's files, and how I could put those pieces together in less than a couple of minutes.

"Persy, I wanted to tell you. I'm sorry."

"I get it," I say again. I squeeze his hand and toss him a resigned kind of smile. I look at his face, and his lovely blue eyes, and his square shoulders, notice how attractive he is. But something inside of me has shifted. I don't fancy him the way

I did. My feelings have changed in some fundamental way. Yesterday, he was a potential boyfriend. Today, he's someone I need to keep close to. He wants to bring Derek down.

FIFTEEN

We wake up in the morning at mine, our legs entwined, his arm draped over my waist, the sun shining through the window. He slept well. His snoring told me so. I tossed and turned, my thoughts hammering in my head. Should I tell Andrew everything I know about Derek? Yes or no? And to what end? At about five in the morning, I finally came to a decision.

Derek is unpredictable; I have no idea what he'll do next. But if the police start investigating him, he won't have time to search through CCTV, pull dumb stunts, or try to prove that Dora is dead. He'll be far too busy for that.

As the scent of freshly brewed coffee fills the air, Andrew gets out of the shower, dresses, and then wanders into the living room. We settle onto the sofa, my legs resting on his lap as we sip our coffee. The question of his lies still lingers in my head, and beneath the surface, the weight of unspoken words and feelings hovers in the air. He's a good man, but caution is required. He lied. He was good at it.

I feel relaxed, and I have a plan.

I stretch, tighten my dressing gown around my waist and walk over to my desk. I pick up the folder containing the spreadsheet from Derek's computer and a typed-up report of my discussion with our insurance broker. I hold the folder close to my chest and slump down next to Andrew.

"What have you got there?" he asks.

Derek's smarmy face inserts itself into my head. "It's something that will help you."

Andrew frowns and looks sceptical, as if whatever I've got can't be that big of a deal. It doesn't bother me; the contents of the folder will blow him away.

"Last night. At dinner. You mentioned looking into Derek."

He taps his feet and gives me a long look. "Okay. But I don't want you to worry about all that, Persy. It's too personal for you; your family is involved with the care home. Let's forget that we ever talked about it."

"I've got information on him. On Derek." I want to slap the file down in his lap and force him to look at everything right away, but seeing me looking so keen, it'll come off as desperate. "The thing is… Marion has been concerned about Derek for a while. She mentioned him to me. I didn't tell her I would look into him because she becomes too controlling. But I did it anyway. On my own."

"Why didn't you tell me last night?" he says bluntly.

"We'd already shared too much with each other. I didn't want to bring this up, come back here and have to go on and on about it all night."

"Or maybe you weren't sure about sharing it at all?" He unfolds his arms, crosses them behind his head. His body language is open and relaxed, but there's a slight tension in his fingers. Is he nervous? Anxious?

"Do you want it or not?" I hold the manila folder towards him and as he goes to take it, I move it just enough away that it's out of his reach. "I need a couple of promises first."

"What?"

I try to read the emotions that flicker in his eyes, searching for any clues as to what is going on in his mind. I can't read him.

"First, this cannot be connected in any way to Marion. The scandal… it would kill her. And Uncle Alfred isn't well; he couldn't take it either."

He nods curtly. "And the second?"

"It didn't come from me."

He rubs the back of his neck and kind of scowls. I know exactly what he's thinking; he's going to come up with all the reasons he can't make that promise because he'll have to find another source of the information. "Okay," he says eventually.

I'd expected him to disagree, and the fact that he didn't it worries me. "I'm serious, Andrew. You've got to promise. No connection to me. No connection to Marion."

"Done," he says.

I hold out my hand for him to shake.

"Really?" he says.

"Really," I say.

"You don't want a pinky promise?"

This time yesterday, I would have found it cute. Now I'm not sure; there's an edge to his voice that I don't recognise.

"Listen to me. The information I have in this folder is exactly the sort of thing you're looking for on Derek. If you take the steps I took, you can confirm all of it. But I'm serious, it can't have come from me."

He sits forward, plants his feet on the floor, rests his elbows on his knees and clasps his hands together. For the first time in this conversation, he looks deadly serious. "Let's do this," he says. "Let me take a look at the file. If I think I can use it, you or Marion won't be anywhere near anything I find. I promise you. And if I don't think I can use it, I'll close the folder and just hand it back to you."

Something about how he acts tells me he thinks he's smarter than me – that there's nothing in this file that he hasn't figured out already. This kind of thinking isn't new to me. Is there a man on this earth who doesn't feel he's better than a woman?

I put the folder flat on the coffee table. "One more thing."

He tosses me a curious glance.

"I don't want to be involved in this. At all. If you take the file, you take the problem. Agreed?"

"Agreed."

"Good." I hand him the file. "I'm making more coffee." I leave him to it.

Outside the kitchen window overlooking the entrance to the old-fashion museum, a mother and her two kids are walking, a little boy on the left a younger girl on the right. The little girl is pulling at the mum's hand. Finally, she gets away and starts running. The mum chases after her, scoops her up before she runs into the road. The mum gets down on her knees, shakes the girl's shoulders, spins her around, spanks her, then pulls her close, pressing her head against her shoulder. The boy looks on, oblivious to the seriousness of what's going on.

It's a picture of Marion, me, and Uncle Alfred. Marion is in charge, and I want to get away. Uncle Alfred is standing in the background, watching as though nothing is really wrong.

"Persy," Andrew shouts from the living room.

I go back in. He was sitting but now he's standing, his back against the window, shaking his head. "If all of this is true?" He presses his fingers against his forehead and grimaces as if he can't take in what he's just read. "He's in a hole so deep, he'll never get out."

"I know."

He runs his hand through his hair. "He's a real piece of work, isn't he? I thought maybe he'd been nicking jewellery, petty stuff, but this… Damn it."

There's nothing for me to add.

The energy in the room has changed. The romance and banter are gone, replaced with a sense of seriousness.

"What are you going to do about it?"

"When did you find all of this out?"

The question catches me off guard. Is he asking because he's trying to figure out how much I knew and when and why I didn't tell him sooner?

"In the last forty-eight hours."

I can see thoughts ticking over in his head.

"The insurance stuff. How did you get it? I mean, you've got a whole spreadsheet."

"You really want to know?"

"*Do* I want to know?"

"If you ask that question, you probably don't."

He sits back down on the sofa, puts all the papers that were inside the folder out on the coffee table. "If this is all true, it's going to be huge." He looks up at me, a mixture of excitement and disgust in his eyes. "I'm just representing three families who thought Derek had stolen stuff. This changes everything. On this list alone, there has to be, what, fifteen elderly, vulnerable people he's screwed?" He closes his eyes, covers his mouth with his hand. "Derek deserves everything that's coming to him."

"One of the policies on the list, it's Dora Haslea. The woman who disappeared recently. You know about her, right?" I try to say it as casually as I possibly can. Like, guess what, isn't that interesting, who would've thought it?

"You don't think…"

I hold up my hand to stop him talking, like I don't want to hear the awful thing that's about to come out of his mouth, like 'you don't think Derek had anything to do with her disappearance, do you?'

"Don't," I say, as if it was his idea. "I can't stand thinking about it."

He looks back down at the file. "Who else knows about this?" he asks.

"Not a soul."

"Good. The less people involved, the better. I'll handle this. Do my own leg work, then take the next steps." He's nodding, biting the inside of his cheek, staring at the spreadsheet. "Do you mind if I head out? I want to get on top of this."

"No," I say. I can relate. The buzz of finding out something important, you don't want to let it go. I walk him to the door and hold it open.

"Persy, I need to thank you for this. You've made my case for me."

"It's not about that, though. Derek is a bad guy. I'm actually kind of ashamed that neither I nor Marion knew what was going on."

"I get that."

"You need to nail this jerk."

"Agreed." He throws his arms around me and holds me tight and I can feel the intensity of what Andrew is feeling right now. If I were Derek, I'd be running scared.

I watch as Andrew bounds down the stairs, two by two. He reaches the bottom and I wait for the sound of the front door. But I hear nothing. I step out to the bannister, look down and see the top of Andrew's head. He's picked up the newspaper that's been shoved through the door and is staring down at the front page.

"Is everything okay?" I ask.

"You've got to see this," he calls up. "You've got to see what he's done."

I run down the stairs and peer over his shoulder. On the front page is a photo of Derek, and next to it, smaller, is a picture of Dora. I read the headline: *Care Home Director fears for the safety of Dora Haslea.*

Andrew passes the paper to me. "He's trying to cover himself, isn't he? He's trying to make himself look good and, at the same time, make the police run in all sorts of directions. I don't believe this," he goes on. "See what he says about the police, 'dereliction of duty'. Unbelievable. They are going to hate him for this."

I read the article. It's written by the local celebrity journalist, Athena Piper. How did she get hold of this?

"What's going to happen when you tell them what you've got on Derek?"

He squeezes my arm. "They are going to go *ape*."

He leaves the building and I stand, leaning against the door, watching. Derek is done for, as good as, and the fog that's been swirling around me for days is finally beginning to lift. The rule of the last inch comes to mind. It's always the last bit that's hard to finish off.

Back in my flat, I jump into the shower and let the warm water flow over me – no cold shower for me today. Things are looking up. I dry off, wrap a towel around me, put on my slippers, and hear the telltale ding from my computer: Derek's spyware. By the time I get to the desk, the conversation has already started.

A woman is speaking. She sounds old. Educated. Condescending. I recognise the voice. Are you kidding me? It's her. Marion.

"I don't think so," she says.

"I really need to talk to you." Derek sounds like he's pleading for his life.

"Isn't that what you are doing right now?" I'd spit out a celebratory laugh if my heart weren't beating in my mouth. The old battleaxe can't stop herself.

"What we have to discuss needs to be in person." Derek's voice has taken on a snotty, superior edge.

"Does it?" She sounds bemused and dismissive. Whatever he wants from her, it's not going to happen. He can be as much of a jerk as he wants; it won't work with Marion.

Then he says something so strange that, for a moment, I think I'm hearing things. He says a few words that sound like German. *Ich weiß, was du getan hast.*

There's a long, long pause. I can hear Marion breathing.

I expect her to laugh out loud, make him small like she does to everyone.

"Very well," she says. "In one hour. Here." She hangs up.

I'm stunned. Why? What? How? Never has she agreed to do something she didn't want to do. It's against her philosophy.

I replay the call and listen to the words he used. *Ich weiß, was du getan hast.* I type them into Google Translate.

I know what you did.

She speaks German, understands what he's said, and feels threatened, or she'd never have invited him to her house. And if I'm right, I know exactly what she's going to do to him.

SIXTEEN

I brick the drive over to Marion's like it's the Indy 500. The roads are narrow, the surfaces slick, and the curves so sharp I have to slam the brakes until the back wheels start to skid away from me. My foot presses down even harder on the gas pedal, the engine roaring as I speed towards Marion's. Ten more minutes and he'll be at her house. I have to get there first.

I speed up the driveway, but no cars are parked in front of the house, so there are no visitors. I rush out of the car, hurry up the steps, and shove open the heavy wooden door with a loud thud. The silence inside is deafening. My footsteps echo through the empty rooms as I search for any sign of movement. The drawing room is eerily still, sunlight filtering in through dusty windows. I recheck my watch; I'm early. Could he have been early, too? I don't want to think about it. I scan the room and check behind sofas and curtains, searching for any clues of something Marion might have done. "Marion!" I shout, my voice bouncing off the high ceilings.

I hear the squeak of a board upstairs. It doesn't sound like someone is walking across the floor; it's just one solitary creak, like someone is up there and trying hard not to be heard.

I take each step one by one. I gently grip the handle to Marion's bedroom door and ease it open, my breath coming in shallow gasps.

Marion is lying on her back, fully dressed, with her arms crossed over her chest, her head slightly tilted, her mouth open, and her skin pale.

My heart races as I rush towards her, my mind filled with panic and desperation. Standing by the bed, I stare at her still form, looking for any sign of life. Deep down, I know she's gone. I stand at the side of the bed, watching her. She's not breathing.

I don't know what to do. I stand back, reach for my phone to call Uncle Alfred, and stop. I have to do it; I have to check her pulse to make sure. I don't want to do it; I don't want to touch her pale, waxy skin, but I have no choice. Whoever I call, they'll ask if I'm sure. It's got to be done.

I lean forward and press my fingers against her neck.

And right then and there, she jolts upright like a bat out of hell. I lurch back with a cry, lose my footing, slip on the rug and fall on my backside.

"What on earth do you think you are doing?" Marion sits up and slides her feet to the floor. Her face is bright red and I can see a vein in her neck throbbing.

I stand up, mouthing wordlessly.

"Get out," she shouts, flinging her arm up and pointing to the door with her crooked index finger.

"I'm sorry," I say. "I didn't mean... I'm sorry."

"Out," she bellows.

I scurry away like a rat down a sewer, dart into the drawing room and pace, listening for signs that she's on her way down. I hear her coming down the stairs. She walks in. She's put lipstick on. Is that a good or bad sign? I used to have a list of things I had to look out for when I was a kid. A smile was terrible. Raised eyebrows were good. A fidgety foot was nasty. Playing with the ring on her wedding finger: I don't want to think about it.

She sits down opposite me. She leans forward, but her black eyes don't move. "What are you doing here?"

"I just popped in." Every part of that sentence is wrong, but the ability to say something sensible has terrified me.

She closes her eyes, sighs, then shakes her head and taps her finger on the table. I remember that. Tapping the table: run away.

"Persephone. I am rather tired. I have just had an unpleasant meeting. I think it would be better if, in the future, you were to call before you arrive."

"Meeting?" Derek must have been and gone. The word 'gone' sticks in my head. She's done away with him. I'm sure of it. "Meeting? Who with?" I don't want to play dumb, but there's no other choice with her.

"With whom? Dear me. Will this torture never end?"

"With whom did you have a meeting?" I spit out, regretting every corrected word that comes out of my mouth.

"Derek."

She's lying. He couldn't have got here so quickly. "But he wasn't supposed to be here until three-thirty." The words slip out before I can stop them.

"How did you know that?"

"Susie," I say, too quickly, "I called her. She said Derek was coming over here."

She knows I'm lying. I can see it in her eyes. "Then, if you knew I was having a meeting, why are you here?" She says every word with a horrid kind of relish. She knows she's got me.

I want to run out of this room, crawl into the coat closet and sit curled up on the floor, my head on my knees, eyes closed, the way I used to as a kid. "I heard Derek was coming here. And… I was concerned."

"About?" She glares at me, baiting me.

"Dora." I stare back at her. "I was worried he knew something about Dora and you. I thought you might… You know what, forget it… I'm sorry. It was stupid of me."

"That is self-evident." She starts to stand up.

"Where is he, then? Derek?" I hold my breath.

"Do you see him anywhere here?" She glares at me and twists her lips into a mean little smile. I've seen this face before. It isn't good. Getting a word out of her when she's in this I'm-ever-so-clever mood will not happen. "I am going into the sunroom. Please do not follow me. Please go." And she leaves.

I wait until she's sitting down, then secretly peer into the sunroom, scanning the corners, searching for signs that I'll spot Derek's nasty trainers poking out from under something. My eyes wander over to her roll-top desk. It's open. A chequebook is sitting on the top. It's never open. She locks it and hides the key in the bookcase, third shelf down, behind a first edition of *Tamerlane and Other Poems* by Edgar Allan Poe.

Her head is back, leaning against a cushion she's wedged behind her neck and her eyes are closed. I wait until I hear the gentle sound of her snoring. I tiptoe in.

"Have you not left yet?" Marion says quietly. Her eyes are still shut.

"I'm going." I grab the chequebook without her seeing it, shove it in my pocket, and leave her there. I hurry down the hall, get out of the house, and slam the front door hard enough to let her know I've gone. As I drive away, I glance in the rear-view mirror and catch a glimpse of her standing by the front door. She's come to check on me, to make sure I've left.

A mile or so down the main road I pull into a small parking area, buy a bacon sandwich from the van and a hot cup of tea.

I put in extra sugar. I'm in a bit of a state, recovering from the shock of what went on in the house. First the fear she'd murdered Derek, then the shock she herself was dead. I can still picture the look on her face as she lurched up at me. It was like something out of *Night of the Living Dead*. I shiver.

I sit in my car, the heat rising, sipping my tea and leafing through the chequebook. What was she up to? As I bite into the bacon sandwich, I spot the carbon copy of the last cheque she wrote.

Today's date, Derek's name. An amount of £100K.

A wave of dizziness washes over me, and I lean back against the headrest and shut my eyes. A yoyo. That's me right now. Pulled and pushed from one moment to the next, always dangling from somebody else's string.

I repeat the sentence out loud because I need to make sure I believe what I've just seen. "Marion has given Derek a £100K."

He's found something on the CCTV – something that connects us to the three missing women. It has to be. It's the only explanation.

SEVENTEEN

Andrew's car is parked outside my place, and he's leaning against it, relaxed, phone in hand, looking every bit the man who has nothing to worry about. I'd prefer it if he weren't there; I need to process that Marion is paying Derek off, which means he's blackmailing her. But I steel myself and raise my hand to wave at him. He's got his role to play, too, and I tell myself it's not time for me to take my eye off the ball, not even for a second.

He strides towards me, grinning. "I've just come from the police station."

I no longer have any idea whether this constitutes good news. "And?"

"And we are going to nail that bastard." He wraps his arms around my waist and pulls me towards him. "They are going to bury him. Derek is as good as dead." He plants a kiss on my lips.

"I don't believe it."

"It's a done deal. I promise you. They want blood."

"Then it's over."

"It is, Persy." He smiles, pleased with himself. "Unless he can give the police something they want, it's over for him; he'll be put away for a long time."

"Something they want?"

"I'm talking about a plea. Come to some arrangement. Something that could potentially reduce his sentence."

"I mean, would they do that with someone like him?" I grab the keys from my bag, fumble at the door to hide my face and shove it open. "What could he possibly have to offer them?" I ask.

"Unless he's got something on someone else who's a bigger fish to fry, there won't be a deal." I pretend to look for something in my bag to give me time to think. "The damage he did with that newspaper article? At the station, they hate the guy. You could feel it. They'll never forgive him. And you know what else? They *already* think there might be a connection between him and Dora. He's made some weird calls to the station. No one trusts him. Persy, it's over for him."

We walk up the stairs. My heart is thumping.

We walk into my flat, and I tell him I will make some coffee. My mind is so scattered, thinking about what Derek does or doesn't know, that I can't hold a proper conversation with Andrew.

He kicks off his shoes, goes into the living room, and falls onto the sofa. "They'll get their ducks in a row, make sure the case is watertight and then act all guns blazing, as they like to say. They'll go after him by the end of the week. Once they're done, he'll be looking at serious jail time."

"What about Dora, then? What are they going to do about her?" I try to put just the right level of concern into my voice: poor-Dora-missing-old-lady type concern, rather than do-they-know-we-fed-her-to-the-pigs voice.

"They'll do their thing. Question staff at the safari park. The other people that were on the bus. Someone must have seen something. If Derek's involved, someone at the home must have their suspicions... And they'll go through CCTV footage. There has to be some footage at home, on the roads, and even on individuals who have home-security cameras. The police will dig until they find out exactly what happened to Dora. Trust me. The British police, they don't come much better than that."

My mind is a jumbled mess. My ever-so-clever plan has completely blown up. It's disintegrated into chaos. What have I done? The police now have more reasons than ever to investigate what happened to Dora. What I've done, it's unforgivable. I can hear Marion's words in my head. *Oh, Persephone, you are such a disappointment.*

"Are you okay?" Andrew asks.

"Yes. Sorry. It's a lot. That's all."

He puts his arm over my shoulder, pulls me towards him, and kisses my head. "This is going to be hard on Marion, but she'll come out of this clean. It's Derek we're after." He rubs my arm. "What happened to that coffee?"

I wrap my arms tightly around him, pulling him close to me, a defensive strategy, a way for me to think without him watching me. My gaze drifts out the window, and my head rests on his shoulder. What am I going to do?

"Did they ask you where you found everything about Derek?" I ask.

"No. I put all the information together and checked out the insurance information. Then handed it all over. The question didn't come up."

He takes a strand of loose hair from my ponytail and gently tucks it behind my ear. "We make a good team. You know that." He squeezes my hand.

I try hard to respond, to smile, to do anything, but it's impossible. There are too many variables and too many unknowns. The answer to everything is what Derek has on Marion and why she paid him off.

Andrew's phone rings. The signal can't be great because he keeps repeating himself and asking if the other person can hear. Eventually, he asks them to hold while he finds a place with a stronger signal and lets me know he's going to take the call outside.

I wait until I see him standing on the pavement, and then I nip over to my computer to see what Derek's been up to. The spyware also records all his internet searches, and it looks like he's been busy. He's clicked on fifteen or sixteen travel sites in the past hour. BA. Airjet. Deutsch Airways. I lean in. He's been searching for flights to Germany. And he doesn't care about the price. He cares about the soonest. Is it a runner he's doing?

Andrew comes up the stairs. Quickly, I close the computer and sit back down on the sofa, yawning and stretching my neck to give the impression that I'm so exhausted I could sleep for a week.

"I feel like crawling into bed. I'm so tired," I say.

Andrew grabs a blanket from the back of a chair. "Here you go."

I lie on the sofa, and he places the blanket on top of me and kisses me on the top of my head.

"You want me to stay?"

"Up to you." But I really don't.

"If you don't mind, I'll head on. That was one of my clients. I need to put a report together. I prefer to get it out of the way." He kisses me on the cheek. "I'll call you later?"

I stay on the sofa until I hear him run down the stairs and the door slam shut. When I hear the sound of an engine start, I throw the blanket off me, jump off the sofa, run to the window and peer out from behind the curtain. The lights of his car disappear down onto Gay Street. Then I open the computer back up. Three flights to Germany today. Five tomorrow. Five the day after. I'm hunched over, eyes centimetres from the screen, watching Derek live, logging in and out, like he's dithering, can't decide what to do.

Finally, he booked his ticket to Germany. Today. My hands are gripped into fists with sheer relief, my nails digging into my palms.

His flight departs in two hours from Bristol. The care home is forty-five minutes from the airport, so he'll leave about now if I'm right. I stand up, pace, go to the sink, pour a massive glass of water, and down it. I pace, check my watch, pace again. I want him to disappear so badly I can't stand it. I grab my coat and head to the coffee shop, where I sit with a cappuccino, my legs jittery and my heart racing. I recheck my watch. He should be on his way by now.

I can't wait any longer. I need to know. I jump in my car.

Susie is at reception.

"Where's Derek?" I ask. I'm too stressed even to bother to make up some excuse for being here.

"Gone," she says, wrinkling her nose.

"How do you mean gone?"

"Vacation. Said something had come up. Weird. Just like that. And you know what, that son of a bitch put that idiot Anita in charge. You know the one. Walks around like she's got something shoved up her you-know-what. Everyone's so damn angry."

"How long's he gone for?"

"A week. That's what he said."

"He just upped and left?"

"Like someone lit a firework under his chair. You could almost smell his car's tyres burning on the tarmac when he drove away from this place." She laughs at the thought. "That expensive car of his. Thinks he's Lewis Hamilton."

"Where's he gone? Did he say?" My thoughts are running away from me, pulling my words with them. They're spilling out too quickly. "Sorry. I'm shocked."

Her voice dips. "One of the nurses said something about Europe somewhere. But he was very quiet about it."

What is Derek up to?

"What's even weirder? He said no one was to bother him." She starts to laugh. "It's like he's buggered off to the jungles in Borneo or the Amazon or Attenborough land. And, get this, he even left his phone behind to make sure we couldn't call him. That made me laugh. When have we ever needed to contact him? This place runs better when he's not here anyway."

He didn't want to be tracked; what other explanation is there for leaving your phone behind?

I've got a reprieve. He's gone for a week.

"At least you'll get a break for a bit; I mean, the boss being away is always kind of nice, right?"

"Ain't that the truth. Even more so when the boss is Derek!"

Conmen like Derek are always pulling some scam. And whatever scam he's pulling now, there's a direct connection between Marion and Germany.

A text comes in from Scooter. *Are you excited for tomorrow? What are you going to wear? Will you call them Mum and Dad as soon as you meet them? Hahahahahah... that last question wasn't real. Please don't call them Mum and Dad when you meet them. But, Persy. Honestly. Good luck.*

Sitting in my car, my mind is shrouded in a thick fog of conflicting emotions. Excitement at the arrival of my parents mixes with fear over the fact that my mother is being blackmailed and might end up behind bars. I can't allow this to go on any further, so I decide to deal with her. I turn on the engine and get ready to do a U-turn. I'm going to deal with Marion head-on. But the truth hits me as quickly as I get ready to speed towards her house. In what world will Marion tell me what I need to know? She doesn't have the gene for honesty.

I call Uncle Alfred.

"I have a question," I say when he answers. "We have a problem. It's serious. Marion has been giving money to Derek. He's blackmailing her. He has to know something."

"Persy," he says with his habitual calmness. "You're sounding rather unnerved. Please don't take all of this on yourself. It is of no significance."

"You know," I spit out. "You know what's going on with her and Derek, don't you?"

"Persy, my dear girl. I would tell you if I thought there was anything to worry about."

"But you wouldn't, would you? You've always protected me, but I'm a grown-up now. I don't need protection. Just tell me what's happening, and I can fix it; I know I can."

"Persy." He says my name with authority as if I need to take what he's about to say seriously. "There is nothing for you to worry about. Are we clear?"

Who are 'we' in this conversation? It feels like he's talking about him and Marion, not me and him.

"Marion and I, we have everything under control. I promise you, Persy, nothing for you to worry about."

"I don't believe you," I say.

"You are very important to me, Persy. I cannot imagine any situation where I would leave you worried or vulnerable. And you're right. You are sufficiently grown up to handle any difficult situation. I believe that without a shadow of a doubt. But now you must trust me when I tell you this whole thing will be dealt with. You do not need to get involved."

He's doing what Marion does – shutting me out.

I go home, take a sleeping tablet, pull an old hot-water bottle out of the cupboard and fill it. I get under the covers, the bottle's warmth against my skin. I'm not sure I exist.

EIGHTEEN

Andrew is calling at eight in the morning, pushing me to join him for breakfast. He's upbeat, enthusiastic, and full of the joys of life; it makes me feel tired. As he speaks, a text comes through from Scooter, saying good luck. Today's the day to meet Mum and Dad. I try to pump myself up to be ready to play the 'here's my parents' game, but too many things are going on.

"Come on, Persy. Look out the window. The sun is trying to break through. And, even better, we're going to go after Derek."

"I can't," I say. "I'm so sorry. I've got a lead on a new job." The always-ready lie. "I'll call you later. When I'm done."

I take a shower, indifferent to whether it's hot or cold. I pull on some leggings and a pale-grey cashmere sweater. On my feet, I wear ankle boots. I should dress up as if I want to make a good impression, but I'm not sure if I can pull it all off. My therapist once told me that my natural disposition is that everything will always go wrong. When she said that, all I could think of was 'no shit'.

I make a cup of coffee, put a lid on the mug, and get into the car. On a better day, it would've been a quick trip to Margaret's buildings, past the pretty glass shop, then to Le Bocage for a pastry. This isn't a better day.

My hands grip the steering wheel as I head out of town. My mind should be thinking about Mum and Dad, what they'll think of me when they first see me, and how I should approach them. Instead, my mind keeps going back to the conversation with Uncle Alfred. He's old. Marion is old. How are they going to fix this? Throwing money at Derek will only correct the problem in the short run. In the long run? No way.

Up ahead, I see the sign for Stonehenge. It's been so long since I've been here that I can't remember what it was like. What I do remember is that we could climb over the fence and sit on the stones. Those times have gone. There is a car park, signposts, and even a change in the direction of the road, which means climbing in like we used to do as kids, we wouldn't get away with it.

I arrive at one-forty-five, fifteen minutes before their bus is expected to arrive.

I lock my car, find the ticket booth, and pay for what the board advertises as 'The Stonehenge Experience'.

I stand at the corner of the building, looking out, shifting from foot to foot, trying to change my mood, but the weather has changed and with the rain pelting down and the wind whipping around the building, it's hard to pull off.

Scooter calls. "Are you there? Just checking in to see how you're feeling."

"Good. I'm early. They should be here soon."

"You don't sound good."

"Sure I do." Other than Scooter, I don't think anyone can ready my mood by listening to my voice. I need to be as positive about finding my real parents as he is. I need to believe it as strong as he does.

"Persy, what's going on? I can tell by the way you sound. Something is wrong."

"It's all this," I say. "Sorry. It's overwhelming."

"Take a deep breath. Now. I'm going to count. Remember, the way we used to. I'm going to count to four, slowly. Please listen to my words; breathe in for four. Hold it for three, breathe out."

"It's not about breathing, Scooter. It's about being honest. Come on. Who are we kidding? We don't even know it's them."

"It's them," he says. "What's going on with you? Are you scared about seeing them, is this what this is all about?"

"No. Maybe yes. I don't know. It seems like I'm chasing shadows." I look around the tourist site. Families, children, and people, all with smiles, enjoy their lives. That option doesn't exist for me. "If it ends up being a waste of time?"

"Persy. Listen to me. Now, shut the fuck up. Whether you like it or not, this may be them. Or maybe it won't. It doesn't matter. At least we're trying. Just give it your best shot. Okay."

"Okay," I say.

"No. Not okay. It's pretty simple. No one knows what's going to happen. If it's them. Great. If it's not, we'll keep looking." He takes a deep breath. "Okay. Listen. If you promise to give this your best shot, and you think it's them, I'll come over."

"To England?"

"To England."

"You're kidding?" I ask.

"No. And I'm sorry, Persy, I know how you get when these things happen. You talk yourself out of anything good happening to you. I should've come over to be with you. But I promise. I'll come."

"When?" I say.

"I'm finishing up a job here. If you think it's them, I'll get over to you, maybe a week?"

He's such a good guy I can barely cope.

"Will you give this your best shot?"

"Yep," I say.

"Good. No telling yourself it's not them. Get your act together. Assume this is going to work."

"You sound pretty convinced."

"Best foot forward and all that, right? I'm not going to let you wimp out on this. Man up."

"I get it," I say.

"I hope you do because if you don't, I'm going to come find you and whip your ass."

"Really, that's what you're going to do?"

"You betcha," he says. "Now, most women would probably love it if I whipped their ass. You, I'm not so sure; I seem to remember you were more interested in—"

"Got it," I say quickly. Now I'm laughing. "Thanks, Scooter. Really."

"You are welcome." His voice is softer. "You let me know how it goes."

"I promise," I say.

I spot a bench, sit down with my hands under my thighs, and jiggle my legs. Five massive coaches drive into the car park. Some of the names written on the side are familiar to me; Bath is a major tourist city, and everyone there is used to them rumbling past. It's the fourth one that causes my heart to race. Brightness Coaches is the name printed on the itinerary Scooter sent me.

The excitement of what's going on starts to build. When I was thirteen, I played the role of Lady Macbeth in the school play. The excitement I felt then is the excitement I feel now. My hands are slick with sweat, and I start to tremble with anticipation. I've forgotten how good this feels. I push off against the bench and stand up. Adrenaline appears out of nowhere and begins to energise me.

The first three coaches take the last parking spots in the far line. Brightness drives past all of them and stops maybe thirty feet away from me. The coach sits there, its engine idling. Inside, a man stands at the front, speaking into a microphone. He'll tell them the logistics: what to look for and when to get back.

A few minutes later, the door swooshes open.

A stream of people slowly steps out, looking up and around as though happy that, for a moment, the rain has stopped.

An older woman gets off the bus first, opens an umbrella, thinks better of it, closes it and pushes it into a large bag over her shoulder.

My heart leaps into my throat as I see them, Mum and Dad, oblivious to me standing there, watching them.

On my phone, I compare the photo Scooter sent. It's them. No doubt. Time to be their long-lost daughter.

I wait, watch them pass by, expect them to look at me, but they don't, too caught up in a map they're looking at. I walk a couple of people behind them.

She has a waterproof coat and a waterproof hat with a narrow brim. It's dark green – the same colour as my coat. We have the same taste. He's wearing a Yankees basketball cap and a navy coat that goes to his knees. Underneath, he's wearing jeans. They both are wearing the same walking shoes, the sensible ones you have to buy from an outdoor shop. He looks like a nice man. The sort you'd be proud to say was your dad. I laugh at the idea. He is my dad. And I am proud.

There's some hold-up at the booth, and the three people at the beginning of the line are looking at the people behind them, who seem to be looking for someone behind *them*. The tour guide, the man I'd seen on the bus with the microphone, bustles forward and hurries to the front. They all go to the other side of the building and wait for the tour bus to arrive to take them closer to the stones. I keep my eyes on Mum and Dad.

I jump on the same bus as they do, hide my face as I walk past, and choose a seat several rows behind. They sit, their shoulders touching as if they need to keep their connection alive. They still love each other; I'm sure of it.

When the bus stops, we all stand in a line and wait to get off. Mum saunters ahead of Dad but turns to look at him and smiles as if she wants to make sure he's close. We all get off the bus and start walking. A gust of wind springs out of nowhere, sending Mum's hat flying like a saucer.

My arm flashes out, and I grab the hat. Our eyes meet. She's smiling and coming towards me.

"I'm so sorry," she says as I hand her the hat. "It's a little on the big side, and I'm not even sure why I brought it on this trip." She puts it back on, squeezing it down as though it will somehow help it stick on her head.

I want to say something, anything, but I can't. The words won't come, and I'm standing there like an idiot, just watching her. But she doesn't seem to notice. She thanks me again and goes back to Dad, who's waiting for her.

She didn't recognise me, but I remind myself, why would she? I remind myself of something else too. Don't get too into this; it will only end up in tears.

She puts her arm through Dad's, and they stroll off together. I keep my distance and stay a good fifty yards behind them. I watch as they look at the stones, stop, and read the different explanations of the history: how old they are, and how the stones got here. Occasionally, he takes his camera and takes a photo of the stones or a selfie together. At one point, he stops, takes a zoom out of a camera bag, and focuses on an object in front of me. He likes to use a good lens. We're on the same wavelength.

Forty-five minutes later, we all walk back to the bus, hair dishevelled by the wind that never really settled down and slightly wet from the light rain that began a few minutes before. Their guide stands in the front and tells them their coach will leave in under an hour. This is enough time for them to go to the souvenir shop and grab some lunch before they head on to Bath.

The bus pulls in, and we all wander into the gift shop. I tuck myself behind a rotating column of floor-to-ceiling cards, calendars and table mats. Mum and Dad walk around the store, picking up things and showing each other the gifts. She shakes a snow globe and shows him, and it must be an inside joke because they both start to laugh. He picks up a T-shirt that says 'Stonehenge. Brought to you by ancient aliens'. She tells him she thinks he should get it, but he knows she's joking because he folds it back up and leaves it on the table.

They buy three postcards, all the same ones: a photo of the stones at dawn. Mysterious, dusky and beautiful. That's the postcard I would've chosen too. She stands at the cash register behind two other people from her group, and Dad stands beside her. I like that about him. He's okay with her paying and taking the lead. The two of them slowly wander out.

They briefly talk to the tour guide, and he points to the café. They go inside. I watch them buy two teas and two sandwiches. They find a seat in the corner, away from everyone, and sit down. I go in, too, and order the same thing they ordered. With the tray in my hand, I walk towards their table, but I make sure not to look at them. I sit at the table next to them.

Mum notices me at once. "You saved my hat." She tosses me a gleaming, lovely, white-toothed smile.

I laugh and nod.

"Are you on your own?" she asks.

I don't know what to say.

"If you are, join us, please."

"Thank you," I say. "That's really kind." And I move onto their table because I don't know what else to do.

"You're English?" Dad asks. He's peering at me closely, frowning. Does he know?

"I am. But you're not. You're American?"

Mum smiles at me. "I told him we wouldn't be able to hide it." They both grin. "Are you from this part of the country?"

I take a deep breath. "I am. Bath. Do you know it?" I feel terrible. I should tell them the truth, right now.

Dad is the one to jump in first. "We'll be travelling there, spending the next two days going around the city. It won't be new to us. We used to work there back in the day."

"Really? Where?"

"The University of Bath," Mum says. "We're not academics. Just spent a year here in England, needed to earn some money."

The moment seems right. I'll mention Marion. Wait for the look of recognition. Then we'll sit at this table, in a café in Stonehenge, talk about how all of this happened. I cough.

"Then you must know…"

The tour guide comes running towards us. "Sorry," he says. "We need to leave early because of a thunderstorm coming our way. Bring your food and drink, and you can finish it on the coach."

Mum starts to stand up, but Dad holds tight. "Really? The weather doesn't look so bad now."

He's not going to be manoeuvred quite so easily. He must know that this moment, us being together, somehow it's important.

"The traffic is backed up. We may not make our dinner reservations if we don't move now. They're at the Royal Crescent Hotel; I'd hate for us to lose them."

"Of course." Mum stands up and starts to put her food on a tray. Dad follows suit. "I'm so sorry," Mum says. "I hope you don't think we're being rude."

"No," I say. "No, of course not." My heart is like a stone, and I'm unsure if the one chance in my life for us to be together has gone.

My phone rings.

It's Marion.

Mum gives me a knowing glance, raises her eyebrows as if to say we always get calls at the wrong time and walks away. Dad is a few steps ahead.

Furiously, I decline and jog to catch up with them. "Sorry," I say. "You said you were going to spend some time in Bath?"

"That's what we came for. To go down memory lane." She smiles at me, but there's something unsaid behind it. Sadness? I like this woman. She really should be my mum.

"Where are you staying?" I ask.

"The Francis Hotel."

"You're kidding," I say. "I have a meeting there tomorrow."

She's watching me, assessing me; I feel it. I know what she's thinking. Could this be her? My long-lost daughter. She looks like me. She even looks the right age.

"I'm thirty-two," I say.

"I'm sorry?" she says.

The tour guide is ordering everyone onto the bus.

"I'd better run, or they might leave without me," Mum says.

"Maybe I'll see you at the hotel?"

"The hotel?" She looks confused as if she can't quite figure out why I'd be at the place where they're staying. Then smiles and says, "I certainly hope so." She leaves me, her hand holding her hat, her coat flapping in the wind, her red hair flying behind her.

I go back to the café and spot my cold cup of tea and half-eaten sandwich on the tray. I've met them. Mum and Dad. I can't believe it. I rest my head in my hands and quietly start to laugh. And tomorrow, I'll see them again. I tell myself that it is better this way, better not to have told them today because it would've been too rushed; Scooter was right.

I know the Francis Hotel. I sometimes go there because it's close to my office, and their chairs are comfy and well-spaced apart, a nice place to work quietly on a laptop. I'll sit inside, in a chair facing the door, to make sure I spot them when they come down for breakfast. It'll be calm and peaceful, and they'll see me, come and join me, and then we can talk.

Marion calls again. I watch as their coach drives away and part of me drives away with it. I look at Marion's phone on the screen. So be it. If Uncle Alfred and Marion want to fix everything, then go ahead. I'm out. I pick up the phone.

"Persephone," she snaps before I say a word. "You need to come to the house. Immediately."

"Because?"

"The police are here. They have a warrant to search your car."

The image of me in the boot of my car, pulling Dora into the back, sends a chill through my spine. Has Marion set this up? It wasn't Uncle Alfred she was putting in the crosshairs. Was it me?

NINETEEN

The ride home is a blur, my heart racing and hands shaking. The streetlights fly by and the sound of cars whizzing past fills my ears as I frantically tap Andrew's number into my phone. He doesn't answer. He always answers. Did Andrew know about this? Is that why he's not answering? On the fourth call, he picks up.

"Did you know about this?" I spit out.

"Persy? About what?"

"My car. They want it."

"You need to slow down."

"The police. They want my fucking car. Why?"

"I don't know anything about this. I promise you. It doesn't make sense. Why would they want your car?"

"Maybe because you told them that I found out about Derek?" That isn't the truth, but I'm angry and telling him what I'm really worried about isn't an option.

"I didn't mention your name. I gave you my word, and I kept it. It has to be some mix-up. I'll make a call. Give me a couple of minutes. Where are you now?"

"Why? Why do you care where I am?"

"Persy. Take it easy. It was just a question."

I hang up.

I reach for the phone to call Uncle Alfred, but fear grips me, and I can't do it. The police could be with him, listening to his every word. My phone could be bugged, too. I try to remember what I might have said, what could be misconstrued, but my recall has gone; I'm too worked up. The crushing weight of what's happening now hits me like a sledgehammer. If I'm arrested, the next time my real mum and dad see me, it could be through the lens of a newspaper headline. They'll label me the 'pig lady' or some other cruel moniker, and Mum will never want to see me again. They'll turn and run, and it'll be a matter of time before our tragic story becomes fodder for a Netflix series. I can't cope.

I pull over, get out of the car, put my hands flat against the metal, dip my head, force myself to take deep breaths, hold them, and then exhale. After a couple of minutes, my heart rate gets steadier, and I straighten up, needing to get as much air as I can into my lungs.

Brightness Coaches is driving past. I see Mum and Dad staring out the window, watching me, a curious look on their faces. This can't be happening. I look like a fugitive, standing on the side of the road, hair in a mess, trying to breathe.

My phone rings, and I jerk open the door to grab it, happy to hide my face so they can't see it anymore. It's Andrew.

"Okay. This is what I've found out. The police have a warrant for the cars. All of the cars. Not just yours. And nothing else. Nothing inside the house and nothing outside in or around the grounds. Not the barns, the outbuildings, the garages."

"I get it. I know what outside means. Why? Why are they doing this?"

"A tip-off."

"A tip-off," I shout. "Who in the hell knows anything about me or Marion or our damn cars? That's bullshit."

"That's what I've been told." He's getting testy. "What else do you want me to say?"

"I don't understand. Okay. I just don't get it."

"Nor do I. If I were to take a guess, this sounds exactly like the sort of bullshit Derek would pull. Please don't quote me on that, but this is what he does. He misdirects."

I can't think straight. Dora was in the back of my car. Her head was on its side, the saliva dripping from her mouth, sticking to the fibres of the carpet in my car. It's all there, the proof of Dora's last moments. But how would Derek know about that? Only Marion and Uncle Alfred knew. Did she spill the beans to Derek?

"And why the hell haven't they arrested Derek? Why are they wasting their time on me? They've left it so late he's probably…" I shut my mouth. I was about to say, 'left the *country*'.

"How far away are you?" Andrew asks.

"Two hours," I lie. I'm about thirty minutes away, but I need to buy myself some time to fix the problem.

"Good. I'll see you at Marion's. I'm on my way there now. And to give you a heads-up, they don't know we're an item. It's better to keep it that way. I don't want them shutting me out."

I stumble back and sit on the grass verge, barely able to keep my head straight. I want to wish all of this away. But I can't. I can't wish Dora in the back of my car away. Her presence there is a cold, hard fact.

I tighten my hand into a fist and punch the damp grass. This needs to be sorted. I'm not going to jail.

I get back in the car. Thirty minutes later, I drive casually up to the double doors of the car dealership. There's Frank at his desk, at the corner of the building, the same desk he's had for the past fifteen years, the same smiling face he's used as we've driven in and out with our new cars. We're his bread and butter. Never haggle, never demand, just request the top of the line every two or three years, and that is exactly what he gives us.

He spots me and jumps up from his seat. "Good to see you, Persy! Marion in the market for a new car? The earliest lease doesn't expire for six months or so."

I skip the small talk. Look serious. "Frank, I've got a problem." I turn and gesture at my parked car. He follows my gaze. "I had a dog in the back, and it was ill. Marion is allergic, and I don't want her to know."

"No problem. Leave the car with us, and we'll give it a good once-over and get it back to you. It'll take an hour or so. You can either wait or come back tomorrow. I can give you a loaner."

"I hate to be a pain. But this allergy of hers, it's serious." I hesitate, hoping he'll come up with the right solution himself. He doesn't twig, though, so I jump right in. "Could you just swap out the carpet at the back? That's the only place where the dog was."

He purses his lips and looks sceptical.

I rush on. "Come on, you know what she's like. Remember when you washed the inside of her car, and she said the pedals sounded squeaky when she pressed the brakes? I don't want to go through something like that again."

"Don't remind me," he says. He looks outside to the cars that are parked next to each other. Some are for sale, some in for service. Then he points to a car exactly like mine. "You see that black one out there. It's the same as yours. Same year. Same everything. It even has the same carpet at the back."

"You can swap mine out for that one?"

"Sure," he says. "For you, Persy, anything."

"I can't tell you how grateful I am. Honestly. She'd go on about this for years."

"Don't worry about it," he says. "Give me fifteen minutes, and it'll be done."

"Thank you," I say. "You've saved me, you know that, right?"

"I know. And after the carpet is replaced, we'll clean the whole thing. It looks like you've gone through some mud?"

"You know what. Don't worry about that. But thanks. Marion knows I never get the thing washed, and if she sees me driving up in a clean car, she'll start to ask questions." I give him a knowing smile. "Just flip the carpet, and I'll be on my way."

"You've got it," he says. "There's a coffee machine over there. Take a seat. I'll let you know when it's ready."

I sit in the waiting room. *This has to work. No*, I repeat to myself, *it will work*. The cars will be clean – nothing to find. The more I think about it, the more I believe this has something to do with Derek. It's a message from him. He wants us to know that he can screw with the Adelard family whenever he wants.

I check my phone again and again. Finally, a text comes in. It's from Scooter. He wants to know how it went with Mum and Dad, and God knows I want to tell him. But I can't because my brain isn't working properly. I need to think about what's going on at Marion's house. I need to make sure I've left nothing else for them to find. I text back: *All good. I have no time now. I will call later.*

I grab a glass of water that I can't drink. I stand by the door to the service area and peep through the window. My old rug is being pulled out, and the new one is ready to be put in. With a bit of luck, I'll be out of here in ten minutes.

A text comes in from Andrew: *I spoke to the police about Derek. They are going to arrest him.* I look down at my hands, am tempted to say, 'Oh no, they're not. Derek's in Germany'. I'm happy, this news means they think he's guilty.

Frank walks towards me, my keys in his hand. "All done. You can be on your way."

"Thanks," I say. "And can we keep this between us? Marion shouldn't know."

"Done," he says.

I drive out of the dealership, stay on the road for about three miles, pull into a service station, and park by a patchy embankment. I look around to make sure no one is watching, grab a handful of dirt, rub it into my hands, open the boot, and wipe my hands on the carpet.

Now, it looks just like an older carpet should look.

Roger, Marion's lawyer, calls to tell me pretty much what Andrew had told me. Bring in my car. Nothing to worry about. It's procedure. He sounds calm. There's nothing odd about this whatsoever. But his calm isn't mine. Have I done enough? Is it possible that when I carried Dora into the back, I got some of her DNA on my clothes, which was then transported to the front of the car when I drove away? I can't remember my clothes; do I need to go home and burn the darn lot? Should I go back to the dealership and tell him to clean the whole inside of the car?

I think I remember an article I read a few months ago about traced DNA. It has a shelf life, and the chances of them finding anything are minuscule.

TWENTY

Slowly, my car creeps up Marion's drive, my engine barely a purr as if it doesn't want to go there just as much as me. The familiar sight of her house is ahead, but it looks different. It's more chaotic. Flashing lights and several vehicles fill the driveway, like a scene out of a crime drama. The thought isn't without irony. My gut twists, and I struggle to keep going, fighting like crazy not to turn around and get as far away as possible. *You can handle this*, I keep repeating. Uncle Alfred is depending on me.

Pressed tightly against the side of the house is a massive transport carrier, its size making it seem almost impossible that it could have been manoeuvred through the narrow roads. On top of the carrier, three cars are already securely loaded: the Bentley, the Range Rover, and the vintage Porsche that never leaves the garage on account of Uncle Alfred not wanting to spoil it. On the lower tier are two cars: Marion's Jaguar and her Mercedes. There is one open space left for mine.

Four policemen stand together, two other men slightly apart. Andrew is near the front door talking to an older, plump man.

I pull up to the side and park on the large gravel area in

front of the house. It's starting to get dark, and rain has begun to fall, so I climb out, grab a coat from the back, and put it on.

Andrew is hurrying towards me.

He's barely recognisable in jeans, a sweatshirt, a Barbour jacket and a check flat cap. All that's missing is the gun and the clay pigeons.

He doesn't kiss me on the cheek. He's all business. He glances over his shoulder as if to ensure no one is nearby. "The police don't know about you and me."

"Yes, you told me," I say. "Who's in charge?"

He turns and points to the man he was standing with near the front door, who's looking at a notepad in his hands. He looks dishevelled, like he's just rolled out of the closest pub: shirt hanging out, top button undone, trousers baggy. He turns and looks at me, and I swallow hard. *Be careful*, I tell myself. *Looks can be deceiving. Just think about Marion.*

"Let's go," Andrew says. "They know I know you. During my investigation, I told them I'd met you at the care home. Just follow my lead."

We walk past the drawing-room windows, and I sneak a peek inside. Marion sits alone at the table that is set for afternoon tea – scones and all – not the bullshit she put together for Andrew.

I turn to him. "Why have they made her sit in there?"

"They didn't. She offered some of the men tea. They all said no, but she went ahead anyway. I said she didn't have to stay there if she didn't want to; she said she was fine."

"You've spoken to her?" Marion isn't a 'let's have a nice chat' person, even when she knows you. She's more of a 'get out of my face' person.

"Just being polite. And I felt sorry for her. She'd put on a nice table. Some of the lads might've liked to eat but not with their guv'nor within earshot." Andrew slows as we approach the man in charge and lowers his voice. "DI Henderson. He's a ball-breaker, so be careful."

Does he think I can't handle myself?

The air is growing cooler, and I flip up the collar of my coat. Henderson watches.

"DI Henderson?" Andrew's voice, when he speaks, is timid, almost apologetic. "This is Persephone Adelard."

DI Henderson stretches out his hand to shake mine. His skin is rough and firm, and he holds on for a few seconds too long, his eyes unblinking and weighing me up.

"Persy," I say. "Please call me Persy. And that's my car over there." I hand him my keys. He calls a young man in uniform, who comes running towards us, and chucks my keys to him. The man catches them; no smile; no 'thank you'.

"I assume you have no personal belongings inside the car?" His voice is surprisingly soft.

"No, you can take it away." I suddenly remember throwing Marion's chequebook in the glove compartment. My heart quickens. I don't want them looking at that. I apologise, run to the car, grab it and come back. "Sorry," I say, waving the chequebook at him. "Forgot this."

He gives me the kind of smile that says, 'you're here, but you're not important'. I immediately dislike him.

"Thank you, Miss Adelard." He turns and walks away and can't be bothered to give me any explanation as to what's going on. It's so rude I can't let him get away with it. I start to follow, about to demand that he stop and talk to me, but Andrew grabs my arm before I can make my move.

I pull away. "What?" I say, unable to hide my anger.

"Don't. Just let him do his job."

"I need to ask a few questions."

"You don't. Let it go."

I ignore him. "Mr Henderson," I shout. "A word?"

He turns around. "Detective Inspector Henderson," he says. "And yes, how can I help you?" The casual, soft voice is still there, but now it has a hard edge.

"I'd appreciate being given a heads-up."

"I spoke at length with your lawyer. Have you not talked to him? I was given to understand that he would be keeping your family abreast."

"He did. But I'm asking you."

"Your lawyer is best placed to answer your questions."

"Why do you need all of our cars? It's pointless. We have nothing to do with any of this."

"Any of what?"

My mouth snaps shut. I need to hold back. Especially with a man who thinks he's clever, a man with power.

"Detective Inspector. I don't know – that's the problem. I'm asking for a quick explanation of what is happening here."

He crosses his arms over his plump belly. "As I said to your lawyer, this is routine. We were given some information. We need to follow due process." He purses his lips. "It's standard procedure. Again, talk to your lawyer. Or, if you don't feel comfortable taking that route, we can set up a time for you to come to the station. Make it more formal. Your choice."

The implicit threat.

I don't like this man. He's used to getting his way, and worse, he enjoys it. Andrew is standing a little away, hovering on the phone, but his eyes are darting between me and the DI. I think he's faking it. I look at Henderson, then at Andrew. I know when I'm beaten.

"When will the cars be returned?" I ask meekly.

"How long is a piece of string?"

I grit my teeth. "Well, is there a contact number?"

He turns around, looks for someone and shouts, "Brandon." The younger man he threw my keys to is running towards us. "Speak to Constable Brandon. He'll give you all the administrative details you need." And he walks off.

I stand there, alone, Andrew not far away, my coat tight around me, my hair straggly from the rain, and watch the cars being driven away. No one nods, no one asks, no one acknowledges my existence. I'm a bystander in my own life.

As the big truck departs, DI Henderson and the other police officers follow suit. The circus is leaving town.

"What did he say?" Andrew is waiting by the front door, and I trudge over to him.

"Sweet FA." I head for the drawing room, Andrew behind me. He's too close. This isn't a place for him.

"Listen." I feel like a jerk. He's helped me. He's useful. But I can't be doing with him. Not now. "Do you mind if I spend some time with her alone?" I toss him an awkward grin. "I don't know how she's going to react. She's tough. But this, it's a whole new ball game."

His eyebrows shoot up. "No. Of course. Sorry, Persy, I wasn't thinking. Go ahead. Do you want me to wait? I can stay in my car if it's easier." His eyes are almost pleading, and I feel responsible. Maybe even a bit guilty. I squeeze his arm. The one thing I don't need is Andrew, who is in the car waiting and distracting me from what's happening. "Thanks, but no." I kiss him on the cheek. "I'll call you later. Is that okay?"

"But you don't have a car. Let me know when you're done, and I'll come and get you."

"I might stay here tonight." There is no chance of that. Sitting in the back of a cab to get home, no talking to Andrew, that sounds like perfection.

He doesn't move. It's like he doesn't know what to do, has been caught on his back foot and is waiting for me to take the lead. I put my arm through his and walk him to the front door. "Call me later, okay."

I stand on tiptoes and wrap my arms around his shoulders, and he holds me tight. Then I stand and wave and watch as he drives away.

I quietly close the front door and walk into the drawing room. Marion is sitting alone at the party table, all the food still lying there uneaten, except for the bottle of whisky that's half empty. She must be fairly drunk; her eyes are glazed, and her hair is in a bun, but the front is falling into her face like it's escaped a hurricane.

She looks up and smiles. "Persephone. How pleasant that you dropped by. Did you see all the guests we had earlier?"

I pull up a chair. Grab one of her sandwiches. "Yep. I did. And they've all gone."

"That was rather a large vehicle. Wouldn't you say? Were they able to turn it around without much ado?"

I go along with her let's-pretend-life-is-normal routine. "They left without a problem."

"And do we know how long this whole exercise will take?"

I won't repeat DI Henderson's bullshit piece-of-string answer. "A couple of days."

"Excellent. Fortunately, I have no appointments, so this, how should we say, this performance, will in no way interfere with my daily life."

She's got no appointments. Does she have the slightest clue about what's going on here? Or is this all part of the act?

I say, "I didn't see Uncle Alfred."

"I suggested he stay at the farm. It's much better that way. He tends to get flustered. One of the policemen was a young man who was very kind and well-spoken. He volunteered to go down there and picked up Alfred's car himself. Very kind. Don't you think?"

I watch her, biting my lip, trying to figure her out. Why didn't she want Uncle Alfred here? So she could speak to the police alone, maybe plant some horrible seed about him? I look away. I've tried to read her mind all my life, but I've failed.

"Would you like me to stay the night?" I ask.

"And why would I want you to do that?"

The response is a relief. Miserable, horrible Marion is still alive and kicking.

"You probably wouldn't. I'm just asking."

"Clear the table, would you? I used the trolley. It's in the hall. I'm going to bed. My legs have been rather awkward today." She tries to stand but almost wobbles over, and I jump up and grab her arm to support her. "No need, Persephone," she says in her drunken brogue. She leans on her cane and straightens up.

"It's all going to be fine," I say, the words coming out of nowhere.

She stops her back toward me, her shoulders slightly stooped. Then she looks over her shoulder, staring at me with those black eyes, but it's like she's not seeing me. I stand quietly, waiting for the onslaught. But in the end, she doesn't say a word; she carries on walking. I'm left in the drawing room, looking at a cucumber sandwich with the bread curling at the edges. I want to feel sorry for myself, but I can't. Been there. Done that.

I order the cab and tell it to pick me up at the gate at the end of the drive. I don't want to be in this house anymore. I prefer the walk to sitting around waiting, inhaling the misery of the past, and wondering what on earth is about to go wrong next.

On the way home, Andrew texts and says something about getting together later, but I'm too drained. He's pushy and suggests meeting up at a pub, maybe somewhere busy with live music, but I'm just not interested. I'm tired. A pervasive sense of unease has settled in my chest; no matter how hard I try, it won't go away. It sits there, nagging me, reminding me everything is spiralling, and I can do nothing about it.

Back at mine, I order a pizza, settle into my sofa and put on the television. Each show is worse than the one before, but it makes no difference. My thoughts are on the rampage. Is it possible I'm addicted to worrying? I don't like that thought but can't turn away from it. Maybe I worry too much, but even if that's the case, I have every reason to be scared. Every time I go one step forward, I'm pulled four steps back. How does that phrase go? Just because you're paranoid doesn't mean they're not out to get you.

I don't answer when Scooter calls because the more I think about meeting Mum and Dad, the more embarrassed I feel. It was a farce. What must they have thought of me? They're probably in the Francis Hotel right now, talking about that ridiculous woman on the bus, then at the café, waving her hands at the side of the road like a deflating blow-up doll. *Drugs*, that's what they're saying to each other. That girl was probably on drugs.

I want to stop thinking. I switch to Netflix and end up watching a documentary about a man who shoved his wife down the stairs, or maybe he didn't; I don't know; I keep losing track of what's going on. The pizza is eaten without one memory of a chew or a swallow. I turn off the TV, shower, make a cup of hot chocolate, get into bed, toss down a sleeping tablet, and pretend that this is all cosy. But thirty minutes later, sleep is still playing hide-and-seek.

I have to get some sleep because I need my wits about me. If I can't think, I can't even try to stay one step ahead.

I take another sleeping tablet.

TWENTY-ONE

It's eleven in the morning, and I've slept through two texts from Andrew, one call from Marion, and two calls from a number I don't recognise. Doubling up on the sleeping tablets wasn't a smart idea; it's like I've got a hangover.

I make coffee, toast some bread, choose thick-cut marmalade and slather it on. I slump on the sofa in my dressing gown, my feet in their slippers resting on the coffee table. I don't know what's going on with my life.

My phone rings, and it's that strange number again – a marketing call, for sure. I go to do what I normally do and stably decline, then change my mind. This is the perfect day to have a useless call with a telemarketer. Why not?

The voice on the other end is snappy. "Miss Adelard?"

Whatever this guy is selling, his approach isn't the best. I already want to hang up.

"Yes," I answer.

"This is the Bath and Avon Constabulary."

I sit up. "Okay."

"We are calling about the cars taken from the estate of Mrs Marion Adelard. We have your name on file as the primary contact."

"Right." I try to sound upbeat, all in a day's stride, but my heart is beating so hard I can hear it in my ears.

"Of the six cars, five will be released today."

"Five?" I don't know what to think. Frank changed the carpet out. This can't be happening. "What did you find?"

"Stains found in the boot. I'm sure it's nothing, but we will take another look and send the carpet off for analysis."

"What kind of stains?" I feel sick.

"We'll be sending it off for analysis," he repeats.

"Okay," I say. "When will you know the results?"

"Forty-eight hours if all goes well."

I stand. I sit. I stand again. I turn on the shower. Forget it's running. Make a cup of coffee, don't drink it. The shower has gone cold. I jump in, jump out, jump back in.

I tell myself to be thankful. In the States, the death penalty might be up for grabs. Roger, our lawyer, will know the next steps. What will I tell him? None of this was my fault.

Andrew calls. I'm standing naked in the bathroom, shivering.

I throw a towel around me and pick up. "They've released all the cars except mine," I spit out.

"You're kidding."

"Not kidding."

"Did they say why?"

"Stains in the boot."

"What kind of stains?" His voice sounds incredulous.

"No idea," I say. "That's what they're checking."

"It has to be blood or saliva. They wouldn't hold it if there were anything else. Did you cut yourself, maybe?"

"No."

"Let me see what I can find out. Okay? And don't worry about it. They find stuff like that all the time. It isn't a big deal." He doesn't sound like it's no big deal.

I get dressed, dry my hair, and stand looking at myself in the mirror. I can't think straight. Is this it? Is this the moment when everything comes unravelled?

Andrew calls back. "Persy. It's not your car they're holding. It's the Porsche."

I freeze. I am not sure I'm hearing what I'm hearing. "I don't understand."

"They said it was vintage. A Porsche. Yours is a Volvo, right?"

"But no one drives it. I don't understand."

"Let's wait for the tests to come back," Andrew says.

"I just got out of the shower," I say, "I'm dripping all over the floor. I'll call you later."

"Out the shower? You must be naked? Are you sure you don't want me to come over now?"

The playful banter misses the spot and his timing is off. "That's funny," I force out, quickly ending the call. I mechanically make my bed, trying to find some sense of normalcy in this mess. Marion keeps invading my thoughts.

The door buzzes. I see Andrew standing outside the window on the pavement, looking up at me. I open the window.

"What's going on?"

"Come on," he says. "We're going for coffee. You need cheering up, and what I've got to tell you will do it."

"Tell me now." I catch myself. No. I don't want him here. He may never leave. "Okay. I'll be right down. Wait there." He's beginning to get on my nerves.

Sitting across each other. Two cappuccinos and two cinnamon rolls lay untouched on the table. I try to bite, but my stomach churns with worry and guilt. I want to open up and share everything, but I can't; how can I? I pick up one of the rolls, take a small bite, and chew it, unable to swallow.

He grins; whatever he's got to share has overwhelmed his ability to spot the drama I'm going through.

"You want to hear my news?"

I nod, slightly irritated he can't just tell me his news outright.

"You're not going to believe this."

I think I'll punch him in the face if he doesn't tell me soon.

"Derek has done a runner." He laughs out loud. "Can you believe that? That piece of shit. What a coward! He's gone."

This isn't news to me – of course it isn't – I've been tracking Derek. But I can't say anything in case I give anything away. This whole acting stuff is too complicated and takes too much energy.

"What?" I splutter. "No! What? No. I don't believe it. What scum. Are you sure?" I laugh, shake my head, and suddenly I know I'm overdoing it because there's a look in his eyes that comes and goes in a matter of seconds that I'm a bit off.

"They think he's in Europe somewhere. They're in overdrive. A full-scale investigation. His whole scam is tumbling down, and it'll crush him. But skipping the country like this, nothing screams guilty like a man on the run."

"Will they find him?" I pretend a look that I hope shouts how awful it would be for Derek to escape justice. In my head, finding him would be the worst thing ever.

"Don't worry. They'll find him, Persy, I promise you." He leans in and holds my hand. "It could take a while, but they won't give up. For sure."

Again, I try to eat but can't, and I put the pastry back down on the plate.

"And there's another thing – he's got a problem." He brushes some crumbs away that have fallen on his chest. "Money. They've frozen his accounts." He leans back in his chair. "All we need now is for them to let you have your uncle's car, and this whole thing will be over." He sips his coffee. "What's happening with the other cars? When will you get them back?"

I didn't think to ask. "I don't know. I assumed they'd tell me the next steps."

"But you need your car, don't you?"

"Sure. Can I go and get it?"

He picks up his phone and has a couple of conversations. "You can go and pick your car up now if you want; they're done with it. The others they'll drive back in the truck, but it will probably take a couple of days to arrange. Or you can go and pick them up one by one. Or you can make your own arrangements."

"I just want mine."

"Great," he says. "I've got enough time to take you over there."

"No way. You've done enough." All of my life, I've been on my own. Don't get me wrong, having someone who cares is lovely, but it gets on your nerves if you're not used to it.

"Absolutely not." He finishes his coffee and eats the last bite of the roll. "Come on. Let's go."

I'm too tired to argue.

We head out of the coffee shop, walk to his car, and head out of town. That's one of the benefits of him having been in the police. He knows where things are, like the warehouse with the cars. I give myself a mental pat on the back for finding something about him that doesn't annoy me.

A little into the drive, he rests his hand lightly on my thigh. "There is something I've got to ask you." His shoulders are tense, and he keeps checking in the rear-view mirror. He's nervous.

"Okay," I say slowly.

"Marion."

My mouth is dry. "What about her?"

"Are you sure she knew nothing about what Derek was up to?"

"I'm not following," I say.

"I'm just asking. She's been involved with the care home for a long time." He takes his arm away and rubs the back of his neck like he wants to say something that might not sit well with me.

"What's on your mind?" I say.

"You're brilliant. It's obvious Marion is smart. I mean, I know she has issues, but when she's with it, her brain is razor-sharp. And I understand that the family must be kept out of this. You've already made that clear. But did neither of you know what he was up to until the last couple of days?" He throws a glance my way. I keep looking straight ahead. "The Dereks of this world don't do these things overnight. He's probably been scamming money for years."

"I've asked myself the same question. I wasn't at home that much, but Marion, I don't know why she didn't figure it out sooner."

He glances my way. "Why do you think she didn't get it until now?"

"My guess. She thought whatever he was up to wasn't important enough. She did talk to me about it, and I told you that, but not until recently. Knowing her, she probably had an inkling but kept her eyes on what was more important: how the people in the care home were being taken care of. Derek is a good manager. Maybe she dismissed things until she couldn't any longer."

"Have you asked her?"

A burst of surprise escapes my lips in a disbelieving laugh. "You don't know Marion. She's on a need-to-know basis."

"Is it possible Derek has something on her?"

His pushing is getting too close to the mark. My mind propels me back to seeing Marion sitting in the sunroom, me finding the chequebook, me eating a bacon sandwich in the car, me finding out she'd paid him £100K.

"No," I say, trying to keep my voice level. "No way. Marion is cleaner than clean. We went to Paris once, and she bought me this Rolex watch. I don't wear it; it's lovely, but that's not the point. The point is she made me declare it going through customs. It was on my wrist, for God's sake, no box; I'd tossed that; who would've known? But she did, and she made me go through and pay the tax." I rub my wrist as if I remember the moment, word for word. And I kind of am. Except she didn't make me go through customs to pay the tax; she wanted to show off her wealth and had made a big deal of asking for the line to pay customs.

"No, I get it. She's clean. But skeletons? There always are some. Could Derek have found out something?"

"If there are, I don't know about them," I lie.

"You don't think she's got anything to lose?"

"No. I honestly don't. She's rich, she's odd. But Marion. Vulnerability isn't something that she does. Definitely not." An idea to explain the money given to Derek comes out of nowhere. "The only thing that I'm worried about is that she's given money to the home, and he's syphoned it off."

"How would we know?" he asks.

"In theory, quite easily. I'm not exactly sure how it could work, but a quick way to figure it out would be to check her donations to the home against the actual record of receipts by the home. The question is how to get it done without raising too many concerns."

"Her accountant could say they're doing an audit."

"There's probably a lot of things she could say, but it might raise eyebrows."

"You should do this, Persy… he's a con artist."

"I'll talk to her about it," I lie. "But Marion is stubborn. It's not easy."

"There's one other thing I want to talk to you about…"

I smile, a bit out of relief because I know what he will do next. He's going to say something ridiculous to make me laugh. Probably something about the sausage rolls Marion gave him for tea, that seems to be the joke that keeps on giving. "I'm listening." His hand is resting on his lap. I lean over and put mine on top of his.

He quickly looks my way and smiles as if he likes that we're holding hands. "Did you know that Dora isn't the only woman who's disappeared from the home?"

My hand sits right on his, and I daren't move. I pretend to shiver, remove my hand from his, and gently touch the heater.

"Sorry," I say. "I hope I'm not coming down with anything. I feel freezing. Sorry, what were you saying?"

"Women. Missing from the home. There have been others."

"I wouldn't really know. Are you sure?"

"Three of them. Over the past five years. I don't think that happens too often. I mean, I know that many of the patients have dementia, but it's still unusual." He reaches for something from his inside pocket. "Here."

It's brochures from the care home. "What am I looking for?"

"Marion does a fundraiser every couple of years, right? She reaches out to like-minded people for funding."

"Okay?"

"The women, the three of them, take a look, they're in one brochure or another. Do you remember them?"

"Sorry, I have no idea," I lie.

"And this is what I'm thinking. Everything points to Derek. I'm wondering if this happens because it makes him feel important. Like he's needed."

"Not following."

"It would be like a fireman who sets fires. You know what I mean?"

"You may be right," I say with as much conviction as I can muster.

"If I'm right and it all comes out, this could be embarrassing for Marion too. I mean, people give money to the home only because she's put her name behind it. It isn't a good look, is it."

TWENTY-TWO

As we pull into the warehouse, Andrew says he'll wait, but I don't want him to because I don't want him in my space or my head. I stand my ground and tell him it's not worth it and that he has more important things to do. He keeps pressing me, and there's a bit of push and pull. He wants to be with me, but he's getting a bit too precious for my taste. I don't want to be in a relationship that gets this hard. Eventually, he agrees with me and leaves.

I enter the reception area, a sterile space with stark white walls and harsh fluorescent lighting. A police officer sits at a desk, his stern expression softening as I approach and explain who I am. He scans a list on his clipboard, his finger trailing down the names and numbers until he nods, acknowledging the information I'd provided. "Ah, yes," he says, his voice carrying an air of bureaucratic weariness. "You're here for the Volvo, correct?"

The car keys jingle as he gets them from a cupboard behind him, then he stands up and gestures for me to follow. We go down a narrow corridor lined with doors marked 'Authorised Personnel Only', our footsteps echoing off linoleum floors.

Finally, we reach the impound lot, a sprawling gridlock of vehicles, and my car sits in a corner spot. The officer suggests I inspect the car to make sure it looks exactly as it did before they took it away, and I walk around it to check. It looks fine. When I'm done, I sign some waiver that I know better than to sign without reading, but I do it anyway because being in the middle of this police warehouse unnerves me.

I get into my car and leave.

As soon as I feel like I'm far enough away from the police depot not to be noticed, I take a sharp right turn onto a secluded side road. The car bumps over potholes and rocks before stopping in a small clearing surrounded by trees. I call Uncle Alfred.

"They're holding Alfred's Porsche. There were some stains in the back that they want to identify?" I pause, waiting for him to jump in, to give me some explanation like, 'Oh yes, I remember, I drove it once, cut my finger.' Anything. "Do you know what they're talking about?"

"No," he says. "Absolutely not. I'm rather astonished. I don't think I've driven that car more than a couple of hundred miles. How could there possibly be a stain?"

"You're sure?"

"No, Persy. I promise you. Nothing I can think of. And it would be best if you didn't worry, my dear girl. It would be best if you did not concern yourself about any of this, and I need to reiterate that there is nothing for you to fix. Nothing at all."

This is the second time he's tried to tell me it's no big deal, and it bothers me. What is it about this mess that he's not getting? Marion, I understand; her thought process is off, but Uncle Alfred has always faced problems head on. Why is he so calm?

There's a sound of cracking on his end of the line, and something sounds different, like he's no longer in his house and he's outside, in a wide-open expanse.

"Where are you?" I ask. "I can hear something in the background."

"I've had quite a busy day. An appointment first."

"An appointment? With whom?"

"Roger the Dodger. I have to say, I find him quite an understanding sort of a chap."

"Why were you seeing him?"

"And now I'm taking a walk. It's such a lovely day."

He ignored or didn't hear my last question, but I let it go. It's not important, especially given that he's telling me that outside is lovely. It isn't. It's damp and cold, and the dark-grey cloud above tells me it's about to pour. "Lovely day? Where are you, Africa? It's horrible out."

"I'm enjoying the world, Persy." There's a tinge of regret in his voice.

"Are you okay? Do you want me to come over?"

"Not at all," he says. "I'm merely enjoying a moment of retrospection. It's rather uplifting."

We hang up, and a nagging feeling of discomfort sits in my chest, but I can't pinpoint what it is or where it came from. Something about his words or his tone has left me out of kilter. I start to call him back but stop. Badgering him isn't going to help, and, if anything, he'll see that I'm worried about him, and he'll start to worry about me. I check my watch and think about swinging by his place to check on him, but I change my mind. He said he was outside; the estate is vast, and he could be anywhere.

A wave of self-pity washes over me, and I wearily rub my eyes. The shadows seem to lurk in every corner, ready to pounce. I can't pretend that they're just figments of my imagination because every time I approach the shadow, a monster comes out of the darkness and attacks me. Fear and exhaustion are pressing down on me, and I tell myself to be careful; I've been there before, where I can't distinguish between the tricks my mind plays on me and reality.

Uncle Alfred told me he was fine. I have to accept that.

Marion calls; she's the monster in the shadows.

"I don't have a car. How am I supposed to function without a primary mode of transport?"

"Where do you want to go?" I ask.

"I am not sure why your question is pertinent to the problem of not having a vehicle."

I can't stand her.

"Derek called," she says.

I don't know if I'm more shocked about this revelation that a fugitive has been trying to contact her or that she led with her annoyance at not having a car.

"What did you say to him?" I ask.

"Why would I have anything to say to him?"

Has she been drinking again? "Marion. Please give me a straight answer."

"Compared to a wobbly answer?"

My brain can't deal with her. Every conversation ends with me feeling like I have to be the dumbest person in the world. I need to get her out of my life.

"You gave Derek money. Knowing him, he wants more. I don't even know why you did that. Why did you give him money?"

"How would you know about the money? Have you been sneaking around in my things again? You always were a most curious child. Tiptoeing around, getting into things that were none of your business."

"I just want to know why you gave him money."

"And I want to know why I ended up with a daughter who does not show a smattering of respect for her superiors."

This is too hard, too draining. A conversation with Uncle

Alfred makes the day brighter. A couple of sentences with her, and I want to shoot myself.

"Persephone," she goes on. "I'm going to give you this book I'm reading. It's marvellous. A biography on Enheduanna. What a remarkable woman. Among her writings are forty-two hymns and a personal devotion to a goddess. When I am done, I shall pass it on."

"What?" I say.

"Don't say 'what', my dear girl. It doesn't become you." She hangs up.

A gnawing, uneasy sensation starts in my stomach and then spreads in every direction until it consumes my entire body. My muscles tense, and my mind is flooded with painful memories that I can't seem to shake, the thoughts so rapid I have no control over what's going to arrive in my brain and when it will go. It's a highlight of my life. Her shouting, her insulting, her punishing. It's too much.

I get into my car, crank up the heat and turn on my favourite radio station. I drive into town, park on Walcot Street, and head into the cupcake shop. The smell of freshly baked goods wafts over me, and my mood lifts. I find a spot outside, sit down, and sink my teeth into the rich chocolate icing. It's pure joy.

I stand up to leave, and I see them.

Mum and Dad.

Their fingers intertwine as they peer through the clear glass window into the kitchen tile shop. It's a familiar sight because I bought tiles from this very place. I bet they're looking at the same ones I'd chosen. I can envision them entering my flat, their faces lighting up when they see the same tiles in my bathroom. They stroll leisurely my way, their voices carrying on the light breeze. As they get closer, my heart races in my chest, and I'm suddenly rooted in the spot, unable to move or look away. I curse myself for inhaling the cake so quickly, and I try to suck it in my stomach, ready to be who they want me to be.

Out of nowhere, a bus driver slams his hand on the horn and screams at a couple of teenagers running across the road. Mum and Dad turn around to see what the commotion is about. The bus leaves, and there we are. Me on one side of the road, them on the other, and we're staring at each other.

Mum recognises me first. "Stonehenge," she shouts as cars drive between us. She waves and has a huge grin across her face. They both cross the road to come and see me. "We were in the café together," she says, all smiling and light and happy to see me.

I pretend to be confused because I'm trying to look calm and independent and not obsessed with them at all. Then I blink, grin, and start to laugh. Scooter will be so happy when I tell him how I bumped into them. "Of course, sorry, I didn't recognise you at first. How ridiculous to bump into you like this." We hug each other. She's wearing Shalimar perfume. I love Shalimar perfume. At that moment, I make a decision that's almost subconscious. I want these people as my parents. As long as they're here in Bath, that's who they're going to be. My parents.

Dad says, "What a coincidence. This was meant to be." He doesn't hug me, but I know why. He's a bit more reserved. I think that's a good thing; he'll need a bit more time to get used to me.

"It was," I say, gushing. "It really was."

"We were going to stop somewhere for afternoon tea. Why don't you join us?" I manoeuvre myself in front of them so they don't spot the cupcake shop. I don't want to explain that I've just eaten there; plus, I want to go somewhere a little more isolated where we won't be interrupted – our first tea as a family.

"I'm so sorry," she continues, "we Americans tend to be a bit pushy. I expect you have a thousand things to do."

"No," I stutter, "no, not at all. In fact, to tell you the truth, I could kill a cup of tea." Mum laughs and looks at Dad, who smiles back at her, then at me. "And I know a great place," I add.

"Perfect," Dad says. "Show us the way."

And the three of us walk through town exactly as it should have been. Mum, Dad and me. The perfect family. Once they know all about me, about my story, they'll want me to go with them to America. And you know what, I'll be okay with that.

I take them to a fancy hotel on Great Pulteney Street. The place is quiet, with tables spaced comfortably apart, and it is easy to share intimacies and talk about things which shouldn't be overheard. We sit at a round table by the window, chatting and laughing, and I can see they're impressed when the tiered plates arrive with the scones, sandwiches, and tiny delicate desserts. Dad even takes a photo of the food. He loves his camera, and he's just like me. I want to suggest they take pictures of me, with them, all together, but I hold off. There'll be plenty of time for all that.

Dad pours the tea, and I look from side to side. My heart is racing, and the palms of my hands are sweaty. I'm tempted to blurt it out: 'I'm your daughter, how great is that, can you believe it?' But no. The moment will arrive, and I'll know when it's right.

"So, Persy," Dad says. "Tell us a little about yourself." He's staring into my eyes, and I think I know why. He's beginning to figure it all out.

"I investigate fraud." I rarely say that out loud because it's the sort of job that needs me to be able to operate without being recognised. But it's Mum and Dad. They deserve to know the truth. "I went to the best boarding schools in the country. I went to university, although I didn't complete the degree."

"Sorry to hear that," Mum says, and she looks genuinely sad. "Why not?"

I don't want to tell them about the nervous breakdown. It's not fair; they don't need to know that.

"I had an accident. By the time I recovered, I don't know. I'd changed my mind."

"What did you study?" Mum asks.

"Literature."

Mum laughs out loud and puts her hand on my arm. "That is what I wanted to study. I love literature. Actually," she dips her head and speaks a little quieter, "my real love is poetry."

"Oh really?" I can't quite believe I'm here, chatting away with her like she really is my mum.

"I don't like to admit it. It's not very unique. But I love Wordsworth."

I slightly die inside. How could this be? I love Wordsworth. I tell myself to shut up. Loads of people love Wordsworth; we wouldn't even know who Wordsworth was if they didn't. It's just a silly coincidence. It's best to move on to another subject.

My phone rings. I look at both of them because I want them to see that I have good manners and don't want to take a call while they're sitting with me.

"I'll turn this off. I am so sorry."

"Oh, please," Mum says. "Go ahead. It will give me a chance to look at all this wonderful food before we eat it all up. I'd like to have more photos." She gives me a lovely, warm smile. I believe her.

I pretend to look at my phone, but I don't care who it is because I won't answer. Being here with them is more important than anything that's going on in my life. It's her, Marion. She's not going to spoil this for me.

"So sorry," I say. "Not important. You were talking about poetry. Do you have a favourite poem that you love?" I pray it's not one of the poems Marion used for the women.

Mum beams. Then, sadness crosses her face, and she looks at Dad as if she needs his approval. He squeezes her arm. "*Three Years She Grew in Sun and Shower*." She swallows, and I swear she's about to cry. "It's about…" she's struggling to finish the sentence. "The poem is about… Sorry, Persy. Something happened a long time ago. Something that makes us both very sad."

I know the poem. He wrote it about a young girl who had died. He's offering hope and comfort to readers to let them know they are not alone. I want to cry with Mum because I understand completely.

Mum is dabbing her eyes with a tissue, and Dad is rubbing her arm.

My phone rings again. Mum says I should get it because she has to go to the bathroom. I press decline, turn the sound off, and watch Mum walk away. I want to stop her sadness.

The phone buzzes in my pocket. Dad hears it.

"Please, Persy. I think it must be urgent. Go ahead."

Dad is kind. I was not going to answer the phone, but I can see on his face that he wants me to. He's putting me first, and I don't want to turn away from that.

"Thank you," I say.

It's Marion.

Dad is watching me watching my phone. I remove my napkin, place it on my seat, and whisper to Dad that I'll take it in the hall, that I don't want to disturb him. He nods and smiles, but his attention is wandering, and he looks over his shoulder as if he's checking on Mum.

"I need to talk to you." Marion's voice is cold and flat.

I stand in the entry hall, far enough for me not to be

overheard but close enough to be able to see what's happening at the table. Dad has folded his arms and looks down at them as if worried. When I'm done with Marion, if Mum isn't back yet, I'll suggest that I go into the bathroom to check on her. I think he'll like that.

"What is it?" I ask.

"I need you to go to the hospital."

Real Mum comes out of the bathroom. She spots me, smiles and waves and sits down at the table with Dad. She looks better, the tears gone.

"Persephone." Marion raises her voice. "Pay attention. I need you to go."

"What?" Mum and Dad are holding hands, and it's obvious he's trying to reassure her. I'm struggling to understand what Marion says because I want to return to the table. They need me.

"Do you ever listen?" Marion's voice is shrill as if she's accusing me of something horrific.

I wave to Mum and Dad and smile; they nod and smile back. I hold up one finger to let them know it won't be long. I walk a little further away because Marion is beginning to piss me off, and I don't want them to see the possibly horrible expression on my face.

"What?" I say. "What is it?"

"It's Uncle Alfred." The words are said without emotion: "He isn't well."

"Then call a doctor."

"I have. They've taken him to the hospital. That's what I've been saying."

"What do you mean they've taken him to the hospital?"

"Persephone, this repetitive streak you have is tiresome. Your Uncle Alfred has been taken away. By an ambulance. A possible heart attack."

"Jesus," I spit out. "Okay. I'll meet you there."

"You may go alone," she says.

"What do you mean I may go alone?"

"Exactly what I said. You may go alone. I am not a doctor, and I suspect it is best to leave the dramatics to you."

"You're kidding," I say.

"Persephone, please stop this."

"I'll call you when I get there."

"No need," she says.

Mum and Dad are still at the table, shooting curious looks in my direction. Mum still looks sad again, and any other time, I would've tried to perk them up, but I can't. I need to take care of Uncle Alfred.

"My uncle isn't well," is all I say. "I'm so sorry; I need to leave."

"That's awful," Dad says. "Is there anything we can do?"

I love him for that. How different my life could have been if only they'd kept me.

"Thank you, but no. He's been taken to the hospital. I'm sure he will be fine, but I must go. I am so, so sorry." I look for the waiter and call for the bill.

"Absolutely not," Dad says, reaching into his pocket, pulling out his wallet, and laying it on the table. "This has been our pleasure." Mum takes a notepad and pencil from her bag. For the first time, I notice her nails, painted a gentle pink. It's called Petal Pink. I know it because that's the colour I always choose when I have a manicure.

She writes down a phone number, rips the paper from the pad, and hands it to me. "Let us know how your uncle is. Promise?"

I nod.

"And when you call, we'll set up another time to meet. Before we leave."

"That would be great."

Her voice drops. "And then we can tell you the real reason for us coming to Bath."

And in among all my fear and dread for Uncle Alfred, those words, coming from her, warm me, fill me with hope. I remind myself to tell Scooter exactly what she said to me.

"I'm going to keep you to that," I say.

She holds both my hands in hers. "Do you ever feel that meeting someone was meant to be?"

Tears start to well up in my eyes. "I do," I say. "I do." I hug them both and leave the restaurant.

When Uncle Alfred is better, I'll tell him all about this. I promise myself, that is exactly what I will do.

TWENTY-THREE

Thirty minutes later, I'm staring at Uncle Alfred lying in the hospital bed. He's asleep or unconscious, but I'm not sure which. I can't tear my eyes from the tubes and the drip and the echo of his heartbeat that ticks across the screen next to his bed. He looks deathly pale and still, and the nurse doesn't want to discuss how he is and tells me I need to talk to the doctor. I'm picking up from her that it doesn't look good. I cover my mouth with my hand and take a few steps back.

I head into the corridor and call Marion. She answers on the fourth ring.

"You need to get here," I say.

"Have you spoken to a doctor?" Her tone is calm.

"I will. But I think you should be here. For him."

"And this opinion is based on your own medical experience?"

I bite my lip and look up at the ceiling. "He looks awful. I'm scared," I whisper. I wipe away the tears that are rolling down my cheeks, trying like hell not to let her hear I'm crying. "I don't know what's going to happen."

"None of us know what's going to happen. He is well taken care of, and the two of us sitting around wallowing certainly isn't going to help."

"Are you going to come or not?"

"Not."

A silence sits between us.

"I just think… honestly, he's not…" I can't finish the sentence.

"Call me if you have any news." She hangs up.

A man is striding down the corridor towards me. He's confident, tall, in scrubs, and I'm standing outside Uncle Alfred's room, and he's looking at me. It's his doctor, it has to be. He smiles, and I shake his hand. It feels odd, as if we're introducing ourselves before we go into a meeting.

"I'm Persy Adelard, his niece. That's my Uncle Alfred." My lips start to quiver, and I know that if I say any more words, I'll break down. I cough, look at the floor, and tell myself to get my act together.

He squeezes my arm. "It's okay," he says. "Come on. Let's sit for a moment." He looks over to a reception area staffed by a few people, all busy on the computer or the phone. A couple of empty chairs are shoved randomly against the wall to the left. He leads me to them, and we sit.

He shifts his chair, so it's angled directly towards me and quietly explains what's been happening. A TIA, a mini-stroke, causes a temporary disruption in the blood supply to the brain. The thought of losing him chokes me up.

"Why did it happen?" I ask, my voice trembling with worry.

"Could be any number of reasons, usually linked to lifestyle. Has he been under additional stress lately?"

"Not that I'm aware of." My mind thinks about Dora, her little legs falling out over the side of the wheelbarrow. I shouldn't have left him on his own with her. And his car, why did I tell him about the stain in the back? He didn't sound worried, but he must have been.

Suddenly, the doctor's beeper goes off, and he stands up abruptly. I follow suit. "We'll continue to monitor him and see how he fares, okay?" His words are a mix of reassurance and caution.

I go back into Uncle Alfred's room and sit next to him. His once rugged and weathered face is now drained of colour, his body lying still on the sterile, white hospital bed. I grip his warm hand and watch the rise and fall of his chest as he breathes, willing him to open his eyes and give me that big smile to let me know he's going to be okay.

A nurse walks around the door, asks me if everything is okay, takes his vitals, and then disappears. She returns four or so minutes later with a cup of tea and a biscuit for me. "Here," she says. "You look as though you need it."

I want to hug her.

Memories flood back to the day at university when I'd had what Marion calls 'The Episode'. In real words, it means the time I didn't think it was worth sticking around in this life. I'd aced my exams; Uncle Alfred called to congratulate me. She'd called too. Said I should've taken more subjects. I'd put the phone down, too upset to talk to her any more. Then, in a moment of confidence, I called her up. She didn't answer. I left a message, my words clear, telling her just how awful she was. She called me back about a minute later and I remember relishing the moment because now we would have a real conversation. All she said was something was wrong with the message machine and she was going to turn it off and just wanted to let me know. She was lying; of course she was. And she'd won. Yet again. So, I got into my car and drove it into a tree.

When I woke up, Uncle Alfred was beside me in the hospital. Marion never showed.

I gently pat his forehead with a damp cloth, squeezing his

fingers, hoping for the tiniest response. His eyes flicker. I'm sure of it. I hold my breath. His little finger moves. It's slight, but it moved, I'm sure of it. I stand up, turn around, and find the nurse, happy to tell her Uncle Alfred is awake.

But she has a worried air about her, so she grabs his chart and studies it. The crease on her brow deepens. She moves to Uncle Alfred's bedside and takes his hand, and I automatically look at the monitor where the line that traces the rhythm of Uncle Alfred's heart seems to be fading.

"Is everything okay?" I ask.

She looks up at me, her eyes soft, her manner controlled. "If you'd like to sit outside, we need the doctor."

She guides me out of the room with her hand on my back. I hover at the doorway, watching the nurses hustle about Uncle Alfred's bed, their movements frantic and precise.

The doctor arrives in a rush. He doesn't waste a second diving in. "What do we have?" he demands, as his hands are already checking pupils, pulse, and the rhythm of Uncle Alfred's life struggling to return.

"A possible response," one nurse answers, her voice a mix of caution and hope. "Finger movement on the right hand."

He takes Uncle Alfred's hand gently, watches the monitors, and asks questions that seem to hang in the air unanswered. I try to read his expression, looking for clues in the lines on his face, but he is an unreadable novel written in a foreign language.

Uncle Alfred opens his eyes. He looks to the doctor and the nurses. I'm sure there's a twinkle in his eyes as he spots me standing there. The heart monitor picks up, the doctor relaxes, and the nurses smile at each other. I walk closer to his bed.

"You're here," he whispers, his voice barely audible.

I nod, tears brimming in my eyes. "Yes, I'm here. Don't try to talk too much. You need your strength."

"Marion…" The doctor asks him not to speak, that he needs to rest. I feel the shame of Marion not being here; she should be sitting by his side, too. How could she do this to him? He coughs softly, and the nurse immediately steps forward to adjust his pillows and give him a sip of water. All the while, his gaze never leaves my face.

"This is very good," the doctor says, confidently smiling.

Uncle Alfred is asleep an hour later, his head slightly tilted to the side. I'm sitting on a comfy chair they wheeled in from another room, a blanket over my lap and the pillow under my head. I've called Marion three times, but she hasn't answered. As I slip my phone back into my pocket, I feel a scrap of paper and take it out. My parents' letter, the old one Marion gave me when I was thirteen.

As I reread it, a wave of guilt washes over me. I should have spent more time with Uncle Alfred, and I might've seen this coming and taken some steps to prevent it. Instead of being focused on me. In high school, he stood by me after I'd given the matches to the new girl and she'd burnt down the science lab. It was he who argued with the school. I was kicked out and had a nervous breakdown, but it was he who insisted on a private facility in the hope that no one would ever know.

He was my mother and my father combined into one. I think about Mum, the one Scooter sent me; she would never have treated me so badly, I know it.

I send a text. *My Uncle is doing better. It was great to meet you. I hope you enjoy your visit.* The last part makes it clear that I have no expectation or intention of ever seeing them again. I read it again and again, not sure if what I'm doing is right, then make up my mind. I have to move on.

I press send, look up at Uncle Alfred, and he's snoring away. I feel good because I've prioritised who is important in my life and who is not. I've done the right thing.

A text comes in from Andrew. *Marion's car. Animal blood. Did she ever have a lion??????*

I laugh out loud. I text Andrew back. *Believe it or not, Uncle Alfred did.*

Your family gets weirder and weirder, he texts back.

TWENTY-FOUR

When I open my eyes, I'm not quite sure where I am. The vinyl of the chair sticks to my body, and a blanket is over me.

Uncle Alfred is awake, sitting up and smiling as the nurse straightens his sheets. They must've heard me move because they both look in my direction.

"I think you were in a deeper sleep than me," Uncle Alfred says with a big grin. "I hope we didn't wake you."

"I'm so sorry. I went out like a light." I stand, stretch, and crane my neck from side to side, kind of grimacing an apology to the nurse. She smiles, fills a plastic cup from Uncle Alfred's water jug, and hands it to him.

He takes a sip. "I'm hungry," he says. "It's a shame they don't have room service." He's chatting easily with the nurse, and I can see they've already figured each other out.

"How are you feeling?" I ask. "You look almost like your normal self." A peg is attached to his finger, and the tubes from the night before are all gone.

"Absolutely fine, I'm glad to say."

"You gave us quite a fright."

"And for that, I am sorry." The nurse asks him to sit up a little straighter, then she fluffs his pillows, and he relaxes back onto them.

I take his hand and feel the thinness of his skin.

"You should call Marion. She will be worried," he says. It's on the tip of my tongue to say that she didn't give a damn, couldn't even be bothered to come to the hospital, but I swallow it back in one huge gulp like bad medicine. Why would I hurt him like that?

The nurse says a few words about needing to go out, but she'll be right back.

When she's gone, I lean in towards him and say, quietly, "Your car is clean. It was lion blood in the back."

He starts to laugh.

I laugh with him. "How in the heck did that happen?"

"No idea, Persy. Absolutely no idea at all."

We smile at each other, an unspoken message sitting between us. We're safe.

"Can I get you anything?" I ask.

"Not a thing. In fact, I am going to take this opportunity to completely relax. This very nice nurse has taken excellent care of me." He nods to the nurse who's just come back in. "And it is very much appreciated."

"How long will Uncle Alfred have to be in here?" I ask her.

"Best talk to the doctor," she says. "If I were to guess, forty-eight hours. Maybe even a week."

"Nonsense," Uncle Alfred says robustly. "One day, maximum."

The nurse turns to me with a mischievous grin and raises her eyebrows.

"You need to listen to what the doctor says, okay?" I rub his arm. "They know what they're doing."

"Understood." He rests his head back on the pillow. "I think I need to sleep again. You go off. I'm sure you have things to do. Your life shouldn't revolve around taking care of me and Marion. You know we won't always be around."

I feel a vague flutter of unease. This is the first time he's said something about his mortality to me. Is it because he's in hospital? Whatever it is, I don't like it.

"I'm staying," I say.

"If you do, I shall worry, and I won't be able to relax. Off you go. You know where I am."

I plonk myself mutinously on the edge of the bed.

"Persy. I am being serious. Go."

"I don't want to."

"If you're here, I won't sleep. I won't allow myself to."

I look at the nurse. She nods. "It really is best if he gets some sleep," she says. "And I'm on a twelve-hour shift. I promise I'll keep an eye on him."

She has kind brown eyes that crinkle at the corners.

"I've been voted out. But I will come back in a few hours. No question."

"Understood," he says. "What about supper time? Bring me some ice cream. Vanilla."

"Done," I say and kiss the top of his head.

Outside the hospital, the air is cold, but it feels fresh, and the early morning sun is high, and birds are singing in the trees. It feels good. Everything is going to be fine; my bones are telling me so.

A text comes in from Mum. *We are off to Blenheim today. We will be back around six. Tomorrow is looking crazy already. Let us know if you could make dinner tonight.*

I think of Uncle Alfred, in good hands with the nurse, the prognosis rosy. Should I take the ice cream over and then head back into town to meet them? I'm not sure that's the right thing to do. Uncle Alfred won't want me hanging around, but I think I'll feel guilty, like I'm sneaking off to do something secret while he's in the hospital.

Another text comes in. *We've booked a table at Côte for*

seven. It would be wonderful if you could join us. If not, it's no problem.

I don't text back because my mind is too muddled.

I sit on a bench facing the sun, my phone cradled in the palm of my hand, more and more convinced to tell Uncle Alfred about them as soon as he gets home. I'll also tell him more about Scooter and how we were once an item when I lived in the US. I think he and Scooter would get along. He's a bit of a chip off the old block. I'll explain I kept it a secret because I didn't want to hurt him, and, quite honestly, I never thought I would find them. He won't be angry. He's too kind for that.

I text Andrew. Tell him about Uncle Alfred, how he had a stroke. He calls me as soon as he reads the message.

"I'm so sorry, Persy. Why didn't you let me know?"

"Too much was going on," I say.

"Are you at the hospital? I'll come and get you."

"Thanks, but no. Honestly. My car's here, and I'm exhausted. I need to go home and shower; I stayed here last night. I wouldn't be leaving now if it hadn't been for Uncle Alfred making me."

"You want me to meet you at yours?"

A bus pulls up less than ten feet away, and the engine racket and the people getting off force me to move. "Sorry, too much noise. What were you saying?"

"Do you want me to come by?" His voice sounds, I'm not sure, a bit fed up.

"Are you okay?" I ask.

"I've just come back from the police station."

His words upset me. The drama with Uncle Alfred had given me a slight reprieve from the reality of the Derek and Marion saga. "Okay," I say, with a feeling of impending doom.

"I'm furious. They're scaling back on the search for Dora. Other priorities. There was a shooting. Early hours of this morning. At a nightclub. Seven dead. Drug related. Everyone's on overtime dealing with it."

"And Derek?" I cross my fingers and hold my breath.

"He's nowhere to be found. They said they're going to keep looking. But I'm not so sure they'll go after him. It's about resources, and at the moment, those resources are stretched thin."

With my eyes closed, I tilt my face towards the sun and feel the warmth spread across my cheeks. Is it really possible that everything I need to happen actually could happen? That the search for Dora is winding down, that Uncle Alfred is on the mend, and that Derek has disappeared?

"I honestly don't know what to say." I try to sound disappointed, but I can't quite keep the happiness out of my voice. The sky is blue, and the world is a clean slate.

"I know," he says. "I tried. I even told them that Derek might also be involved in the other three missing women."

My chest tightens. A little claw of fear hooks into my gut because I want this all over.

"I'm not sure they believed me. I swear they thought I was playing an angle to keep their eyes on this case. I mentioned it to my clients, the families of the patients I've been working for. They want to help, but the idea of murder is too much for them to get behind. I understand it. I do. But I can't do this on my own. I feel like giving up. What other choice do I have?"

"Nothing," I say. "You've done your best. And, Andrew, I just want to say that I don't know how I would've got through this without you."

"I hope it's not over yet."

I want this to be over now. "I don't know about you," I say, "but I'm done. I'm exhausted. I want this all to go away. I hate Derek, but with Uncle Alfred being so sick, it's put everything into perspective. I'm done."

He doesn't answer.

I carry on. "You know, what goes around comes around. He'll get his comeuppance. For sure." My fingers are crossed. In my experience, karma doesn't happen. Look at Marion.

"But what would you think of me if I walked away from this? You wouldn't feel like I let you down?"

"No. Of course not. If you don't let this one go, I would worry that Derek has got the better of you. It's time to move on. He's a conman. One way or another, he'll get caught. Let's move on."

When I look at the ground, weeds are creeping through the cracks in the paving, and insects are bustling around, bumping into each other and then scuttling away in the opposite direction. Is that what we do, too? Run around, hoping for the best, constantly trying to correct our own mistakes.

"What are you doing now?" Andrew asks.

"Uncle Alfred fell asleep. I'm outside, getting some air."

"You want to catch dinner later?"

I think about Mum and Dad. No. I'll go and meet them – time to put everything to bed.

"I'll be here at the hospital. Sorry. Tomorrow, maybe?"

"Sure. If you change your mind, call me."

I hang up and text Mum and Dad. *I look forward to seeing you tonight at seven.*

Inside the car, I press the number for my hairdresser, arrange to have my hair done and get a manicure and pedicure while I'm at it. I can't remember the last time I felt this optimistic about the future.

Marion calls. "I've just spoken to the nurse." She sounds pleased with herself, as though she's taken over a vital task and completed it far better than I ever could have. "She tells me Uncle Alfred is much better."

"He is." I bite back the words 'no thanks to you'.

"She also said he needs sleep. I suggest you don't bother him anymore."

"Whatever," I say, gritting my teeth. "Are you coming in to see him then?" I know the answer; I don't even know why I'm asking.

"Whatever? That's rather an odd expression. Whatever what? Whatever the weather? Whatever you are wearing? Whatever your state of mind."

"Are you coming to visit him?"

"Good gracious, no. Uncle Alfred wouldn't want that. And besides, we have other plans."

I'm so furious with her for telling me I shouldn't be visiting Uncle Alfred that it takes a minute for me to register what she's said.

"What plans?" I say. "A cruise on the Nile? What about parachuting over the Grand Canyon? How does that sound?"

"What an odd suggestion. I presume this is a sorry attempt at humour? If it is, I suggest you stop. As your guardian, I feel obliged to tell you this is not one of your strong points."

The word guardian sticks in my throat. She has no right to allow such a word anywhere near her mouth. "Talking about guardian." I ask, "Why won't you tell me about them, the real ones, the biological ones?" If no none knew about the way she's treated me, they'd think it was cruel. It isn't. I'm plain old tired of it all.

There's silence on the other end. I don't know what she's going to say, but it will cut me down to shreds, and I brace for the impact.

"Persephone." Her tone is authoritative. I steel myself, and here it comes: Marion's wrath. "The nurse mentioned you were going to get ice cream. I've already taken care of it. That farm shop, they were very kind. Said they'd deliver to the hospital. I didn't like the idea of you picking up something from the

Co-op or some such place. The farm shop's produce is organic. Much better for him." She hangs up.

My head is starting to ache. I wonder what Mum and Dad will say when they discover how horrible she is.

TWENTY-FIVE

I call the hospital and speak to the nurse, who tells me Uncle Alfred is doing great. He gets on the line and is so upbeat that it lifts me up, and I'm ready to go for it, which is perfect because Mum and Dad are waiting.

I wait to pay at reception. A blonde woman, young, in the corner, is watching me, I swoosh my hair, and I leave the salon with my hair shiny, bouncy, and swishy. The stuff they put on it costs an extra hundred, but I don't mind. Mum will like it. She'll probably say it's exactly like the photo Scooter sent me.

I pop into one of the most expensive clothes shops in town. They carry designer clothes, costly brands with an edge, and it's like I'm playing dress up all over again, except instead of pretending to be Marion, I'm pretending to be me, the lucky girl about to meet her ever-so-real mum and dad. The look I'm going for is sophisticated and calm and effortless. I settle on a cream turtleneck sweater and a fitted skirt that falls just below the knee in the same colour. I bought the crazy expensive coat that's a shade of the sweater and a pair of kitten-heeled shoes with a little bow on the toe. I stand in the shop, looking in the mirror, my hands in the coat pockets, chin up, a touch of attitude, my hair cascading in pretend-it's-effortless waves down over my shoulders. The look is perfect. At £3K, it should be.

I walk home, shoulders back, bags swinging in harmony with my girl-about-town, going-somewhere-important, new look that's folded up in tissue paper to make sure the get-up doesn't crease. Inside the flat, I toss the bags onto the floor and kick off my shoes. Three hours before I meet them; I've got time to relax. I wander into the living room, toss the throw over me, and, with no effort at all, gently fall asleep.

The inky blackness of night lingers outside my window as I slowly open my eyes, woken by the shrill ring of my phone.

"Persy," he says. "It's me, Scooter." It's six in the evening. "Where are you? At home?" He sounds odd and tired.

"I'm in my flat. Just come back from the hospital."

"You're sick?"

"Uncle Alfred is in hospital, and he's going to be fine, don't worry about it."

"What happened?"

"Stroke. But honestly, he's stable. It couldn't be better. I slept there last night. He woke up before I did."

"But you're okay?"

"I'm absolutely perfect." I can't wait for him to ask me why I'm so happy because I'll get such a kick out of telling him I'm about to have dinner with Mum and Dad. As I talk, I open the bag with my new clothes. They're neatly folded, the hangers tucked in beside them. One by one, I remove them, hang them up on the door, and set them side by side so I can appreciate how good they will look when I put them on. "I've just had my hair done. Can you guess why?"

"Persy, just stop a minute—"

"You don't want to know why?" I ask.

"Okay, sure. Why'd you have your hair done?" He still

sounds strange and distant. It's like he's trying to force himself to be interested.

"I'm meeting Mum and Dad later." I know Scooter is going to be so happy to hear me say this.

There's silence.

"Scooter. Did you hear me? I'm meeting them for dinner. We had tea yesterday. It's a long story; we had to cut it short because of Uncle Alfred, but I'm meeting them again tonight. They texted me. They'd never met me, but there was such an instant connection, and they wanted this to happen. I still can't believe it." I start to laugh. "Honest to God, I keep thinking, any moment now, I'm going to wake up." I take a huge deep breath because I'm working too hard at this and I think I'm overdoing it. "Anyway, before you get all sad that this project is over, I've got a great idea. They live in the States, so I'll be spending a lot more time on your side of the pond. What about opening up a PI company together?" I laugh out loud again. "Can you imagine? Think about all the disguises we could use. And don't worry about the money, I'll fund it; it'll be great."

"Persy," he says.

"All you have to do right now is think of a name. And don't say anything stupid like Sherlock and Holmes, Prudent PI, or Sly Sleuth. Something catchy. What about 'S' for Scooter and 'AD' for Adelard? SAD Investigations." He's not joining in. "Oh, come on, Scooter, you've got to admit, it would be fun."

"Persy," he says. "I need to tell you something."

I stop laughing.

"What is it? What's wrong? Are you sick?"

"I'm not sick."

"Then what?"

"I'm sorry, Persy. I don't know how to tell you."

"Just say it," I whisper.

"They're not your parents."

I'm standing in the bedroom, looking at my reflection in the mirror. It's like I'm observing myself from an outside perspective. My bouncy hair looks silly and out of place, utterly foreign on my head. The new clothes hanging up have been chosen for another person, not me. I'm an imposter in my own life and I can see it.

"Persy. I'm so sorry. When I met them, I did something and didn't tell you about it. I took their DNA from an old napkin. The tests have just come back. I'm sorry. They're not your parents."

I take a breath. Of course they aren't. Why did I do that to myself? "The last time, you were furious that I'd taken the DNA." I'm angry for the wrong reasons but I need to be angry at something or someone.

"I'm sorry," he says. "This is all on me. I honestly thought we'd found them. I was more convinced than you. I overreacted. I'm so sorry."

I can't seem to get out of the role I'd created. "The photo. She looks like me. Her hair, her smile, the same pink nail polish. How could that be? I mean, DNA or not, it was like we were meant to be."

He's quiet on the other end and the silence just sits there like a spent bullet.

"It's okay, Scooter." My voice quivers as I struggle to let him know that it's okay, that it's not his fault.

"What can I do?" he says.

"I don't know. I don't know."

"It's not over, Persy. We'll keep looking."

"I think I'm done," I say.

"This is all on me. If you don't want to keep looking, that's fine; I'll keep on without you."

"I need some time. I'll call you later." I hang up.

The memory of the three of us, walking through town, me

pretending that it was really them, Mum and Dad; maybe, for a while, it was worth the pretence?

Scooter calls me back. "I know you need space; I get that. But like I said, I'm coming over. Okay."

"Really?" I say.

"Really."

TWENTY-SIX

Scooter calls. I let it ring because I opened a bottle of wine and, without paying attention, drank the whole thing. It's better not to talk to anyone when I'm like this because I'll get everything all muddled. The phone stops and I close my eyes, my head resting against the side of the sofa, and fall asleep.

An hour later, I wake up, still groggy, still thinking bullshit and with only one thought in my head. I need to get to Uncle Alfred. Once and for all, this has to be straightened out.

I call the hospital. The lovely nurse is there and wants to chat. I listen, happy to hear someone rattle away as she tells me Uncle Alfred is so much better, how much he's eaten, and how he managed to get himself out of bed and take a few steps with the help of two nurses. I dig my nails into the palms of my hands; I need to feel pain.

She passes the phone to him.

"Persy." His voice is cheerful and strong. "I hope you're not calling to tell me that you are going to stay here tonight again, are you? Because I'm very well. I've been running up and down the stairs, so I won't hear it."

I don't want to say what I need to say, but it's time to start clearing all of this mess up.

"The letter," I say.

"What letter is that?"

I don't know if I've got the guts to go ahead. I purse my lips. Tell myself it's time to face the truth. "The one Marion gave me when I was thirteen. She said it was from my parents. But she wrote it herself. I know that. The question is, did you know?"

The phone line is deathly quiet save for the sound of my own breathing. My throat constricts with emotion, and tears well up in my eyes. I fight to hold back the sobs as I take a deep breath and muster the courage to speak. "I already know the answer, don't I?" My voice quivers with sadness and resignation.

"I'm sorry, Persy. It wasn't done to hurt you."

Shame washes over me. Shame for him, Marion, and most of all for me for believing the lies. "Why?"

"To help you move on."

The absurdity of his answer sickens me. It never allowed me to move on. Instead, it kept me rooted in the same place, unable to live my life until I figured out what was going on. My heart pounds in my chest. But the worst of it: I would expect this type of deceit from her, but not from him, my Uncle Alfred. It breaks my heart.

"Do you want to tell me who my parents are?"

Again, there's silence on the other end, which tells me everything. He was part of the secret, too.

"Please. Say it." My voice is gentle, willing him to tell me the truth. *This is the moment*, I keep telling myself, *please, Uncle Alfred, now is the moment.*

"You need to speak to Marion." His voice is breaking with emotion, and as much as I want to feel sympathy for him, I can't. Even now, he defers to her. How pathetic we all are.

"She'll turn the whole conversation into another one of her games. Please, it has to be you."

There's silence.

"Now is the time," I say. I'm begging now, gulping back the tears flowing freely down my face.

"Talk to Marion. That's the only thing you can do."

"I can't believe you'd do this to me. Marion, but not you." I cover my eyes with my hands and sob, imagining him lying in his hospital bed, the look of pain on his face, hating to have this conversation. But I can't bring myself to say any words of comfort because my hurt is too deep. "Who decided to lie first?" I ask. He's on the edge of telling me, I'm sure of it. "You said you'd never lie." I'm not sure if he's ever said that to me, but the words feel right.

Quiet hangs in the air. "They died in a fire when you were weeks old. Everyone thought you had died with them."

I cover my face with my hands.

"What Marion did was wrong, but what she did was for the right reasons. It was something that happened out of the blue. She saw the house on fire, you outside, she grabbed you and brought you home. Every day she looked in the newspapers; nothing. By that time, she wanted to keep you. So she did."

"That's not true," I say.

"It is, Persy. All I know is she arrived here with you in her arms. In the back of the car was her old sweater that she'd wrapped you up in."

Lies, lies, lies.

"Persy, I'm so sorry."

"Why the story about Americans working at the university? Was that supposed to amuse the two of you?"

"Persy, I'm sorry. I understand why you—"

I hang up. I no longer exist.

I sit on the edge of my bed, the phone slipping from my fingers and landing with a soft thud on the floor. It's late; the sky outside has turned dark, and, somewhere in the distance, an ambulance siren wails. My mind races through the years of memories and secrets, knitting together pieces of a puzzle I never knew I was a part of. Marion's evasions, Uncle Alfred's half-truths. Did they talk about it? Together? Sitting in the sunroom over a nice glass of port?

A text comes in from my parents, who are definitely not my parents. It's almost eight, but I said I would be there at seven. I don't have the energy to pretend that anymore.

I'm so sorry to have missed you, she texts. *We hope all is okay. We're about to leave the restaurant. We're on our way back to the US tomorrow. It was a pleasure to meet you.*

I text three words back. *I'm so sorry.*

She immediately comes back to me. *Not necessary. We know how life can get in the way.*

I answer with an emoji of a sad face. She doesn't text back.

I step into the steamy shower, and the hot water cascades over my stupidly styled hair. I carefully wash and condition it, paying attention to the scent of lavender that fills the air. I put on the new clothes I recently purchased, and I appreciate the tailored fit and the neutral colours that make me look sophisticated. The warm and elegant coat adds the perfect touch to the cashmere turtleneck. I slip on the kitten heels with the pretty bow.

I make my way to Marion's. I will make her tell me the truth.

I ease my car into the driveway, gently come to a stop, look straight ahead, and take in the spectacular view of her home at the end of the tree-lined road. The majestic grey-stone house, its intricate architecture lit up by the full moon and the large windows that glint in the sunlight, is a grand home that hints at the loving family that must live inside. The lie.

All those years, that fake letter, did she really think she'd fooled me? Was it funny to her? Did she go to bed thinking about it, smirking, telling herself how clever she was?

I press my foot onto the gas pedal, push harder, and feel the smooth surface of the drive slipping under my wheels. My heart races, and I pump up the speed. Twenty-five to thirty-five to sixty, then seventy. Adrenaline courses through my veins as I reach eighty, the house less than a hundred metres away. I see it all unfold: crashing through the front door, pieces of glass and wood flying in every direction, and Marion's terrified face as she witnesses the destruction. I'm getting closer. The house is getting nearer. It will soon be over. I want to see the shame on her face. I need to see it. I slam on the brakes, and the car screeches to a halt, sending gravel flying all around the car. My body jerks forward, straining against the force of the seatbelt digging into my collarbone.

A wave of fear and determination rushes through me and leaves me breathless as I sit in the stillness. Every muscle in my body is tense. I take a deep breath to steady my nerves and look at her bedroom. Is Marion there, watching me?

I slowly get out of the car, and my hand rests on the open door for support as I try to shake off my nerves. I look around the sprawling estate, taking in every detail, imprinting it into my memory, knowing that this will be the last time I will ever be here, the last time I will ever see Marion.

TWENTY-SEVEN

Inside the house, the place smells empty. The thought strikes me as odd because I'm unsure what I mean. It's never been a vibrant place, but today, it feels barer and more lifeless than ever before as the shadows lurk in the corners and the gentle tick from the grandfather clock echoes through the dark. Where is she?

I hover, expect a chair to move, a foot to fall or a door to shut. Nothing.

It's nine at night. She usually goes to bed anywhere between nine and eleven. Either way, at this time, she will only be in one of three places: the sunroom, the kitchen or her bedroom.

The hall has a soft glow inside, coming from the moonlight filtering in through the window. The lamps have been turned off. The smell of eucalyptus triggers memories steeped in misery and betrayal – memories steeped in Marion.

A newspaper is on her chair, open, half-read. I pick it up. It has today's date. Marion's been sitting here. Her pen is sitting on top of the crossword page, and the top has fallen off and rolled under the coffee table. Without emotion, as if time is standing still, I bend, pick it up, and slip it back on.

As the hardwood floor groans under my weight, I walk back out and down the dimly lit hallway. In the kitchen, empty plates are stacked haphazardly in the sink, still stained with the remnants of a meal as the smell of cabbage and beef wafts through the air. I spot the tiny bottle of Nembutal next to the kitchen window kitchen with some still in there. I grab a glass, pour the liquid in and top it up with water I take from a jug in the fridge. I take the glass with me back up the hall. I go into the drawing room and put the glass on the table. When I find her, this is where we will sit, in a civilised place to have a civilised conversation. And I will drink it, all right, there in front of her. She can win. This will be my final gift to her.

I pause at the foot of the stairs and look up. The door to her bedroom is slightly open. I slowly walk up, every step more cautious than the next.

Outside her bedroom, my ears strain to hear the sound of her breathing. Nothing. With a light touch, I push open the door. It's empty. The bed is neatly made, untouched, with no signs of sleep. Where is she?

I walk from one bedroom to another, kicking open each bathroom door, pulling back curtains, and opening wardrobes. She's not here.

The shed?

I head down the stairs, go back into the sunroom, throw open the doors and cross the patio. The garden is littered with leaves and branches, and I'm careful to navigate around them as I feel the dampness from the sodden lawn soaking into my shoes.

The shed is empty.

There is only one place left – Uncle Alfred's. I go back through the garden, then the house, then the front door, get into my car and head down to his cottage. The tyres kick up dirt as I speed down, and I grip the steering wheel as every bump and dip in the road jolts my body.

At the front of his house, I hesitate and look around. I see nothing. I go on in.

It's empty. Marion has gone.

I stand in his living room, looking out at the pigs as they sleep. Under the coffee table is a receipt. Uncle Alfred buys everything online, so he doesn't have receipts. I pick it up. It's payment for the delivery of a hire car. It's today's date. I grab my phone and call the hospital.

"Alfred Adelard. Please." He knows where she is, I'm sure of it.

The woman who answers puts me on hold. Less than a minute later, she comes back on the line.

"Alfred Adelard, you said, correct?"

"Correct."

"Right. Yes. Got it here. He left. Maybe an hour or so ago. Signed himself out."

"That's not possible. The last time I spoke to him, he could only take a few steps." I struggle to remember the exact words spoken by the nurse, but whatever she told me, I have a picture of him in my mind, trying to take some steps, holding on to her arm. Had I made that up? "He can't walk," I say. "I'm sure of it."

"A Marion Adelard accompanied him. He wasn't alone."

"You're sure?" I don't believe what she's telling me. Marion had said she didn't want to go near the place. "Marion Adelard. Did you see her? I mean, did you, personally, actually see her?"

"An older woman, slightly wobbly on her feet. Tweeds. Hair in a bun. Very polite. I only know that because I helped her find a wheelchair."

"Where was she taking him?"

"I apologise," the woman answers. "That's not the sort of question we have the right to ask."

"Could they be in the café?"

"I wouldn't think so. That closed two hours ago."

I hang up. Calculate the time it should take them to get here. Marion drives slowly; at a guess, ten minutes, and they'll be making their way here, to me, waiting. I get back into the car and drive back up the dirt track. I leave my car around the side of the house because I don't want her to be prepared for me being here. I sit in the dark. I am waiting and watching.

Another hour goes by.

Marion must be driving; she's not used to a hired car or used to being out late at night. Anything could've happened. A skid on that horrible turn by the pub; a young boy racer, going too fast, overtaking, forcing her to brake and ending up in a ditch.

I call Andrew. "Can you check on something for me? Marion is bringing Uncle Alfred home, and they're a bit late. I'm sure it's nothing, but I was wondering if there is any way of finding out if there's been an accident."

"Give me fifteen minutes."

At the front door, I look into the night, willing them to return. *Any minute now*, I keep repeating. The rain starts to fall, and I step back, grab one of Marion's old coats, throw it over my shoulders and stand outside as the trees sway in the eerie silence that creeps into my bones.

My phone rings, and I grab it. "Anything?" I say to Andrew.

"Who is this?" It's a man's voice.

My heart sinks; it's the police, it has to be. They've found Marion. "What has happened?" I say.

There's a pause. "Persy?"

The voice is familiar, but I can't place it. The cop from the warehouse? "Yes?"

"It's me, Derek. I need to speak to Marion." His words tumble out so quickly that it's hard to understand what he's saying.

"Join the queue."

"I need to speak to her, please. She needs to hear what I have. I know everything, Persy. I know it all."

A wave of nausea overwhelms me, and the memory of it all comes rushing back – the images of the bodies, the wheelbarrow, the sickening ear-splitting squeal of the pigs.

A call is waiting. From Andrew. "Get lost, Derek. And if you're smart, you won't bother any of us again because if you do, I swear I'll hand you over to the police myself." I hang up, switch to the call on hold.

"Persy, I'm sorry," Andrew says. "There have been no accidents. I even got them to call the AA to see if there had been any breakdowns. There hasn't."

"I don't know what to do."

"They'll turn up. They're fine. I know it. I called every hospital in a thirty-mile radius. No one has been admitted."

"I just don't know why she picked him up. It doesn't make sense."

"Why? She's his sister, isn't she?"

"You don't know her."

There's a pause. "You're right. Okay." The tone of his voice tells me I was a bit too sharp.

"Sorry. I didn't mean to come off that way."

"This is what I'm going to do. I'm going to jump in my car. Follow the road Marion would have taken from the hospital to where you are now. If something has happened to them on the road, I'll spot it."

"Thank you," I say, trying to keep my voice steady.

"Try not to worry."

I wander back into the house, turn on the lights in the drawing room, and sit, my body stiff, arms wrapped around me, legs pressed together, feet flat on the floor, gently swaying back and forth. I catch sight of myself in the mirror. My hair is plastered to my head, my face is tired and drawn, and I look twenty years older. I look tired and miserable like horrible Marion.

My eyes scan the room, landing again and again on items of pain. The fireplace with the dead animal and the books were things I wasn't allowed to touch. I don't know who I am. Did I ever exist? Everything about me is a reflection of her. A long-ago therapist used to ask me questions I didn't understand. Was I happy? How did I feel? What was my favourite pastime? I'd struggled with the answers. I would be happy if Marion were happy with me. My hobbies revolved around what Marion told me they should be. And now. Here I am. Waiting for her.

I call Andrew. "Anything?"

"Nothing at all. I took the main road and am at the bottom of your drive now. But I'm going to go back to Bath again, but this time I'll take the other way, the side roads, to make sure. I'll call you when I get there."

"Thanks," I say. "Really."

"Do you have any idea where she would have taken him? Is there another property somewhere? A place in Bath?"

"Only my flat. They'd never go there. She wouldn't get him up the stairs."

"I'll call you in a bit. Try to think if there's anywhere else they could be."

Could she have taken him somewhere? Something she said, I hadn't taken much notice, made a joke about it. Something about a plan? She would've packed if that were true and she was going somewhere. I hightail it upstairs, rush into her bedroom, and open the doors where she keeps her luggage. They're all there. Stacked on top of each other like luxury building blocks. I check her meticulously organised medicine cabinet, searching for her meds that she would have taken if she was going somewhere. The statins are there, and the pills for her acid reflux are there, too.

I stand transfixed, staring into her bedroom. On the bedside table is the old tin where she keeps her spare bottle of Nembutal. I stroll forward and open it. It's empty.

TWENTY-EIGHT

Andrew keeps calling. I can't talk. Not to him. Not to anyone. I know what Marion is going to do and I have to stop it. The plan, the missing bottle of Nembutal, taking Uncle Alfred away, it's as clear as black on white. She's going to kill him.

The world blurs around me as I frantically head towards the mausoleum, my foot shoved against the gas pedal, my white-knuckled fingers gripping the steering wheel as my tyres skid and slide and the gears grind as I try like hell to maintain control. My brakes lock up as I veer past Uncle Alfred's house, and the car almost turns over. I drive parallel to the cluster of trees. The terrain gets rougher and rougher, and the steering wheel vibrates so much that it's hard to hang on to.

In the distance, my headlights pick out the polished granite mausoleum with its columns and steps set behind decaying trees. I squint, lean forward, and tense my arms. A car is parked outside; I don't recognise it. The rental; it has to be.

I jam my foot on the brake, fling the door open, and run like hell into the place of the dead.

Marion is sitting in the middle of the stark, bare room, leaning against a giant statue, her legs stretched out in front of her. Uncle Alfred is lying next to her, his head on her lap. She looks up at me and smiles. A cold, calculating smile.

I take a step towards them, my legs threatening to give way.

"What have you done?"

She doesn't answer. She looks down at him and strokes his face with her horrible, gnarled fingers. Is he dead?

I crouch, press my fingertips against his neck, search for a pulse; it's there, he's still alive.

"Persy…" she says. My nickname has never passed her lips before.

"No," I say. "Don't." I turn my back on her, grab my phone, call emergency, demand an ambulance. I can't let her win.

"He's gone, Persy; I had to do it," she says. "Let him be." Her voice doesn't break. There's no emotion. I kneel by Uncle Alfred. His sterling-silver hip flask, with its beaten-up leather cover, lies on the ground next to him; it's empty.

I snatch it up and shove it in her face. "Why?"

She doesn't blink or flinch. No emotion.

"Now," I say. "Tell me now. My parents? Tell me?"

Her eyes start to close, and her body slumps. I grab hold of her shoulders and shake like hell. "You're not going to die," I scream.

Quiet fills the air. No siren. No ambulance just seconds away. I'm running out of time. I frantically drag her across the floor, down the steps, and into my car. I place her in the boot, the same as Dora. I go back in, drag Uncle Alfred too. He's heavier, it's taking longer, but I can do this. I pull him into the back seat, get into the car and drive like hell to the hospital.

I call ahead, tell them what's happened, ask them to be waiting for an elderly couple who've taken poison and that if they're not ready, they will die.

Andrew calls, and I decline.

Scooter calls, and I stab decline.

My foot slams on the brake pedal outside the hospital, and I burst through the emergency room doors. The scent of antiseptic and chaos fills my nostrils as I frantically call for help. Nurses rush to me as I babble and explain in panicked words about the two people in my car. Gasping for breath, I take them to my car where Uncle Alfred and Marion lay, their faces pale and eyes closed. I plead with the nurses to hurry, to make sure a doctor is ready, as seconds tick by.

Marion and Uncle Alfred are taken away, and in the sterile, fluorescent-lit waiting room, I'm left alone, not knowing what to do. I pace and inhale the smell of antiseptic, mingled with fear and sickness. Panic begins to claw up my throat. I shiver and draw my stupid, expensive jacket around me.

I sit in one of the hard plastic chairs lining the room. My fingers grip the hem of my skirt. Time stretches out ahead of me.

Across the room, a vending machine hums, and I ache for that feeling of hunger or thirst. I glance around. I'm not alone. Five or six other people, worn out by worry or exhaustion, sit and wait. An older man has a newspaper on his lap. He's not reading. He's just staring blankly at the top of a page. A young woman with red-rimmed eyes taps incessantly on her phone.

My name is called. I rise, smoothing out my skirt as if looking tidy has suddenly become one of the most important things in my life. The doctor, a middle-aged man with kind eyes framed by square glasses, nods at me to follow. I step forward, my legs carrying me as if they know the way, even though my mind can no longer think. His face is a mask of professionalism, giving nothing away. I search his eyes for a clue, a hint of what's going on, but his face tells me nothing. He leads me through the swinging doors that separate what feels like my past from my future. "Come with me," he says.

His office is sterile and comforting in its orderliness. Diplomas line the wall, and bookshelves are filled with medical texts and journals. He gestures to a chair opposite his desk, and I sit down. With his door half-open, I hear the muffled sounds of distant beeping monitors and the shuffle of nurses' shoes on the linoleum floor.

"Persy, may I call you Persy?"

I nod.

"Persy, this is a tough conversation to have. I am so sorry. They died. There was nothing we could do."

"But they were breathing."

"It was too late. There was nothing we could do," he repeats. "They were dead before we took them into the emergency room. I am so sorry." He gives a solemn nod, his face etched with professional empathy.

His words sit in the space in the room, the finality of the situation impossible to comprehend. The weight of his words presses down on me, but inside, there is a strange void. No tears come, no gasp of shock, just a numbness that seems to extend beyond my body.

"What happens now?" My voice sounds foreign to me, detached and hollow.

He clears his throat, shifting slightly in his chair. "There will be some formalities to take care of, of course, arrangements to be made." He takes a breath. "And I'm afraid the police will have to be informed."

I can't understand what he's saying, but he must know because he comes around from his side of the desk and sits next to me, leaning in as if he thinks I'm having trouble processing it all.

"Nembutal. That is a controlled substance. We are obliged to report its usage."

"I understand," I say.

He pauses, watches me, nods like he's showing me he knows what I'm going through, and then stands up.

"I'd like to see them. Is that okay?"

He nods. "Stay here, and I will ask one of the nurses to take you."

"Thank you," I say.

A middle-aged nurse arrives, gives me a solemn smile, leads me down a couple of halls, and then takes me into a hospital room. Two beds are inside, about six feet away from each other. Uncle Alfred is on the left, and Marion is on the right, and crisp white sheets cover their bodies. The nurse folds the sheets back just enough so I can see their faces.

"Take as much time as you like," she says, leaving me there with them, the three of us, just like always.

Uncle Alfred's face is relaxed, and a slight furrow on his brow is the only sign that anything was ever amiss. Marion's features look softer now; her lips slightly parted as if she might speak at any moment with some smart-ass comment that will piss me off. I brush a hand over Alfred's cold forehead and tuck an errant strand of hair away from her face.

Memories come flooding back. Marion sewing my name into my school uniform before it was packed in my school trunk. Uncle Alfred letting me hide near the coal shed, making sure Marion didn't find me.

I stand between them, then go to the side of Uncle Alfred's bed and push it so it sits right next to hers. I take her hand from under the sheet and place it on his. The two of them, together, with me looking on, make the picture more honest.

A pile of clothes sits in the corner. I suppose they were cut off their bodies in an attempt to save them. Uncle Alfred's jacket is on top, and the corner of something is sticking out. It's a letter. I take it, open it, and read it.

My name is on the top, and his words are clear and to the point: *I understand. None of this was your fault.*

My body shakes with sobs as tears stream down my face. My chest feels heavy and tight like a boulder is weighing me down. I crumple to the ground. They left me behind, alone and abandoned. Even in their final moments, they chose each other over me.

TWENTY-NINE

A numbness has taken up the space where predictable misery once lived. They've been dead seven days.

In the sunroom, without Marion sitting in the corner, the room feels like it's lost its purpose. I close my eyes for a moment, allowing myself to imagine Uncle Alfred wandering in from the dirt road, walking across the patio and opening the doors, a big smile on his face, and telling Marion and me it would be nice to light a fire.

Marion's house feels larger now, as if her passing has emptied the place. I wander from room to room, a ghost among memories, trailing my fingers over the dusty book jackets and the mantelpiece with their bronze statues. The table where Marion served tea sits in the middle of the room. Those absurd sausage rolls; why did she do that? I can almost hear the clink of china and the smell of her mothballed clothes. The glass of water with the Nembutal inside sits on a side table by the door. Most people would freeze at the idea of poison, sitting there, looking harmless. They'd feel the need to grab it, throw it away, do anything to get rid of it. For me, it's a reminder of how awful she was. When I was sitting here, waiting for her, with this glass, I'm no longer sure what my intentions were. Was it for me or for her?

The sound of a car's engine comes up the drive and Roger's sleek red jaguar pulls up. His face looks different at this moment; he is older, tired; it's hard to tell. He was so intertwined with her life. Will he still be as connected to mine? He gets out of the car, dressed in a sombre black suit and tie. He looks serious and sad. It dawns on me that I may need him more than he needs me.

He strides towards me with his arms outstretched. As he wraps his arms around me, I can feel his strength and comfort pour into me.

"I'm so sorry, Persy," he says. "Very sad. Very sad indeed."

In the drawing room, we sit at the table with no tea, no sandwiches, not even a starched white linen, just a polished mahogany table. He sits down, rubs his hands, shivers a little and glances around, a questioning look on his face. "You don't have the heating on?"

"No, sorry." I don't tell him it makes the place smell worse. I wonder if that's why Marion never bothered with it. Not for the first time, I have a horrible vision of her hovering just over my shoulder, lipstick marks on her teeth.

Roger sets his briefcase down on the wooden table with a practised grace. The hinges snap open, and inside is a pile of documents for me. I watch him, noting the crisp lines of his suit and the confident way he carries himself. "I have the papers for you to sign," he says, his tone professional.

"I'm sorry, Roger. You must think me so rude. Would you like some tea?"

"You know, Persy, hearing you say that, you sound so much like Marion."

The taste of bile pricks at my throat.

"But no, thank you. This won't take long. As I explained when we went through the agenda in my office, everything is in order. Marion was meticulous in her planning; it's just a matter of you signing the necessary documents."

The papers have small, brightly coloured stickers. He carefully rearranges the stack so that each document is aligned neatly and perfectly. He hands me a pen with such professional grace it's like he's presenting me with a prized possession.

"Please initial and sign with your full name," he instructs, sliding one set of documents after another towards me. After a deep breath, I begin filling in the blanks. Fifteen minutes later, we're done, and he shuffles the neatly signed documents back into his briefcase. With a small smile, he nods at me, satisfied that all the loose ends have been tied up.

"As you can imagine, I have helped many clients who have gone through similar situations. And I tell them all the same thing. Take your time before you make any major financial decisions."

"I understand," I say. "And thank you."

His hand gently pats mine. "I will continue to serve and support you for as long as you need." His voice sounds sincere, and I'm sure I see a determination to do what's right in his eyes. His words bring a sense of calm and stability. "And, Persy, if there is anything you need, any information you'd like to go over, please let me know."

"There is one thing," I say.

"Of course, go ahead."

"Do you know the truth about my parents?"

Roger's eyes narrow as he studies me. I can almost see the gears turning in his mind, trying to decipher my thoughts. His gaze is intense and searching.

He leans back and folds his arms. "There is nothing I can tell you, Persy. I am so sorry."

He hasn't answered the question.

"She must have said something to you?"

"I am so sorry," he replies, his voice calm and professional. "There was mention of a fire, that is all I know, and that was said over twenty years ago. Marion was ruthless with her privacy, you know that. The only discussions I had with her regarded the disposition of her and your uncle's assets."

A tense silence hangs in the air. With my voice strained with emotion, I keep pushing, not wanting to believe that she didn't say something, a clue, a slip of the tongue.

"You spent a lot of time with her. She never said a word? I mean, you must have wondered?"

Roger's face remains unchanged. "My expertise only extends to the law."

"But you must have asked yourself, didn't you?" My words are almost pleading.

He straightens up a little, his eyes squarely on mine. "I did wonder, you are correct, but that wonder was quickly dismissed. It was none of my business. And if I delved into areas where I shouldn't, I could not continue as a trusted advisor." His face looks apologetic, as if he wishes he could answer my questions. "I'm afraid I have no idea. The subject of your birth, Marion kept that close to her chest. Sorry." The silence sits between us, and he moves uncomfortably in his seat. He coughs. "Should we review the inventory of all your inherited assets?"

He wants to move on from this discussion; I'd be offended if I didn't know him better. "Just leave the list with me. I can take a look later."

We leave the drawing room, me walking a little ahead, out the front door and to his car. He gets in, pauses, rolls down the window and gives me a reassuring smile.

"One last thing, Persy," he says calmly. "The police have contacted me. They will not be pursuing the question of where the Nembutal came from. Nothing to worry about there at all."

"Good," I say.

"I'll see you at the crematorium." And with that, he starts the engine and drives away.

I cross my arms over my body and shiver.

My phone rings, and my knee-jerk reaction is that I'm irritated because it's bound to be Marion. There is no caller ID.

"Persy. It's Derek. We need to talk."

His voice is like a hook pulling me back to a place I don't want to go. "They're dead," I say. "Marion and Uncle Alfred. It's over." I hang up.

Exhaustion overwhelms me. My mind and body are drained and I've reached the last bit of a long road that went straight to a dead end. It's time to face the truth. I'm on my own. I'll never know my true identity, and all the money in the world isn't going to help.

Scooter calls. He's called a couple of times already, but my head wasn't in the right place to answer; too many questions and thoughts, shifting like a kaleidoscope with every tiny movement. I answer it now because he's the only person who knows me and I need some reassurance that I'm still here and everything that's happening isn't just an illusion.

"I know about Alfred and Marion," he says.

"Sorry, I haven't been in a good place."

"You need to see a shrink."

"That's what Americans do," I say.

"Sure. And that's why we're all so well-adjusted."

The surprising snort of laughter that comes out of my mouth feels good.

"And before you go all ape on me, I've found you one, a therapist. I've just sent you an email. I've already spoken to him and when I get to London, I'll come with you. But for now, you need to see him. Okay. His name is Chris Gates. He's one of the best there is. Harvard, Johns Hopkins, the lot. He spent a lot of time working with people with PTSD. He's American but spent all of his working life in London. He's at the top of his game. I've told him you'll go and see him."

"I don't have PTSD."

"That's what all the PTSD patients say."

"I'll look at your email." And maybe I will. I don't know.

"I've made an appointment for you. Next week. And I've paid upfront. And he's expensive, so don't make me waste my money. I work too hard for it. You're not going to get away without speaking to him."

"Let me think about it."

"I get that. But you're going to see him whether you like it or not. I told him you live in Bath, he loves the place, and he's willing to come see you. I'm not budging on this."

"Don't you have other things you're interested in?"

"Sure," he says. "How much are you worth?"

I laugh again. "I don't know. A lot."

"Will you marry me?" he says.

My laugh is so loud it echoes around the hall.

"We'd make a great couple," he goes on. "Think about it. Our kids would be perfect. Your brains. My looks. No, that's not right. My brains, your looks. No, that's not right either. Now I've got it. Your brains, your looks; there we go, they'd be perfect."

"I'm in," I say, hoping that he knows I mean it.

"I've gotta ask. Marion and Alfred. Did they give you a heads-up? A secret letter with the names of you know who?"

"Nothing." Saying it out loud makes me feel ashamed. If they'd loved me, wouldn't they have told me everything? If they'd cared, they would have. There you have it. I'm uncareable. The word is interesting, but I don't think it exists. Marion would love to correct me on that one.

There's a pause on the other end. "Maybe they were trying to protect you."

"Right. I'm sure that's what it was all about."

"I mean," he continues. "There could be any number of

things. Maybe your parents were drug addicts. Maybe they had genetic diseases that they didn't want you to know about. What about FFI? You know what that is? Fatal familial insomnia is rare; you end up not being able to sleep, and it kills you." He pauses. "You know what. Forget that. I don't want to put ideas in your head. My bad."

"Just to let you know, I'm pretty sure I don't have FFI. Plus, my blood tests say I'm quite healthy."

He changes tack. "What are you going to do with the house?"

"Not sure," I say.

"Going through everything. I don't envy you."

He's right. The idea of trawling through the house is exhausting. There's nothing in here I want and having to look at everything and decide what to do with it is too much. Most people go through their parents' home with a sense of nostalgia, finding things they did as a family and looking at old photos. For me, it's not going to happen.

"I've got to go, Scooter," I say. "I'll call you later. Okay? And I'm sorry. I'll get to you as soon as I can. I promise."

I want to go home. To my home. To my flat.

I lock the house, get in my car and take the long route home. The woods, trees, and shops all look the same but somehow different. I turn on the radio and switch to the classical music station. An opera is on, Donizetti, *L'elisir d'amore*. Uncle Alfred's favourite and I can't remember why for the life of me. I can remember going to the Royal Opera House with him and seeing his intensity as we watched. We were supposed to stay at a fancy hotel nearby, but when Marion found out, she went crazy, insisted we came home. The memory brings with it such a sense of hopelessness it could destroy me. I pull over, unable to stop the emotion. I shut off the engine and let my forehead rest against the steering wheel as sobs shudder through my body.

The emotions slowly pass and I wipe my eyes, tell myself to expect all of this. Like a therapist once said, embrace it all. I get back on the road and drive home.

The stairs up to my flat seem harder to climb than before. Should I keep this place? Something inside tells me I need to erase everything from my old life. Sure, it would seem like I was running away, but right now, with all the misery I've carried with me, it sounds about right. A villa in Italy, maybe. Something Uncle Alfred said he always wanted to do. I stop, tightly shut my eyes, and lean my head against the wall. My brain must stop connecting every thought I have to him and her.

With my computer on, I search for the contact number of Sotheby's in London. Marion knows them well and bought a lot of art and antiques through them. I'm connected to the estates department and end up talking to a man, probably around his early forties. I explain who I am and about Marion and Marion's house. The sound of him tapping on his computer echoes through the phone.

"Got it," he says. "Impressive."

"I've just inherited it. I don't want it, and I don't want anything inside."

He sucks in a sharp breath. "Are you sure? I've just brought up your mother's name. Marion Adelard, correct?"

"That's her."

"She's brought some quite valuable pieces from us."

"And she's never sold a thing. It's all there, in the house."

"Do you have any idea as to the value of everything?" he asks. "I'm assuming there's more than the items purchased from Sotheby's?"

"There's an inventory. I'll send it to you."

"Excellent." He sounds excited, like he's sitting at his desk, rubbing his hands together. "Given the estate's value, I suggest we send someone down."

"I'll give you the name and number of our family solicitor. You can get in touch with him."

"Good enough," he says. "And thank you."

I check my watch: there is an hour until the cremation. I start to choose something black and formal, then stop and change my mind. I will wear the clothes I have brought to meet my parents. The logic makes sense. I'm letting go of all of them.

When I arrive, the crematorium is quiet, its solemn facade offering no solace. I slip inside and sit in the almost-empty space. Roger is already there, standing, talking to the vicar or the priest or whoever Marion chose and Roger arranged. He comes towards me, hands stretched out.

"There will be a short service. I followed Marion's instructions regarding the flowers, music, and a psalm."

"Thank you," I say.

Someone hovers behind me, and when I turn around, I see Andrew, dressed in a black suit, looking slightly sheepish. I didn't tell him about the funeral because I didn't want him here. I don't want his pity.

He reaches out and touches my arm. "Would it be better if I left?"

"No. Stay. It's fine."

We sit side by side, silently watching as the coffins are solemnly transported forward. The creaking of the wheels and the shuffling of feet echo through the room. Andrew's hand grasps mine, but it feels lifeless. The heaviness in the air is suffocating. The scent of flowers fills the room, and my heart aches.

I want to say I felt a surge of emotions or had an uncontrollable need to weep, but I didn't. I try to think about Uncle Alfred in his deckchair, but I hear the pigs squealing every time I picture it. I try to think about Marion sitting in the sunroom, but when I picture that, I see a pair of dead ankles peeking out from behind the sofa. Will those memories ever become so distant that they disappear?

The ceremony comes to a close, and we make our way back to our cars. As we leave, the rustle of footsteps and the murmur of voices fill the air. No casual detour to a friend's house for snacks and catch-up conversations, no lingering with the vicar for small talk, and no swapping stories with others who attended the service.

The sun dips low on the horizon, and a fierce wind whips through the air, sending chills down my spine. Andrew gets closer, puts his arm around my shoulder, and pulls me towards him.

Roger catches up with me.

"Call me later, Persy. We should get together to discuss your plans. I had a call from Sotheby's?"

"Good," I say. "I want them to come in and value everything."

"Before you make any major decisions, let's discuss?"

"I want all of the stuff gone." Marion would be so angry about me using the word stuff.

"I understand the instinct to move on, but as I've mentioned, I strongly urge you to resist making any major decisions."

"I want it all gone," I say again.

"So be it." He shakes my hand, then gets into his car and drives away.

I turn to Andrew, and I feel like I owe him something. I didn't want him here, but now I'm glad he is here.

"I'm hungry," I say. "You want to eat?"

"Sure," he says with a big smile. "I have some news."

"Sounds exciting. What is it?"

"Let's talk about it when we eat." He squeezes my arm, kisses me on the cheek, and waits until I get into my car. "I'll follow you in mine, okay."

Instead of heading into the town, I opt for a more scenic route and drive up the hill towards Lansdown. Eventually, we arrive at the Hare and Hounds pub, nestled among rolling hills and picturesque countryside. We are lucky to snag a table by the large window and look at the breathtaking views of the expansive landscape stretching out for miles. We both know what we want to eat. Comfort food. Fish and chips.

"How are you feeling?" he asks.

"I'm not sure."

"Give yourself some time." He rubs my arm. "I overheard what your lawyer was saying to you. He's right, Persy. Don't make any decisions yet. It's too early."

Another person's opinion is of no interest. "You said you had some news."

"I've been offered a new job. In Amsterdam." His eyes flicker with anticipation, searching for a response that I'm not sure I can give. His gaze remains fixed on me, waiting for some reaction. "I think you should come with me."

The food arrives before I can answer, and we smile at each other and awkwardly mention how good the food smells, the colour of the crispy batter, and how the fries have to be the best.

I take a deep breath and finally find my words. "Good for you. You should take it. I don't know if you know Amsterdam, but it's fantastic."

"You don't want to come with me?"

His eyes are earnest, and I can see the pain on his face because he's forcing himself to ask a question that he already knows the answer to.

"Give me some time," I say. "Can I think about it?"

"Sure," he says. "All the time you like." He smiles up at me, picks up a chip and eats it. "If I take it, I'll have to drop the whole Derek thing."

"I thought you'd dropped it already."

"I have, but part of me doesn't seem right that Derek will get away with this. And there's something else. I also think I'm letting you and Marion down too. A part of me would like to finish it all up."

I move the fish around on my plate. "Marion wouldn't thank you," I say. "If anything, she'd end up blaming you for ruining the reputation of the care home. If I were you, I'd push the thought of Marion as far away from you as possible."

"Is that what you're doing?"

"Maybe."

"Persy, nothing is keeping you here. Come on. It will be an adventure."

A clean break, a move away from all the miserable memories? I picture walking along the canals, riding bikes over pretty bridges, sitting at sidewalk cafés sipping espresso. The problem is that I can't see Andrew in the picture.

The waiter clears our plates, and we sit silently at the table.

"When will you have to be there?" I ask.

"Soon. I'm heading there tonight. I need to look around, get the lay of the land, see what I might be signing up for."

"You'll love it," I say.

We pay the bill and walk out of the restaurant. The chilly air nips at our skin as we silently stand by my car. He breaks it first, touching my arms and meeting my eyes with sorrow and longing. I nod, unable to find the right words, and climb into my car. As I drive away, I steal one last glance at him standing tall, arms crossed, watching me leave.

A sense of unease settles in my chest as I trudge up the stairs to my empty flat. I'm lost, unsure of myself, a puzzle with missing pieces. It's time to find those pieces and put the complete picture together. I go to my desk and sit down. I start making a list with a pen, ready to create who I am. I like tennis, especially singles because I can only rely on myself. People make me laugh, not by telling jokes but by banter that riffs off one another. Like Scooter; his humour is irreverent, but it's funny, as if he's unguarded. I want to be unguarded. Andrew is kind, which is clear to me. And kind is nice, but not nice enough to spend the rest of my life with him.

Scooter is right. I need to talk to someone who can help me find me. In a split second, it hits me. Everything about my life leads back to Marion. That's where it all started, and if I'm going to erase the past, I need to face her head on, at her house.

I slip into soft, black leggings and pull on a cosy sweatshirt with a faded logo across the front. The fabric is worn from years of use, but it feels good. The sky is already beginning to darken, and rain is falling, leaving puddles on the sidewalk. It would be easy to change my mind about going out in this weather now, but I tell myself, *no, not this time*. This is my choice, and I need to follow through.

I head outside. The city is quiet and there's a peacefulness that comes with being alone in the darkness that feels good. By the time I get there, it will be darker, colder, damp, and mouldy, but it's the right thing.

It's time to get rid of her for good.

THIRTY

Outside, by nine in the evening, the flickering glow of a roaring bonfire spits out ember as it lights up the sky like it's Guy Fawkes Night. The flames dance and leap and the air is filled with the smoky scent of burning wood as the blaze casts gold shadows across the drawing room window.

The roaring fire consumes all the papers from every room in the house. Anything to do with my past was non-existent among the scrap. No school reports or medical files, no keepsakes or mementoes. Not even the birthday, Christmas, or Mother's Day cards I sent her every year. Marion had already disposed of them, deeming my past unimportant and insignificant, as if she got rid of anything to do with me before she died, leaving me nothing but a blank slate and a nagging sense of emptiness.

I go to my bedroom, grab all the clothes I can manage, and take them down. Clothes that once held sentimental value now feel meaningless. Shoes that wandered down countless paths now seem worn and tired. It all goes on the fire.

Then it's up to Marion's bedroom. I fill the suitcases with everything inside her wardrobes. I drag them on down and stare as her Hermes, Gucci, or Versace clothing goes up in smoke. It's cathartic.

Exhaustion begins to drag me down, and I head into the drawing room and pull out a small, plush armchair. Carrying it outside, I put it on the grass, then return for the footstool and bring that out, too. I sit down, kick off my shoes, prop up my feet near the crackling fire, feel the warmth spread through my body and drift off into a gentle slumber.

My eyes open at the sudden, sharp sound coming from nowhere. Scared that someone might be in the woods, I sit up, my heart racing as I try to see where it came from. In the distance, the rustling of leaves and the cracking of branches echo through the woods. Finally, I lie back down, my head resting on my arm as I watch the embers start to die down, but I can't shake the feeling of being watched.

The twigs snapping echoes through the air, gradually growing louder and closer. I rise to my feet and spot a shadowy figure emerging from the trees, heading towards me.

A man walks closer. He's dishevelled, bearded, hair covered in leaves and twigs. It takes me a moment to realise who it is. Derek.

"We need to talk," he says. He looks around as if to make sure there is no one else here. He walks closer, and I subconsciously step back. The mud on his shoes tells me he's been in the woods for a while.

"You were watching me."

"Just wanted to make sure no one else was here. Don't get excited."

His cheap innuendo sickens me. "What do you want?"

"I know Marion and Alfred are dead. I know the police are after me."

"What do you want?" I say again.

"Money. I need money."

"Okay?"

"And you're going to give it to me." His eyes are mean and

desperate, contrasting with the person he pretended to be while managing the care home.

"And why would I do that?"

"Because I fucking want you to."

I watch him.

"You still don't get it, do you, Persy? I'm the one who knows everything. I know about the women, I know about your Uncle Alfred and Marion and, most of all – you'll find this funny – I know about you. Where you came from."

"What do you know about me?"

"Seriously, you think I'll fall for that one? I want a million. You give it to me, I'll tell you everything. If you don't, no problem, I'll give it to the press."

"You've got nothing," I say.

"Shut the fuck up." He's getting more and more agitated.

"And the scam you pulled at the care home; you should be ashamed of yourself," I say, enjoying seeing his face redden and his body tighten up.

"You think I give a shit about any of that? What else was going to happen to their money? Their families never gave a shit. And, trust me, it wasn't as though they knew what I was up to." He's got a cocky grin on his face. "Of course I took their money. Now shut the fuck up or the press will know all about you."

A sharp, sudden gust of wind rushes through the air, making the embers fly past us. We step back so quickly to get out of the way, we gulp in the smoke and end up coughing our guts out. I recover quickly, but he doesn't; embers must be stuck in his throat because he's almost doubled over, gasping for breath. We hurry into the house for water. I go into the drawing room, spot the glass with the poison in it. I look at him and look at the glass. He pushes past me, picks it up, takes a couple of gulps, wipes his mouth with the back of his hand.

I stare at him. Don't move. Don't try to grab the glass.

"What are you staring at me for?" he shouts.

I don't move. It will start any moment now.

He comes towards me like he's going to hit me. I shove him hard; he stumbles back, trips over the fender, smashes his head against the marble fireplace and goes down hard. His head cracks as it hits the ground, and a pool of blood appears around his head. He opens his eyes and reaches out to me. Then, they close, and he lies there. Dead.

The smell of burning wood from the bonfire mingles with the metallic tang of blood. He shouldn't have lied.

I walk down the hall into the sunroom, sit on Marion's chair and stare out into the blackness of the night, exactly as Marion must have done.

Andrew calls from Amsterdam and wants to tell me how great a city it is, and I listen but I have no idea what he is saying. I tell him I have to go, and I hang up. I wander into the kitchen, make a cup of tea, and hold the hot mug between my hands.

I go back into the drawing room and look at Derek sprawled on the floor. I drag his body out of the house, back my car up so it's as close as possible to the front door and pull him into the boot. I drive around to Uncle Alfred's, back up to within inches of the sty. I get into the boot with him, put my hands under his arm, and throw him so his body can balance on the fence. For a moment, it feels like he's breathing as he see saws from one side of the fence to the other. I push his feet up and over and his body lands with a thud. I drive back to Marion's as the sound of squealing pigs shouts into the air.

Derek's blood lies in a pool on the marble floor. I soak it up, dump bleach on it, wipe it up again. I don't know much about blood splatter, but the movies I've seen make it look like blood can always be found even after it's been cleaned.

In the barn, I grab a hammer, go back in, hit the hell out of the marble. It starts to shatter until the original flagstone base is uncovered. I pile the marble into a four plastic carrier bags and put them in my car. I leave the estate, take the back road into the city, dumping bits of marble on the side of the road, in the ditch, at regular intervals.

I get home, take my clothes off, shower, get dressed, take the old clothes I'd worn at Marion's, and drive to the charity bin. Back at home, I change into my pyjamas, fill a hot-water bottle, put it in the bed and get in. If he'd only been honest with me, none of this would've had to have happened. With the duvet pulled up over my shoulders, I fall asleep.

At nine in the morning, the door buzzes. It's Andrew. I don't understand. He's back from Amsterdam too soon. With my dressing gown wrapped tightly around me, I let him in. He comes up the stairs with a puppy in his arms. I pray like crazy that it isn't for me or that he thinks this will make us a couple.

"I'm going to stay. In England." He hands me the puppy. "Amsterdam wasn't for me. And this is for you."

"I can't look after a dog," I say, nuzzling my nose against the tiny ball of fur in my arms.

"You don't have to. It's mine. You can move in with me if you want to see him."

"Wow. You're using a dog to blackmail me into a relationship…"

"You say blackmail. I say woof."

We sit in the living room on the sofa, the little puppy jumping from sofa to chair, then back to the couch. Rolling on its back, letting me rub its tummy. I'm not sure, but I think maybe I'd like to keep it. Andrew said it was for himself, but I don't believe him. I think he's trying to show me his softer side. It's working.

Roger calls and tells me he's heard from Sotheby's. One of their people is on their way to Marion's. He'll let them in if I can't make it. The thought of Derek sprawled out on the floor freaks me out. I need one more look around Marion's house and the sty just to make sure there's nothing there that will indicate something bad has happened.

"The train arrives in Bath at around eleven-fifteen. They'll get a taxi to Marion's. They should be there around noon," he says.

"I'll be there, and thanks."

"What's going on?" Andrew asks.

"Sotheby's are going to Marion's. I need to be there."

"Perfect," he says. "We can bring Hannibal with us. He'll love the place. Can you imagine him out on the grounds? He'll go nuts."

It's too big a risk for Andrew and the dog to be there. What if the dog smells something?

"It's okay," I say. "I can handle it."

"No," Andrew says. "Absolutely not. You're not going there on your own after everything has happened. If you want to drive on your own, fine, but I'm going to follow you. Plus, Hannibal here, he said he wants to see your gardens."

I can't argue with him and I figure maybe it's best that a puppy might find something rather than a police officer. "We are not going to call that dog Hannibal." I smile.

"I'm not," he says, laughing. "But you said 'we'; it's a done deal, *we* have a dog. Get dressed, and I'll come with you. Buster here needs to get out."

"It's not Buster," I say.

"Lancelot? What about that?"

When I go into the bedroom to get dressed, with my door slightly open, I see Andrew on all fours, crawling after the little puppy as it runs and jumps. Maybe this is the new me – with a proper boyfriend and a dog.

I pull on some leggings and ankle boots and head into the living room. Andrew is lying on his back, laughing, and the puppy is playing on his tummy. "I'm good to go," he says. He picks up the puppy and rubs his nose into the soft fir, and the puppy yawns. We head out down the stairs. I'm holding the puppy now, and it's licking my face. We get into Andrew's car, and we head out. When we arrive at Marion's, the puppy is asleep on Andrew's lap. I get out and open the front door. Andrew gets out after me; he's cradling the puppy in his arms.

Andrew is playing with the puppy outside, so I head into the drawing room. I take a good look around for anything that might look odd. The smashed marble fireplace looks as if it's waiting for a stonemason to come and fix it. Under the coffee table is a small Persian rug, and I grab it and put it over the stonework.

The half-empty glass of water is still sitting on the table. I grab it, turn to go to the kitchen but the puppy has come in without me seeing it and it's under my feet. I trip, the glass falls out of my hand and the puppy starts licking it up. I scream out, Andrew comes running in. He takes the glass of water from me and tells me not to worry. I'm still screaming, my eyes on the little puppy knowing exactly what's going to happen next. Andrew grabs me, tells me it's okay, it's not a big deal. He picks up the glass, tells me water won't harm the dog, tells me to look, and he puts the glass to his mouth and drinks the last bit of liquid.

I can't breathe. Can't speak. I turn away, close the drawing room door, walk down the hall, out through the sunroom and into the garden.

What have I done?

I hear someone shouting my name. Andrew is walking towards me a big smile on his face, the puppy is running and jumping behind him.

"What was that all about?" he asks. "What's going on?"

I'm staring at him, unsure if this is reality or illusion.

"Persy," he says. "Are you alright?"

I walk towards him and wrap my arms around him. The puppy is jumping up against my leg. I pick up the puppy and cradle it in my arms as it licks my face. There was no poison in the glass; there couldn't have been. I remember the bottle in the kitchen, the liquid in the bottom; she must've washed the whole thing out. It was bits of water left, nothing else. I stand, my arms wrapped around Andrew, the puppy licking my ankles. This is good. This is all really good.

By the time Sotheby's arrives to value Marion's things, Andrew has fashioned a piece of rope into a lead and is outside playing with the puppy, who showed no interest in the broken fireplace at all. After an hour or so watching a couple of men going through the items, I call Roger. I need to leave. I never want to come back.

THIRTY-ONE

Andrew has gone to the pet store with Puppy, the name we've given him. Puppy. It doesn't make much sense to me, but Andrew thinks it's funny, so Puppy it is. Roger is on the phone.

"The inventory is done," he says. "As soon as they have an estimate, they'll send it to me. I'm heading on home. I'll close the house up."

The flat is silent, except for my tapping at the keyboard. I'm determined to remove every last trace of Derek from my computer, and every file, every document, and every link that gave me access to his world has to go. Thirty minutes later, I'm done and finally close the laptop and, sat back in my chair, stare at the blank screen. Done. Derek is gone in the real and the digital world.

Andrew calls and I take a deep breath before I answer. He's gone to a pet store; why is he calling? He's a good guy and would be a great partner, but more and more, he's starting to feel like a responsibility. The problem isn't him; it's me. I like privacy. I like my space. I'm beginning to even like my thoughts.

"Persy, I've had a call from Athena Grace, a journalist. Do you know her?" he asks.

My stomach drops. Athena Grace, how could I forget her name. The woman who wrote that article about the police and how they were not doing enough to find Dora. A friend of Derek's, no doubt; how else could she have written that piece?

"She called me and wants to talk to you."

"Why did she call you?" My tone is too defensive.

"She was talking to the police, and they gave her my name."

"If it were that important, I imagine she would've called me directly."

"I don't know. She said she wanted to talk to you but wouldn't tell me why. She just said it would be better if you went on the record."

I feel sick. "The record for what?"

"No idea; I told her I'd tell you; if you wanted to get in touch, you would." He takes a breath. "What's wrong? Did I do something to offend you?"

I don't want to deal with his insecurities. "Sorry, no. I just woke up from a nap. I'm still a bit groggy. Give me her number, and I'll call her. And thanks."

My head is beginning to ache. Her needing to speak to me, it's got Derek's fingerprints all over it. I can see his face now, demanding money, that smug look. What was he thinking? The questions are piling up in my brain and I'm rattled. It's impossible that she knows anything new about the dead women, plus Marion and Alfred are gone and they were the ones really implicated in their deaths.

I call Roger. "A journalist is sniffing around, and she's asking questions. I don't know what I should do."

"Don't worry." He almost sounds indifferent. "You know, I managed several of these issues for Marion and Alfred in their time. It's usually nothing, but it does need to be dealt with promptly. Let's schedule a meeting with her in my office to make things official. It sounds like she's picked up a story related to your wealth and what happened to Marion and Alfred. From her perspective, their double suicide is quite sensational. Let's try to address this issue proactively. Persy, let me call her and arrange everything."

"How would she have found out about them? Would she know about the Nembutal?"

"Anything is possible," he says.

I end the call, my fingers itching to learn more about her. I quickly pull up a search engine and find her biography. Eight out of ten stories are about celebrities and their fall from grace. If she finds out the truth about the Adelard family, she'll have won the lottery.

Andrew's name flashes on my phone screen. It's eight in the evening; he'll want to come over or have dinner or want to manage my time. I don't want it. I text him back, tell him I'm not feeling well.

I crawl into bed, my bones aching and my muscles exhausted. I prop myself up with pillows, trying to find a comfortable position that will get rid of some of the tension, but nothing is working. I'm drained and depleted and scared. What does this journalist know?

Tears prick at the corners of my eyes. No matter what went on in Marion's house, the three of us, her, me, Uncle Alfred, we were in it together. Overwhelming feelings of despair wash over me. I take two sleeping tablets, close my eyes and try to focus on my breathing. Before I know it, I'm fast asleep.

The next day, Roger calls and wakes me up. "We have a meeting in my office in an hour with Athena. Does that work for you?"

"Okay," I say.

"And a word of warning. She's young and tenacious and charismatic, a worrisome combination. I suggest we consider her questions thoroughly before we answer. It would be a shame if what happened to Marion and Alfred was splashed all over the newspapers. They spent their whole lives successfully achieving privacy."

"Got it," I say.

I sit down to a breakfast of boiled eggs and toast. I sift through the rows of clothing, can't decide on what I should look like. I end up with black leggings, a dark-brown sweater, turtleneck, and dark-brown ankle boots. I throw an oversized camel-coloured cashmere coat over the top. I grab my laptop.

I walk into Roger's conference room and see Athena Grace sitting to the side, her golden hair catching the light and framing her face in a halo. When she sees me, she stands up and extends a hand, and something about her radiates warmth. It's no wonder she's so successful at her job; she could probably charm blood from a stone with her smile.

After a brief introduction, she gets straight down to business. "Can this conversation go on the record?"

I look over at Roger.

"Absolutely not. You cannot attribute anything that is said in this office to Ms Adelard or myself. I would also like to remind you that while this agreement is not legally binding, if you do attribute anything we say to either one of ourselves, we will sue."

"Understood," she says. She places a writing pad on the table, a pen beside it.

"Let me give you some background." We both nod. "My grandmother was a resident at Meadow Bank Care Home." I start to feel sick. "It was obvious to us, her family, that Derek Pringle took one of her rings. I confronted him, he denied it, of course, even threatened to kick my grandmother out." She raises her eyebrows, makes it clear that she thought this was reprehensible. "But, he suggested we could have a beneficial relationship." She looks down at the table and I'm not sure if what she's doing is well-rehearsed or authentic. "It was a bribe, clearly, but I went along with it because it meant my grandmother could stay there."

I nod. "You broke the story that the police were not doing their job looking for Dora."

"I did. And I'm not proud of it. In retrospect, working with Derek, it wasn't my smartest move. In a way, I'm glad he left the country."

I look away.

"You know, that story, the one I wrote about Dora, I've made a lot of enemies in the police department."

She scratches her shoulder and moves her sweater just enough for me to see a thick red mark around her neck and shoulder. I know that mark. A camera strap.

"Do you drive an Alfa Romeo?" I ask.

She smiles. "Busted. I'm not very good at following people. And you almost caught me, I had to get out of that car park so quickly I almost crashed my car." She looks embarrassed. "My editors tell me I'm too impatient. And I'm sorry. I was trying to get background on the man you were following."

"You weren't following me?"

"No. I think we were following the same man."

I smile. "What did you find on him?"

"Nothing. We had a tip off, but he's clean." She frowns, stares at me. "Did you find anything?"

I shake my head. "Nope. Nothing at all." I start to relax; she's not as smart as she thinks she is. I'm about to ask another question but Roger spots it, puts his hand on my arm. He's reminding me to be on my guard.

"Again," he asks Athena, "why are we here?"

She gives him one of her sparkly smiles but his expression doesn't change as if he's immune to her charms. "Can I show you what I've found out?"

"Of course," Roger says.

"Derek gave me some clues; I just ran with it." She looks at Roger, me, then back at Roger.

"Do you know where Derek is?" I ask.

"No idea." She says, her palms up, facing me. "I promise you. If I knew a thing, I'd go to the police. He deserves to be put in jail."

"You were going to tell us what you found out?" Roger says.

She apologises then looks straight at me.

"Persy, how much about your family do you know?"

I look at Roger. "Very little, why?"

Roger coughs. "Athena, if you would show us what you have, I would be very grateful."

She's got papers in a folder, one on top of each other with little stickers. She glances at the clock and then selects a single piece of paper, lays it on the table and pushes it towards me. It's an aged photo of the remains of a once-grand country home, now nothing but charred wood and ash. The story of me being taken from a burning house. I want to laugh out loud. How deep did Marion go to make people believe this story.

She takes out a second photo, her eyes on me as if she's assessing what my next reaction is going to be. It's unnerving. I take the photo. The condition isn't great, it's old, but the people in the photo are easy to see.

Four people, two parents and two children. The man is tall and carries with him an air of authority with his squared shoulders and strong jawline. The woman next to him looks elegant with her hair in a bun and a serene expression on her face. At the front are the two children standing hand in hand – one a boy and the other a girl, the boy looks older and they look happy, their eyes sparkling with mischief, as if they're hiding a secret.

"Do you recognise them?" Athena asks.

"Me?" I look at Roger. "No. Why would I?"

She taps at the two teenage children. "These two? You don't recognise them?"

"Athena, please get on with it," Roger says.

"The children at the front, they are your mother and father."

"What?" I say.

"The two younger people in the photo. Cousins. They are your parents."

I spit out a shocked laugh. "Don't be ridiculous. How could they be my parents?"

"They came to this country and they changed their names."

I daren't speak.

"They changed their names to Alfred and Marion Adelard. Persy, you were not adopted by Marion. Marion was your biological mother. Alfred was your biological father."

Time slows. The whole world will know.

"We need some time," Roger says to Athena. "Could you do that, please?"

Athena says something, then leaves the room.

"Persy. Are you okay?" He's twisted his body so he's facing the side of me. I don't want to look at him. I'm a freak. "We need to check everything she is saying. For the moment, I suggest you ignore everything you've been told today."

"Did you know any of this?" I ask.

He shakes his head. The look on his face is confusion. "I knew nothing of this. I promise you."

I squeeze my eyes shut and bury my face in my trembling hands. I'm no longer in control. I'm not safe and I have nowhere to go.

"Persy, let's finish this off another time."

"No." I wipe the tears from my eyes, press my lips together

to stop the scream coming out of my mouth. "I need to know what else she has."

"I'll want proof from her. You know that."

Athena comes back in and the look on her face tells me how awful this news has to be for me because she can barely look at me.

"The news gets worse. I think we should do this another day," she says.

"Let's do this now," I answer.

She looks at Roger, who looks at me.

"Please," I say.

She removes a newspaper cutting. It's in German. "I'll make a copy for you to get translated but I'll give you a brief summary. This was a major case in Germany. The parents of Marion and Alfred died when the house burnt down."

I nod. It doesn't matter anymore. Nothing matters.

"This newspaper article is clear. Marion burnt the house down knowing their parents were still in there. Marion had locked them in the cellar. Then they fled. Were never heard from again."

I spit out a laugh as if this is too preposterous to even think about.

"I'm sorry, Persy, it gets worse. The older man in the photo, your grandfather, he had a history of abusing women and children."

"No," I say. "No, this can't be possible."

Roger leans forward. "Marion had substantial wealth?" It's clear what Roger wants to know. Where did she get all of her money?

"They came from generational wealth. Trust funds were set up before they were even born. They also came into money when the parents died. Alfred moved everything to England and the US."

She takes back all the papers she's put in front of us and puts them back in her folder. "I'll leave all of this with you."

I nod.

"And you're sure, of all of this?" Roger asks. He's in a state of shock. "Marion and Alfred were Persy's biological parents?"

She sits at the table, the folder closed, the flat of her hand resting on top. "Full disclosure," she says. "We have DNA proof. DNA taken from Alfred and Marion, Derek obtained it. We also have DNA from you, Persy."

"How?" I ask.

"I'm ashamed to say this was given to us by Derek. All of it was taken illegally."

Roger steps in. "You don't have authority. This is out of order, completely—"

"It's okay," I say. "It doesn't matter anymore."

"I advise you to do your own testing, Persy. But I can assure you, this is all real." She looks from Roger to me, lets the weight of the news sink in. "I've been researching this story for the past six months. There is no doubt."

The reality that my whole messy life will be splashed across every newspaper in the country, it's too much to think about.

"You're going to print all of this?"

She nods.

"Is there anything more?" I ask.

Roger interrupts. "Persy, I think this is quite enough for one day."

I keep my eyes on Athena. "Is there?" I ask.

"Meadow Bank Care Home."

I keep my eyes steady on hers. This is it. The moment when she tells me she has proof of what happened to those old women.

"I'm not sure if you're aware, women have disappeared from there."

"I'm aware," I say.

Roger again tries to interject. "Persy. This is enough."

"Go on," I say.

"I checked the dates of their disappearance, I checked any available CCTV footage from the roads in and out of the home, from the roads when a coach trip took place, from any point that I thought might be helpful in us finding out what happened."

I nod.

She puts another photo on the table. It's Marion's Mercedes. I stare in; the photo has caught an image of two people inside. The sunlight is glaring on the driver's side, impossible to see who was driving. On the passenger side is a woman. Dora Haslea? The photo isn't good enough to see.

"What does this prove?" Roger asks.

"It doesn't prove anything," Athena answers, "but it does suggest an interesting story."

I watch her, the confidence in her eyes, the certainty in her words. "Go ahead," I say.

"Marion or Alfred picked up those women from the home. Then killed them."

"No," I say. "That's ridiculous. They would never do that. I knew them."

"Actually, you didn't, Persy. I apologise for being so blunt, but your family, your lineage, I don't know how to say this gently, but you're from a long line of people who felt comfortable hurting others."

"Why?" I whisper. "Why would they want to kill those women?"

"I don't know," she says. "I honestly don't know. I can't find a connection." She takes out more photos. Again, Marion's car. Again, women sitting in the passenger seat, although the photos are too blurry to prove a thing. "These photos were taken on the day the women disappeared. Other than that, we can prove nothing."

"This is of no value," Roger says. "It's impossible to ascertain who was in the car. You can't even see who's driving."

"You're right," Athena says. "But it's compelling, isn't it."

I can't breathe.

Roger steps in. "Athena. We have to stop this now. I'm sorry, but this is all too distressing for Persy. I'm sorry."

"I understand," she says. "One last thing. I have a source at the hospital; I know that Marion and Alfred committed suicide by ingesting Nembutal."

"Where does your paper stand on this story?" Roger asks.

Athena nods. "First, I have to admit that some of the information obtained doesn't reflect well on me. In fact, you might think it morally and spectacularly dishonourable. But the fact of the matter is that Marion and Alfred killed their parents and fled. It is also likely that Alfred or Marion killed women from the care home. All of this information will be published with or without your approval. I also suspect that the police will need to take the investigation further."

"What do you mean by that?" Roger says.

"Within twenty-four hours, they will have a warrant to search the house and the gardens and the outbuildings looking for any proof."

"I could take out an injunction against you publishing this."

"You could. And you would fail."

"It will damage Persy's reputation; this is defamation."

Athena snaps her folder shut and pushes it towards me. "This has nothing to do with Persy. Everything points to Alfred and Marion. If you wish to pursue a legal route, go ahead, but in my view, you don't have grounds. And, Persy, I'm sorry."

I bury my head in my hands.

"I'm sorry, Persy. It's a lot. But in my experience, knowing the truth is always better."

"Not if you're sitting in my position," I say.

"I will be putting a story together. If you want to sit down and discuss it, I'm ready. I will also give you the courtesy of showing you the story at least a week before it runs. If you believe any of it is wrong, I'll be happy to listen and to correct if necessary."

I stand up. Roger stands up. Athena leaves.

"I don't know what to say," Roger says.

"I don't either."

THIRTY-TWO

I sit in Roger's office, in the conference room. Roger is sitting on one side of the table, Scooter on the other. I told him I didn't need him to leave the US and come to England, but he wouldn't have any of it, said he was going to be here with me when the newspaper article came out whether I liked it or not. Andrew wanted to be here too, but I said no, that we didn't have a future. He seemed fine with it. I think only the puppy gave a damn.

The draft of Athena's story is laid out in front, each one of us has a copy.

Athena has done a convincing job. The photos of my parents, grandparents, even great-grandparents. Thoroughly awful people. She's got the proof. She's also got photographs of the police scouring every inch of Marion's estate, looking for some connection between the Adelard family and the missing women and the details of where they searched on Marion's estate and how they'd found nothing. The one point she agreed to was to go with the story that I was adopted. I think she felt sorry for me, knew how telling the world that I was the daughter of a line of psychopaths wouldn't do much good. Plus, Roger had done a deal with her. She had complete access to Marion's estate, as many photos as she liked, as long as she didn't mention my genetic background.

I can't bear to look at the article any longer. The words on the page are like poison, seeping deep inside of me. My whole life. The big lie.

I push the paper away. Scooter does the same thing.

"The only missing link," he says to Athena, "is Derek. Does anyone know where he is?"

"Nope," she says. "It's in the hands of the police."

Scooter looks at me. "Are you worried Derek has something more to tell?"

"Like what?" I ask. The image of Derek's body wobbling on the fence pops into my head.

"Well," Roger says, before Scooter can answer. "As much as I enjoy this line of discussion, I'm happy to say this whole affair is over and I have another meeting to go to." He smiles at us both. "Please stay here, if you wish." He smiles at Athena. "Shall I show you the way out?"

She nods. Shakes my hand. Then Scooter's.

"We're heading out too," I say. I fold up the draft and toss it into the bin. Scooter does the same. We all walk out of the conference room, down the stairs and into the car park.

"Where to now, Persy?" Roger asks as we watch Athena leave.

"The States," I say. "Scooter and I are going to fly to Chicago then drive Route 66. Two and a half thousand miles, right across the country."

"Rather you than me," Roger says. "Keep in touch."

I nod.

Roger looks at Scooter. "Take care of her. She's one of the good ones."

Scooter puts his arm around my shoulder and I lean my head against it. "I will," he says.

We get into the car with Scooter driving and me sitting beside him as the engine hums to life. Roger stands by the kerb, his silhouette shrinking in the rear-view mirror as we drive away. The sky is a watercolour wash of grey, and there's a mist that clings stubbornly to the world as the houses and shops of my old life blur past as Scooter navigates the car through familiar streets.

"We should probably make a playlist," Scooter suggests, breaking into my thoughts. "You know, for the road. Classic American tunes, some rock, and definitely some guilty pleasures."

"You are definitely not putting one together. We'll end up with that yellow ribbon song or 'Country Roads' or something."

"Hey, could be worse. What about Elvis? Who doesn't love Elvis?"

"And we'll take turns driving, right?" I say.

"Sure, whatever you say, honey."

We both share a knowing smile and I can see that we're getting close to where I've always wanted us to be. A couple.

"One thing I don't understand," he says. "Those women disappeared. I mean, where did they go? Who would want to hurt them?"

"I've no idea," I say.

"Bullshit," he spits out. "Come on. I know the way you think. Give me what you've got and I'll tell you why you're wrong."

I watch the subtle movements of his face as he focuses on driving, the way his brow furrows in concentration and his lips purse in determination. My mind races with thoughts; should I tell him? The urge to open up and share my feelings is strong, but I know it's just my head toying with me. This isn't the right time. It will never be the right time.

"I think they just walked away. Nothing more. Nothing less."

"Come on. Work with me. Why would anyone want to hurt some vulnerable old women?"

I don't answer.

"I'll keep asking," he says. "Why hurt some old women?"

"Okay. You want to know what I think?"

"Sure," he says, giving me a sly glance. "Baffle me with your brilliance."

"Punishment," I say.

"You've got to give me a bit more than that."

"I think Derek killed those women to punish Marion."

"Wow. That's really out there. Your mind is more warped than I thought." He looks and smiles at me. "But I'll go with you. Now, why would Derek want to punish Marion and how would spiriting them away even achieve that? And how did he get Marion's Mercedes to do it?"

"Marion was nasty," I say. "I mean, she was my mother, I get that, but what she did to me…"

He must hear the upset in my voice because he puts his hand on my thigh. "Sorry, Persy. I didn't mean to upset you."

"It's alright." I cough, get my act together. "Marion was an awful woman. Maybe she hurt Derek too. By getting rid of some of the women in the home, the home that she managed and financed, maybe that was his way of getting her back. And remember, the women who disappeared, they were Marion's favourites. I think he was trying to tell her you can do whatever you like to me but I will make sure I hurt you back."

"But if that were true, he would've had to have let Marion know, right? I mean, it's hardly revenge if the person you're trying to stick it to doesn't know."

"She would've known," I say. "Come on. She was sharp enough to have figured it out."

"And how did he get Marion's car?"

"He had meetings with Marion at the house. The car was parked most of the time; she wouldn't have noticed it gone." I kind of grimace. "I didn't say I had all the answers."

He looks ahead as we drive closer to my flat. He parks. "Okay, we're here. And by the way, your story is crap. I think you know nothing." He ruffles the top of my hair. "You want me to come in and help you grab your bags?"

"Bag," I say. "I'm bringing one bag. And no thanks, you wait here. I'll be right back."

I jump out of the car, my steps quick and urgent as I hurry towards my flat. I take the stairs up to my front door two by two, eager to get in, even more eager to get out. I fumble with my keys, push open the front door, stand inside and breathe the smell of my old life.

I go to the window to check on Scooter. He's still there, in my car, playing with the controls, oblivious to me here, in my flat. I check my watch. A couple of minutes is all I need.

I go into the bedroom, push the bed to the side, get down on all fours, and remove the loose wooden floorboard. I put my hand inside the hiding place and remove three bottles of Nembutal, the German newspaper article, and the photos of me, the ones I cut out from the photos, all taken from under Marion's bed.

I head into the kitchen, pour the Nembutal down the sink and wash them inside and out to make sure no remnants still exist. I stamp on the bottles until they crack, then put them into my pocket.

I take a lighter and burn the newspaper article with the cut-out pieces of my face in the same sink and wait until it turns to embers. I pick the pieces up and flush them down the toilet.

Back in the bedroom, I replace the wooden floorboard and push the bed back.

With a swift motion, I hoist my packed bag onto my

shoulder, the weight of it feeling familiar and comfortable. My gaze sweeps over the neatly organised space of my flat one last time, to the cozy sofa where Andrew and I had sat together, to the window where I'd watched the world go by, to the shelves of books now collecting dust. I go down the stairs, push open the heavy door and step out into the sunlight, ready for the adventure with Scooter to begin. I head to the rubbish bin a few feet away and throw away the broken plastic bottles that had the Nembutal inside. I head towards my car with the answer that I was throwing away an old tissue, just in case he saw me going to the rubbish bin, but he's not even watching. He's looking at something in his lap. I get in the car.

"What's going on?" I ask.

He pushes his hand towards me and opens it up. Sitting in the middle of his palm is a set of keys. Car keys, the familiar Mercedes keyring glistening against the light.

"I found these in the glove compartment?" he says. "Why would you have these? Keys to Marion's car. The Mercedes, right?"

I snap on my seatbelt. Rookie mistake, stashing them in my car after I'd picked Dora up, given her something to drink, then taken her to sit down in Marion's sunroom. The moment flashes in my head, as clear as day. I'd driven the car back into the barn, shoved the spare keys into the back pocket of my jeans. They'd prodded my ass so I'd shoved them into the glove compartment without thinking.

"I'm selling it," I lie. "On the way out of here, we need to stop off at our dealer to give him the keys. And before you whine about it, the dealership is on the way. I never want to see that damn car again. In fact, I'm going to get rid of all of their cars. But he's got a buyer already."

"You didn't mention that before."

"Wow. One road trip and you're already upset because I don't share everything?"

Scooter watches me. "You're sure?"

"Come on. Let's go. Of course I'm sure." I sound defensive. I need to tone it down. "Why wouldn't I be sure?" I smile, try like hell to look and sound surprised, innocent, somewhat confused.

"It's a vintage car. Maybe I'd want to buy it," he says.

A wave of relief washes over me. He's bought what I said. He isn't suspicious at all.

"Do you want to buy the car?" I ask.

"Not really," he says. "But you could've asked me first."

"Sorry. Think about the others. Whatever you want is yours."

"The vintage Porsche?"

"Done," I say. And he smiles. "Good," I go on. "Let's get rid of the keys then Heathrow it is."

We drive away with a flutter in my heart and a twinkle in my eye. I settle into the leather seat next to the man who I know will fall in love with me. I imagine running my fingers through his dark hair, feeling his lips on mine.

We'll live in a house that's filled with laughter and love and I think about what I'll cook when he's rolling around with our two children, their laughter bouncing off the walls, and how we'll spend lazy Sundays cuddled up in bed, talking and dreaming of all the adventures we'll embark on.

"Have you thought about what you're going to do when this trip is done?" he asks.

"What do you mean?"

"I've got this contract going on in Abu Dhabi."

"Really? I was thinking we could start a business together in England. It could be fun."

"You're not worried about coming back? About people looking at you and thinking about your family?"

"Nope," I say. "Why should I be worried? I'm nothing like them."

This book is printed on paper from sustainable sources managed under the Forest Stewardship Council (FSC) scheme.

It has been printed in the UK to reduce transportation miles and their impact upon the environment.

For every new title that Troubador publishes, we plant a tree to offset CO_2, partnering with the More Trees scheme.

MORE TREES
LET'S PLANT A BILLION TREES

For more about how Troubador offsets its environmental impact, see www.troubador.co.uk/sustainability-and-community